"Julia." His voi...

"Yeah?"

"If for some reason I don't come back from that op tomorrow…"

Panic constricted her heart. "Hey, don't say that. You're not going to get blown up, damn it."

"I know." Sebastian paused. "At least I hope not." Another pause. "But just humor me, okay? If I don't come back, there's something I need you to know."

Unsettled, she moved onto her side and studied his profile. She couldn't decipher the strange expression on his face, and that only troubled her more. "What is it?" she asked.

After a long moment of hesitation, he breathed in deep, then exhaled in a fast rush. "If I could offer you more than a casual affair, I would."

Surprise lifted her eyebrows. Okay. Well, she hadn't been expecting *that*.

But he wasn't done surprising her.

Sebastian sighed. "I'm not making any sense, am I? I…I'm cursed, Julia. I can't love you. Do you understand?"

The Hunted: A band of brothers out for justice…and love.

Dear Reader,

I fall a little bit in love with every hero I write, so picking a favorite is a darn near impossible task. But I can honestly say that Sebastian Stone, the hero of this story, is in my Top Three list of *Gosh, I Love You So Much Why Can't You Be Real?*

Sebastian has all the qualities that the perfect hero embodies. He's alpha to the core, sexy and magnetic. But he's also sweet, vulnerable (something he doesn't show very often) and kind. Flirty. Compassionate. Protective. Yep, he's very protective, especially of Dr. Julia Davenport, the sassy doctor Seb teams up with in order to stop a deadly virus from infecting thousands of innocent people. This story was incredibly fun to write.

I hope you guys enjoy Sebastian and Julia's story. This is Book Two of The Hunted miniseries, but you won't be lost if you haven't read the first book, *Soldier Under Siege*. However, this book does expand on plot elements introduced in the previous one, so if you're interested in what led to Sebastian and Julia's adventure, check out Tate and Eva's story, too.

I love hearing from my readers, so don't be shy—stop by my website, www.ellekennedy.com, and send me a note!

Happy reading!

Elle

ELLE KENNEDY

Special Forces Rendezvous

HARLEQUIN® ROMANTIC SUSPENSE

Recycling programs
for this product may
not exist in your area.

ISBN-13: 978-0-373-27819-0

SPECIAL FORCES RENDEZVOUS

Printed in U.S.A.

Books by Elle Kennedy

Harlequin Romantic Suspense

Missing Mother-To-Be #1680
★Millionaire's Last Stand #1686
★The Heartbreak Sheriff #1690
Colton's Deep Cover #1728
★★Soldier Under Siege #1741
★★Special Forces Rendezvous #1749

Silhouette Romantic Suspense

Silent Watch #1574
Her Private Avenger #1634

Harlequin Blaze

Body Check #458
Witness Seduction #637

★Small-Town Scandals
★★The Hunted

Other titles by this author available in ebook format.

ELLE KENNEDY

A RITA® Award-nominated author, Elle Kennedy grew up in the suburbs of Toronto, Ontario, and holds a B.A. in English from York University. From an early age she knew she wanted to be a writer, and actively began pursuing that dream when she was a teenager. She loves strong heroines and sexy alpha heroes, and just enough heat and danger to keep things interesting.

Elle loves to hear from her readers. Visit her website, www.ellekennedy.com, for the latest news or to send her a note.

To the most amazing plot-buddy on the planet,
Travis White. And my equally amazing editor,
Keyren Gerlach—you will be missed, K!

Chapter 1

"Are you lost, Blondie?"

Sebastian Stone killed the engine of the Jeep and glanced over his shoulder, ready to work the charm on the female whose tone had been more mocking than welcoming. But when said female strode up to the driver's side, the flirty remark died in his throat. The girl couldn't have been older than fourteen or fifteen, which rendered any flirtatious exchanges absolutely inappropriate.

Still, he couldn't resist a little mocking jab of his own. "Actually, kiddo, I'm right where I'm supposed to be."

He knew no self-respecting teenage girl would respond well to being called *kiddo,* and sure enough, he got the reaction he'd expected. The girl's brown eyes flashed with indignation, and her mocha-colored cheeks took on a reddish hue.

Shooting him a sinister look, she crossed her arms over her chest. "Seriously, dude, what are you doing here?"

Sebastian hopped out of the Jeep and nodded at the ramshackle brick building twenty feet away. "I have an appointment with Dr. Davenport."

Those dark eyes narrowed. "Are you a patient?"

He cocked a brow. "No. Are you?"

"No." She huffed out an annoyed breath. "Fine. Come on, I'll take you to Julia."

"How gracious of you, Miss…" He waited for her to fill in the rest.

"Simone," she said grudgingly.

"Pleasure to meet you, Simone. I'm Sebastian."

Grabbing his canvas messenger bag from the backseat, he trailed after the teenager, who, despite the sweltering heat, was surprisingly energetic as she led him toward the covered porch of the clinic.

It was a disgustingly hot day, and the sun had been beating down on Sebastian's head during the entire drive over here, bringing beads of sweat to his forehead and making his threadbare T-shirt stick to his chest. Eventually he'd taken off the shirt and made the rest of the drive shirtless, drawing uneasy glances from several of the local women he'd passed on the side of the road.

The folks around here weren't used to seeing strangers in cars roaming the area. Valero was one of the poorer towns in San Marquez, just a small settlement at the base of the mountain. Lush greenery, rocky slopes and an abundance of tangled shrubbery marked the landscape, with gravel and dirt roads winding their way through the terrain like unwanted intruders. With a population of barely a thousand, the town of Valero was nothing more than dilapidated brick houses scattered about, isolated farms, a surprisingly busy marketplace and this Doctors International clinic located on the outskirts of town.

"Julia's in the back," Simone said as they stepped through the paint-chipped double doors at the building's entrance.

The girl stuck to a brisk pace, but Sebastian still had enough time to scope out his surroundings as they ventured deeper into the medical facility. Although Doctors International specialized in visiting areas in dire need of medical care, setting up makeshift hospitals and then packing up and moving on, the organization did have some permanent clinics in place all over the globe. This was one of them, and Sebastian noted that the operation they had going here was professional and efficient.

The hallways were dimly lit but clean. The waiting room hc and Simone passed was small and cramped, but offered rows of plastic chairs and toys for the children waiting with their parents. Because the building was L-shaped, they had to take a sharp left and ended up striding down another long hallway. This one featured several closed doors, most likely exam rooms. Through a pair of swinging doors with small square windows, Sebastian glimpsed a large room containing dozens of hospital beds.

"You get a lot of overnight patients?" he asked the teenager.

She spared him a glance over her shoulder. "Sometimes. There's always a few patients in the AIDS wing, but the general wing isn't usually so full."

"But it is at the moment because of the malaria cases that have cropped up, right?"

Simone tossed him another look, this one laced with suspicion. "How do you know about those cases?"

"I'm a journalist," he answered. "It's my business to know everything."

The teenager halted, her hands landing on her slender waist. "You're a journalist? No way."

Despite the fact that he was lying through his teeth, he stared at the girl with nothing but sincerity. "Yes way."

"Who do you write for?" she challenged.

He shrugged. "Everyone. I'm a freelancer, so I'm constantly traveling the world, searching for stories."

As of three days ago, anyway.

He decided to keep that to himself. He couldn't very well come out and say, "Hey, guess what? I used to be Special Forces, but now my own government wants me dead." The kid probably wouldn't believe him anyway. It did sound farfetched as hell.

Unfortunately, it was the cold, hard truth. For the past eight months, he'd been hiding out with the two remaining members of his former unit. What had once been a nine-man team had been reduced to a paltry three. Six dead—one during that ill-fated mission to San Marquez, but the five that followed? Those deaths were no accidents. After the unit had been recalled back to the States, those men had been systematically killed off, presumably because they'd seen too much during that last op.

Sebastian had nearly died himself, which was why he'd promptly connected with Nick Prescott and their commanding officer, Captain Robert Tate, and the three of them had gotten the hell out of Dodge.

Up until two months ago, he would've insisted there

was nothing off about that mission to rescue Richard Harrison, the American doctor who'd been held captive by rebel fighters. But as it turned out, nothing was as it seemed—the doctor hadn't been a hostage at all, and the dead bodies Sebastian's team had found strewn all over the village? Those villagers hadn't died at the hands of the rebels but from a virus Dr. Harrison was testing on innocent people.

Unfortunately, that was about all Sebastian knew. The key to finding out who authorized the killing of his unit was in discovering who authorized the manufacturing of a virus he still knew nothing about.

Hopefully that would change today. For the last couple of months, he and the others had kept their eyes and ears open to any unusual medical developments in San Marquez, and last night they'd hit pay dirt.

He didn't know if these malaria cases in Valero were related to Richard Harrison's virus, but he was damn well going to find out. Tate and Nick had agreed it was worth the risk for Sebastian to leave their safe house in Ecuador to investigate, and although he hated being out in the open like this, he was determined to make use of every second.

"So what are you doing here, kiddo?" he asked in a conversational tone. "You're clearly too young to be a volunteer."

"My dad works here." Simone stuck out her chin proudly. "He's a surgeon."

"Impressive." Sebastian smirked. "So he just lugs you along during his travels? He doesn't think school is important?"

She glared at him. "I'm homeschooled. But FYI,

there *are* more important things than school. Like saving lives."

He couldn't argue with that. Saving lives was important. So was *staying* alive, which was his one and only goal at the moment.

Simone led him to the very end of the hall to a door that swung open the second they approached it.

The slender brunette who'd slid through the threshold stumbled in surprise, then let out a laugh as her gaze met Sebastian's. "Mr. Stone, I presume? I was just coming out to meet you."

"No need. Simone was gracious enough to escort me to you," he answered with a charming smile he'd perfected over the years.

The brunette snickered. "Simone, gracious? I'd like to see that."

Rather than object, the teenager simply shrugged. "You know me too well, Doc." Then she lifted her nose up and frowned at Sebastian. "Later, dude."

As Simone bounded off, Sebastian gave the brunette a wry look. "Nice kid."

She grinned. "She can be a handful, but her bedside manner is surprisingly remarkable. She's wonderful with the patients." The brunette stuck out a hand. "I'm Julia Davenport."

"Sebastian Stone." He leaned in for the handshake, and the firmness of her grip surprised him, especially because her hands were so small and dainty.

In fact, everything about this woman was dainty. Delicate, even. She was average height, but skinnier than she ought to be. He didn't mind a willowy figure on a woman, but Julia Davenport could definitely afford to put on a few pounds. She wore a blue tank top that clung to a pair of small breasts and outlined the unmistakable ridges of her ribcage. Her legs weren't quite scrawny but, again, could have benefited from some extra curves.

Though she did have a surprisingly plump ass, he had to concede, his gaze honing in on that round bottom when Julia turned to reenter her office.

Because he'd always been an ass man, the tantalizing sight stirred his groin, serving as a reminder of his eight-month-long stint of celibacy. Getting laid wasn't something he'd given much thought to since going into hiding. Granted, it was easy not to think about sex when your only company was two bad-tempered soldiers and a case of watery South American beer.

"How was your flight?" Julia asked.

"Uneventful." And nonexistent—he'd arrived on the island by boat after bribing the captain of a cargo vessel to give him a ride and drop him outside the harbor where he wouldn't encounter any customs officials.

"Have a seat," she said, gesturing to a very small, very uncomfortable-looking plastic chair.

While Julia rounded a narrow metal desk and sat down, Sebastian crammed his six-foot-two-inch frame into the tiny chair and tried to get comfortable.

His shifting and sliding earned him another grin from Julia Davenport, and now that he focused on her face rather than her too-skinny frame, he realized just how pretty she was. Not classically beautiful by society's standards, but her features were interesting. A wide, generous mouth that seemed to contradict with her slightly angular jaw, a straight aristocratic nose and a pair of big hazel eyes that gave her that perpetually fragile and doe-eyed air.

But he suspected there was nothing fragile or doe-eyed about this woman, which was confirmed when her expression suddenly turned shrewd. "Okay, what do you want to know?" she asked, getting right down to business.

"Eager to get rid of me?" he couldn't help but tease.

"Actually, no. I would love nothing more than to sit here with you for the next two frickin' weeks. I'm exhausted, hungry, cranky and I can't remember the last time I had a conversation with someone who wasn't sick or dying." She let out a heavy sigh. "But what can you do? I knew exactly what I was getting into when I signed on for this gig."

Her blunt tone and frank words intrigued him. When he'd set up this bogus interview, he'd expected to hear a bunch of praise for the Doctors International organization and heartfelt speeches about saving the world and making a difference and all that jazz.

"Sounds like running this clinic is a tough task," he remarked.

"Tough is an understatement." A beat. "Aren't you going to take notes?"

Right. Notes. That was what journalists did.

He bent down and removed a notebook, ballpoint pen and mini tape recorder from his messenger bag. Holding up the recorder, he met Julia's big hazel eyes and said, "Mind if I record this?"

"Not at all."

As he set up the recorder and opened his notebook to a fresh page, Julia shot him another one of those no-nonsense looks. "I read some of your articles online this morning. You're a good writer."

Thank you, Eva.

Sebastian made a mental note to be nicer to Tate's fiancée next time he saw her. He hadn't been Eva Dolce's biggest fan when the woman had come into their lives. Then again, when a mysterious chick showed up asking your commanding officer to risk his neck and kill a man for her, were you really expected to bust out the trust parade?

But in the end, Eva had proven to be trustworthy, and thanks to her, Hector Cruz, the leader of the rebel group currently terrorizing San Marquez, was out of commission.

Also thanks to Eva, Sebastian had a fake writing career all over the internet. It had only taken Tate's hacker fiancée a day to establish Sebastian Stone as a bona fide freelancer, mostly by hacking into newspaper sites and changing the by-lines. The story wouldn't hold up under deep scrutiny, but they'd figured Julia Davenport and her colleagues wouldn't have time to do a thorough background check on the man who was coming to write a glowing piece about their organization.

"Thanks," he said, hoping Julia didn't ask him any specific questions about his "work." "Though I'm surprised to hear you have internet access here."

"We do in the clinic, but it's expensive, so we only use it for work purposes. Communication-wise, we've got a radio we use to connect with other clinics on the island, and a sat phone for emergencies."

"What about cell phones? I noticed mine kept losing its signal the closer I got to the mountains."

"There's a cell tower somewhere around here, but my phone rarely gets a signal either. Last night the signal lasted for almost an hour, and the midwife we have on staff actually got to talk to her grandson for more than five minutes." She flashed another one of those dry grins. "I swear, we throw a party every time someone sees one bar on their phone display. It's like frickin' Halley's Comet just flew overhead."

He chuckled, and for a moment, he totally forgot he was supposed to interview her. He was enjoying simply talking to Julia Davenport. It had been so long since he'd had a conversation with someone other than Tate or Nick, about something other than the damn targets painted on their backs.

"Anyway, off-topic again," she said with a chuckle of her own. "Interview away, Mr. Stone."

"Sebastian."

"Sebastian," she echoed.

"All right, well, why don't you start by telling me a bit about the setup you folks have going here."

With a nod, she leaned back in her chair and gave him a quick rundown of the Doctors International organization. She described their goals, the way the organization was structured, the equipment they had on hand. Every now and then, Sebastian interrupted with a question to give credibility to the whole interview thing, but in his head, he was trying to figure out the best way to broach the dying patients in the next room.

"So you do have an MRI," he cut in, pretending to be fascinated.

She nodded, her dainty fingers toying with the end of her long brown braid, which fell over one shoulder. "We do, but we don't have an on-site expert to handle the results. The scans are sent to the central lab in Merido, and the diagnoses and results are emailed back to us."

He asked a few more questions without really caring about the answers, except he found himself incredibly fascinated the more he listened to Julia Davenport talk. She wasn't like any doctor he'd ever met. She actually spoke English, for one, and not that complicated medical jargon that made people's heads spin like merry-go-rounds.

And he liked the sound of her voice—it was soft but controlled, husky enough to be sexy but still professional. A rush of heat skated up his spine as his gaze moved to her mouth, those pouty lips that pursed each time she paused to organize her next thought.

Damn, he was getting all sorts of turned on courtesy of Dr. Julia Davenport. He definitely needed to nip this strange attraction in the bud. Now.

"So what you're saying," he said with another laugh, "is that you're overcrowded, understaffed, short on equipment and pretty much doing the best you can by the skin of your teeth."

Her answering laughter summoned another jolt of heat. "Pretty much," she confirmed.

He studied the random questions he'd scribbled down in his notebook, pretending to think about his next line of inquiry. "What about the rebels?" he asked. "Are you getting any resistance from the ULF soldiers in the area?"

"Actually, no."

Sebastian was surprised. It was no secret that the United Liberty Fighters resented the alliance between San Marquez and America. For the past ten years, San Marquez had seen nothing but strife and turmoil thanks to the ULF. What started out as an admirable movement to fight a genuinely oppressive government had transformed into violence, unrest and borderline terrorism.

"I've been here for six months and so far the rebels have left us alone," she went on. "They might not appreciate American interference in their political affairs, but I believe that many of these rebels truly care about the country's citizens. They won't achieve anything by causing trouble for the medical workers who are attempting to help the people the ULF claims to be fighting for."

"That's a good point." Readjusting in his unbelievably uncomfortable chair, he carelessly crossed his ankles together. "Let's shift gears for a moment. Tell me about the inpatient care you offer. Simone said you have several AIDS patients staying here in the clinic…" He feigned ignorance. "And something about malaria?"

Julia nodded. "We do treat a handful of AIDS and HIV patients, but as you probably discovered in your research, this area isn't heavily afflicted by either one. We tend to see more outbreaks of cholera and malaria."

"So at the moment you're dealing with a malaria outbreak?" he asked casually.

To his frustration, she smiled and shook her head. "No. We're keeping about a dozen or so patients for observation, but only until their blood test results come back. It's a precaution to test for malaria if the patients exhibit any of the symptoms, but I'm fairly certain none of the folks here have the parasite."

"But a few patients did recently have it, right?"

"Yes, but those were just isolated incidents and not indicative of a major outbreak."

"Can you tell me more about the cases? Without revealing names or private details, of course."

Julia twirled the end of her braid around her finger. "They were all from the same family, which is why I don't believe we have a malaria problem on our hands. It's been cooler here in the north, so the mosquitoes haven't been too brutal. The family in question neglected to take the preventive measures we encourage the locals to employ."

"Mosquito netting, repellents?" he prompted.

"Exactly." Her tone became soft, regretful. "They didn't protect themselves and unfortunately, they didn't come in for treatment right away either. By the time they did, it was too late."

The pain in her hazel eyes told Sebastian that she was the kind of doctor who actually gave a damn about her patients. Then again, that shouldn't surprise him. If she'd gotten into medicine for the money, she would be back in the States, running a cushy practice and counting her pile of cash. Instead, she'd chosen to work for peanuts in isolated, needy areas of South America and Africa.

He found himself curious about that, and had to fight the impulse to ask her why she'd gotten into foreign aid in the first place. But he couldn't get off-topic, not when they were on the very subject he'd come here to talk about.

"How many dead?" he asked gruffly.

"The mother, all five of the children and the grandparents who were living with the family. The father didn't get sick." Another flicker of pain crossed those big eyes. "He's devastated, to say the least. Lost his entire family in less than a week."

Something hot and unwelcome squeezed Sebastian's chest. He knew all about loss, didn't he? Seemed like he'd been losing people his entire damn life.

But now wasn't the time to dwell on painful, unwanted memories. He'd come here to figure out if those malaria deaths were connected to the virus Harrison had been testing in Corazón, but it looked like this was nothing but a false alarm.

Unless… Was Julia Davenport in cahoots with the people hunting him? Was she continuing Harrison's secret project by killing her own patients?

He let the possibility simmer for a moment, then dismissed it. Nah, he seriously doubted that. He prided himself on being a good judge of character, and it had taken only a few minutes in Julia's company to decide that the woman didn't have a malicious bone in her body.

"I wish there was more we could do for these people," she said, a wistful note entering her voice. "But it's tough. The organization gets most of its funding from private donors, and with the recession, we're not seeing as many donations as we used to. Less money means fewer supplies, fewer staff to hire, less everything."

"But it's better than nothing," he pointed out. "You're doing what you can, Doc, which is more than what other people are doing."

"You're doing something, too," she said with a warm smile. "You're shedding light on the issues, forcing the people back home to open their eyes to the conflicts and inequality and inferior health care others are struggling with."

An arrow of guilt pricked his chest, and for a moment he wished he *was* writing an article, just so he could put another one of those beautiful smiles on Julia's face.

This was damn perplexing. When it came to women, he didn't have a type, per se, not unless *temporary* counted as a type. He didn't do serious or long-term, and Julia Davenport had serious and long-term written all over her. She was a doctor, for chrissake. Doctors were notoriously serious.

And why was he even thinking about this, anyway? He'd come here to interview the woman, not to sleep with her.

His body, however, clearly hadn't received the memo. His cock was semihard beneath the zipper of his cargo pants, and his palms tingled with the urge to undo Julia's braid so his fingers could dive into all those silky brown tresses.

"Sebastian?"

Her amused voice jerked him out of his tasteless thoughts, and he nearly dropped his notebook on the linoleum floor. He made a mad grab for it, only to end up with a paper cut as the notepaper sliced into his thumb.

"Damn," he mumbled, lifting his thumb to his mouth and swiping his tongue over the line of blood forming there.

Julia's hazel eyes sparkled with amusement. "Paper cut?"

Something about her teasing voice snapped him into flirt mode again. "Yup. Wanna patch me up?"

She laughed, but he noticed a light flush rising on her cheeks. "Really? A big tough guy like you is worried about a measly little paper cut?"

"Deathly worried." He slanted his head. "So what do you say, Doc? Will you kiss it and make it better?"

Chapter 2

Julia's heart actually did a somersault. She'd thought that once you turned thirty, your heart didn't do silly schoolgirl things like somersaults, but sure enough, it was flipping around in her chest like an excited dolphin.

Of course, how could her heart *not* turn into a dolphin when the sexiest man she'd ever met was flashing that gorgeous smile at her?

Sebastian Stone was not at all what she'd expected him to be. First of all, he was much more *fit* than she'd pictured, his long, lean body clad in green cargo pants and a thin gray T-shirt that couldn't hide the tight six-pack of his abdomen. He wasn't pretty-boy attractive, but ruggedly handsome, hard lines and angles creating a stark, masculine face that was more Marlboro Man than movie star.

Everything about him teased her senses. His playful gray eyes, the dark blond stubble coating his strong jaw, the woodsy scent of him.

"Cat got your tongue, Doc?"

Jeez, even his voice was sexy. Deep, with a slight rasp to it.

Blinking out of her stupor, Julia glanced at the thumb he'd been holding to his lips. "Sorry, but kissing boo-boos is not part of my job description," she said, making an attempt to keep her tone dry. "But I should probably clean that up for you."

He let out a low laugh. "That's not necessary. It's just a paper cut."

She was already heading for the small cabinet next to the door. "We're in Valero," she replied. "Even paper cuts get infected, and around these parts, infection can lead to some pretty nasty stuff."

She appreciated that Sebastian didn't argue, not even when she rummaged in the cabinet and pulled out a small bottle of antiseptic, a piece of gauze and a bandage.

Heading back to the desk, she hopped up on the edge and gestured at his hand. His dark blond eyebrows quirked for a moment, and then he willingly gave her his hand.

"I know it seems extreme," she admitted as she poured some antiseptic on the gauze and wiped the thin cut on the pad of Sebastian's thumb. "But just suck it up and say thank you."

His eyes twinkled. "Thank you."

A smile lifted the corners of her mouth. "Huh, I didn't think it would be that easy."

"What?"

"You dropping the macho man protests and just accepting my authority."

The grin he flashed her made her heart skip a beat. "I know when to pick my battles."

"Meaning?"

"Meaning you strike me as the type of woman who likes calling the shots and who gets ornery as hell when she's challenged."

"I am," she confessed with a sheepish laugh.

"Like being in control, huh?"

"Of course." She wrinkled her forehead. "Who wants to feel out of control?"

A seductive glint lit his gray eyes. "Lots of people like relinquishing control every now and then." He arched one brow. "Especially in the bedroom…"

Heat scorched her cheeks. God, had he really just said that?

Averting her eyes, Julia swiped the gauze over his thumb one final time before unwrapping the bandage and sticking it on him. In an unnaturally high voice, she squeaked, "All done," and practically vaulted off the desk like she was competing in the Olympics.

His soft laughter tickled her back, which she kept turned as she shoved the supplies into the cabinet. Her heartbeat was going haywire again, and she had to take a moment to collect herself.

What was up with the sexual awareness rippling over every inch of her skin? And she could swear she felt that same awareness being radiated from *him*. Which made no sense.

Sebastian Stone was sexy as all get-out, and a man as blatantly sensual as him would never be attracted to someone like her. She didn't suffer from low self-esteem—she was perfectly content with the way she looked—but she also wasn't delusional enough to think she was a supermodel or anything. Average features, frizzy hair, small breasts. And after six months of working herself ragged in Valero, she was now officially ten pounds underweight. It was hard to find the time to eat when you worked twenty-four hours a day, seven days a week.

Gorgeous and glamorous she wasn't. Nor was she overly feminine. She didn't wear a lick of makeup, kept her hair braided most of the time, and she only donned the professional white coat for patients; the rest of the time, she wore faded jeans, tank tops and beat-up sneakers.

So why was Sebastian looking at her like he wanted to eat her up?

"Sorry, Doc, I don't mean to make you uncomfortable."

His rueful voice stilled some of the butterflies floating around in her stomach. "You didn't," she assured him, finding the courage to meet his eyes.

The second their gazes locked, that hiss of attraction coursed through the air again.

Holy cow. What was going *on?* She'd never experienced this kind of instant, visceral chemistry with a man before, and though she wasn't the type of woman who fell into bed with complete strangers, she honestly couldn't see herself protesting if this man made a move on her.

God, if he marched over and kissed her right now?

She'd probably *let* him.

Swallowing, she broke eye contact and fiddled with

the end of her braid. "Anyway, do you have any more questions? Because, er, I should check on my patients."

With a knowing smile, Sebastian stood up. He rolled his shoulders for a moment, as if being stuck in that tiny chair had done a number on his back. Hell, it probably had, seeing as the man was built like a linebacker.

"I think we're all good." He reached for the tape recorder he'd left on the desk. He clicked it off, then shoved it in his canvas shoulder bag, along with the notebook he'd been scribbling in during the interview.

"So when's the article coming out?" Julia asked, trying for some casual conversation.

"Not sure yet. I don't work for a specific publication, remember? So I'll need to shop the piece around first. I still have your email address, though, so I'll keep you updated."

"Thanks, I'd appreciate that."

They slid out the door and fell into step with each other in the corridor. When they passed two of the volunteers on staff, Julia quickly introduced them to Sebastian, noting how both women cranked their flirt meters up a notch or two in his presence. Apparently she wasn't the only one affected by the waves of magnetism rolling off that big, strong body of his. And he reeked of confidence, walking in a measured gait that was almost a swagger, offering that charming smile to everyone they encountered on the way out of the clinic.

When they finally stepped onto the pillared porch, Julia stifled a sigh of relief. The clinic wasn't tiny by any means, but Sebastian seemed larger than life, and it had been getting hard to breathe walking side by side with him in that narrow hallway.

She inhaled the humid, late-afternoon air, her gaze

sweeping over the dusty courtyard that housed a few rust-covered pickup trucks, the two vans they used for transporting supplies, and the crappy old moped she rode when she visited the more remote settlements to see patients who were too old or sick to travel, or who refused to come into town.

For the past six months, this had been her life. Waking up in the canvas tent she shared with three other female staff members. Treating the patients who came to the clinic and visiting those who couldn't. Sitting inside the mosquito tent with her colleagues every evening, listening to Simone's father strum his guitar, or Kevin Carlisle, the British physician, tell dirty jokes.

At the thought of Kevin, a frown marred her lips, reminding her that the Brit still hadn't returned from his visit to the north. He'd been gone for several days and was due to return sometime this morning, but he'd yet to make an appearance.

"Everything all right?" Sebastian asked, evidently noticing her frown.

"Yeah, it's fine," she said absently. "I'm just making a mental note to radio one of our doctors. He was seeing patients in some neighboring villages, and he was supposed to be back by now."

"Is there reason to worry?"

"Not yet. Kev notoriously loses track of time, so we usually adjust for his tardiness—we take the time he says he'll be somewhere, add five hours, and if he exceeds that, then we're allowed to worry."

Sebastian chuckled. "Sounds like you Doctors International folks are pretty close."

"We are. It's bound to happen when you spend every

waking hour with the same group of people. We're like a family now."

"I know exactly what you mean." He paused for a beat. "In my line of work, you tend to run into the same journalists and media folks and a sense of camaraderie develops."

A short silence descended, during which Julia tried to come up with a way to ask him if he was sticking around for a while, without sounding like she *cared* if he was sticking around for a while. After a moment, she gave up. Screw it. She hated playing games, or saying anything less than what was on her mind.

So she opened her mouth and said, "Are you sticking around in San Marquez for a while?"

A regretful look entered his eyes. "I'm afraid not. I'm on a nine-o'clock flight back to Ecuador."

Disappointment skidded through her, but she hoped it didn't show on her face. She trailed after him toward the older-model Jeep parked a few dozen yards away. She couldn't help but admire his taut ass, which looked ridiculously good in those cargo pants of his.

Oh, boy. She was totally lusting after this man.

And he was leaving. Just her luck.

Sebastian opened the driver's door, but didn't make a move to hop into the Jeep. Instead, he offered an awkward-looking shrug. She got the feeling this man didn't feel awkward or nervous often, and she fought a smile as she watched him shift his feet.

"Thanks for taking the time to talk to me, Doc."

"It was no problem at all."

He cleared his throat. "And if, er, if I find myself in these parts again, maybe I can come see you…"

He trailed off, making it unclear whether that was a question or a statement.

She treated it like the former. "Sure, I'd like that."

Their gazes collided, and there it was again, the crackle of heat, the sizzle of awareness. Her nipples promptly puckered and strained against her white cotton bra, and that spot between her legs throbbed with anticipation. Jeez. You'd think she hadn't had sex in two years or something.

Oh, right. She *hadn't* had sex in two years.

Pushing aside the sarcastic thoughts, she focused on Sebastian, who looked ready to say more. Julia held her breath, waiting for him to speak, but then an indefinable expression washed over his face. She glimpsed reluctance, regret, even a cloud of torment, and before she could try to make sense of it, he slid into the driver's seat and shoved a key in the ignition.

"Keep up the good work, Doc." He raised his voice so she could hear him over the rumble of the engine.

She swallowed another dose of disappointment. "Have a safe flight," she told him, and then she stepped away from the vehicle and raised her hand in a wave.

The Jeep raised a cloud of brown dust as Sebastian executed a U-turn and sped toward the gravel road that would lead him back to civilization.

"Who was *that?*"

Julia turned around in time to see Lissa Purdue descending the porch steps and striding in her direction. Out of all the staff at the clinic, she was closest with Lissa, the fun-loving Australian nurse she'd been bunking with for the past six months.

"That was that journalist I told you about," Julia answered, her eyes still focused on the Jeep, which was slowly disappearing from view.

"For real? Because that was one crazy-hot bloke."

She sighed. "Yes, he was."

Lissa's jaw fell open. "No way. The perpetually professional Dr. Davenport is showing not-so-professional interest in a bloke? Are you ill, love?"

She rolled her eyes, but she couldn't very well argue. It was true, the opposite sex hadn't interested her much since she'd arrived on the island. While some of the other women—Lissa included—had no qualms about flirting with the single males in their vicinity, Julia made an effort to keep things professional.

There were several attractive men working at the clinic, including Kevin Carlisle and Simone's single father, Marcus, but Julia wasn't one to mess around with a coworker. During her last placement in Ethiopia, she'd watched two colleagues fall in love—and then she'd witnessed the relationship crash and burn, making life downright unbearable for everyone who'd had the misfortune of being around.

Unfortunately, with her coworkers off-limits, she didn't have many other options in terms of sex or romance. Aside from the cute pilot who dropped off supplies every two months, there were no other single, eligible men to lust over.

"You should've asked him to stay for dinner," Lissa added, slinging an arm around Julia's shoulder.

At six feet, Lissa towered over Julia's five-foot-five frame. Some of the men on staff teased the Aussie about her monstrous height, but truth was, everyone was a little bit in awe of Lissa. Now *Lissa* would definitely be

Sebastian Stone's type. A tall, gorgeous redhead with a great rack and endless legs?

Call her selfish, but Julia was kind of glad Sebastian had already left before Lissa came outside. No doubt the man would have been drooling all over his hiking boots.

"He had a flight to catch," she replied as the two women headed inside.

"Pity. You could've benefited from a good shag."

Julia burst out laughing. "Why are you so concerned with my sex life? Seriously, you talk about it a scary amount."

"I just don't like seeing my mates work themselves to the bone, love. I wish you'd let yourself have some fun."

"I'll have fun in three months."

She neglected to mention how incredibly *not* fun the thought of heading home was, but because Doctors International demanded mandatory breaks between placements, she had no choice but to return to Boston when her time was up.

The nine-months-on, three-months-off cycle was liable to kill her. She'd joined D.I. the second she'd finished her residency, and she'd been with the organization for three years now. She was already dreading returning to Boston and twiddling her thumbs for twelve weeks while she waited for her next cycle to begin. She usually spent the time off taking shifts at a colleague's private practice and counting the days until she could go overseas again.

"Anyway," she added as they headed for the small nurses' station past the waiting room, "you can have fun for the both of us." She grinned. "That is, if you're still planning on seducing Kev?"

"Definitely," Lissa declared, her vivid green eyes

shining with mischief. "The second you and Marcus graciously bestow me with a night off, I will be sneaking into Dr. Carlisle's tent and finally putting us both out of our misery."

"You have been dancing around each other for six months now. It's about time."

"Exactly." Lissa pulled out the elastic restraining her hair and retied the curly red strands in a fresh ponytail. "I'll see you later, love. Sally needs help with those vaccinations."

Julia watched the nurse bounce off in her usual lively fashion. Earlier, when she'd told Sebastian that her colleagues were her family, she hadn't been kidding. Lissa truly had become like a sister to her. Kevin was her teasing older brother. Marcus was the father figure she'd lacked her entire life. Helga, the midwife on staff, was the sweet grandmother who handed out endless words of wisdom.

With both her father and sister gone, Julia was all alone in the world. Sure, she still had her mother, but the two of them had never been close, and once Darlene moved to the West Coast a few years back, they'd completely lost touch. Not that Julia was beat-up over it—Darlene Davenport was a cold, self-absorbed woman without a single maternal bone in her body, and Julia was better off without her.

"Jules, I need you in here."

Shifting her gaze, she caught sight of Nadir Patel poking his head out of an exam room. Along with Julia, Kevin and Marcus, Nadir was the fourth physician on staff. In his native India, he had run a thriving pediatrics practice, so he was responsible for dealing with the younger patients in Valero.

"Everything okay?" she called.

"I'm attempting to take a blood sample and our patient is a tad cranky. Perhaps you could lend a hand?"

A loud, petulant wail came from the exam room, telling Julia that Nadir's patient was more than a *tad* cranky.

"Sure thing," she called back.

Ten minutes later, she'd successfully assisted Nadir in drawing blood from the bawling two-year-old. Afterward, she went to check on her own patients, pleased to see that many of the ones who'd come in complaining of malaria-like symptoms were no longer showing signs of the parasite. She still couldn't release them until the blood test results were in, but she was fairly confident they weren't looking at a serious outbreak.

For the next three hours, she bustled around the clinic, doing everything from stitching up patients to changing bedpans. Her white coat might label her a doctor, but the clinic was so understaffed that the responsibility lines blurred significantly, and Julia often found herself being not just a doctor, but also a nurse, a surgeon, a janitor, a cook, a babysitter or any other job that cropped up.

It was no surprise that by the time nine o'clock rolled by she was ready to collapse. Because she was on the evening shift, she hadn't eaten dinner with her colleagues. She'd scarfed down a can of cold beans during a break between patients, and her stomach rumbled with hunger by the time she shrugged out of her coat and left the clinic through the back doors.

The D.I. staff lived in heavy canvas tents behind the building. There were four large tents, two for the men, two for the women, which housed six cots each, and along with those, there were a few smaller tents for people with special circumstances; one for Simone, and the others were reserved for the married staff.

She strode to the tent she shared with Lissa and two other nurses—Kendra, a lovely African-American woman from Detroit, and Marie-Thérèse, a young French blonde right out of nursing school.

Kendra was passed out on one of the cots, so Julia tried to be quiet as she sank onto the edge of her cot. She dimmed the battery-operated lamp so as not to disturb the sleeping nurse, then opened one of the two drawers and pulled out her toiletry kit.

As tired as she was, she wanted a cool shower before bed to wash off the heat and grime of the day. There was a bathroom and shower area behind the tents, which they shared with the men. Not that it mattered much in such primitive conditions, but a schedule had been arranged to preserve the modesty of those who actually still cared about things like that. Julia was always far too exhausted to worry about who might see her naked.

She stood up with her toiletries in hand, then froze when the radio on the night stand began to crackle. Shooting a quick look at Kendra, she grabbed the radio and hurried out of the tent, ducking through the flap.

Outside, the small recreation area was deserted, and she headed for the long picnic-style tables where the staff usually congregated for meals.

"J-J-Julia…c-can…h-hear me?"

She could barely make out the tinny voice emerging from the speakers, but it sounded like Kevin's. Her brows furrowed as it suddenly occurred to her that he still hadn't come back.

As more static hissed out of the radio, she clicked the button and said, "Kevin, is that you?"

"J-Julia…"

She heard him more clearly this time. Relief swept through her. All right, at least he was still in one piece. He'd probably decided to spend the night in one of the villages rather than trek it back to the clinic in the dark.

"Kev, do you read me? Where are you?"

"I…village…Esperanza…"

Julia frowned. "Esperanza? Why did you go so far north?"

More static, followed by what sounded like a round of heavy coughing. "Things…h-here…bad."

For the first time since she'd heard her colleague's voice, a real pang of concern tugged at her gut. "Kev? What's going on there?"

"I…t-treatment…don't know…never seen it before."

Unease circled her spine like a school of sharks. Her palms started to tingle as a wave of panic swelled inside her.

"The water…maybe…don't know." Kevin sounded more anguished, and his British accent grew more pronounced, the way it always did when he was upset. "B-bad, Jules…Don't know wh-what's wrong with me…stay away."

Those last two words sent a chill through her body.

"Y-you hear me, Julia? D-don't come here." He repeated himself, more desperate now. "Don't…come… here."

And then the radio fell silent.

Chapter 3

"You're at a *church?* You're kidding, right?" The incredulous voice of Second Lieutenant Nick Prescott blared out of the satellite phone.

Chuckling, Sebastian swept his gaze over the single-story brick building a hundred yards away. Two simple wooden crosses were the only hints that it was a church, one adorning the door, the other affixed on the roof. A yellow glow spilled out of the window at the side of the structure, telling Sebastian that the elderly priest who'd shown him hospitality was still awake in his quarters.

"No joke," he replied. "Though technically I'm in a barn."

He glanced behind him at the darkened entrance of the little barn he'd be spending the night in. He'd already scouted the area to make sure it was safe, and now he was looking forward to collapsing on the big pile of hay in that empty stall and falling asleep listening to the snorts and neighs of the priest's two Appaloosa mares.

"So you ran out of gas, and instead of hiking to the nearest gas station, you decided to spend the night in the San Marquez countryside?" Nick's confusion only seemed to deepen. "And since when do you not carry an extra gas can with you? You're like the poster boy for *always prepared*."

"I had an extra can," he muttered, swallowing a rush of frustration. "Someone stole it. Most likely one of the patients at the clinic, because I can't imagine anyone on staff robbing the reporter who's there to write a story about them."

And if he hadn't been so distracted by Julia Davenport's big hazel eyes, maybe he would have noticed the missing gas container when he was leaving the clinic.

Fortunately, once the Jeep could no longer run on fumes, at least it had the decency to break down near this church.

"Fine. That doesn't explain why you're not walking to the gas station as we speak."

Sebastian stifled a sigh. He couldn't explain why he needed this respite. It didn't make much sense—he definitely couldn't afford to be lazy right now. Unless he wanted to spend the rest of his life on the run, he needed to find out who wanted him dead, and to do that, he had to learn everything he could about Project Aries and the mysterious virus Richard Harrison had been testing on those villagers.

But this was the first time in a long time he'd been alone. Without Tate or Nick lurking around, without that feeling of urgency weighing down on him. Not that the situation was any less urgent. It was as critical as ever. It just didn't feel so...*smothering* at the moment.

A part of him wished he *had* stuck around in Valero, maybe talked Julia Davenport into having a cup of coffee with him.

Oh, fine, who was he kidding? He would have talked her into *going to bed* with him.

He'd been thinking about the woman all damn night, and he still couldn't figure out how a skinny, overworked doctor could get his blood going like this. Hell, he'd barely even blinked when he'd met the drop-dead gorgeous Eva Dolce last month, and Eva oozed sex appeal. Julia Davenport was pretty, sure, but she wasn't sex incarnate or anything.

So why had he been having *X*-rated thoughts about the woman ever since he'd left the clinic?

A sigh lodged in his throat. It was probably a good thing he hadn't stuck around. Sex had the power to be distracting as hell, and at the moment, he couldn't afford any distractions.

"I'll catch a boat tomorrow morning," he told Nick. "There's no reason for me to rush, anyway. This malaria thing was a false alarm."

"It would help if we knew what symptoms to look for. We don't know a damn thing about the virus that killed those people in Corazón." Nick grumbled in aggravation. "Are you sure Cruz didn't offer any other details about the state of those bodies?"

"You can keep asking that question a hundred more times, Prescott, but it won't change the damn answer. Cruz said the only visible signs of illness were nosebleeds and some foaming at the mouth. That's it."

The irony of the situation didn't escape him. All the

information they had on the virus had come from a source that could hardly be considered trustworthy—Hector Cruz, the former leader of the ULF, who was now very much dead thanks to Tate. But although Cruz had been responsible for killing Tate's brother during that ill-fated mission in Corazón, the rebel leader had insisted that he hadn't laid a finger on his countrymen and women, whose dead bodies had been strewn all over the village.

Cruz and his men had apparently burned the bodies in case they were contagious, but Sebastian still wished he'd seen the evidence of a disease with his own eyes rather than having to take a dead man's word for it.

"Well, it probably isn't something that's found in nature," Nick was saying, still sounding incredibly irritated. "Harrison headed up the biological weapons department at D&M Initiative, so we have to assume the virus he was testing was manufactured."

Sebastian let out a breath. "Yeah, and it's probably a mutated strain of something or other, which means it's doubtful there's an existing vaccine for it."

Nick's answering breath was equally glum. "Can't be government-sanctioned either. President Howard has been firm about his position on the manufacturing of biological weapons."

Unlike his glass-half-full counterpart, Sebastian was far more cynical. "Oh, this is government. But my guess is Mr. President knows nothing about it. I think we've got a bad apple trying to poison the rest of the tree."

"Maybe." Nick mumbled an uncharacteristic curse. "Look, just get your ass back here, Seb. Eva and her hacker friend are looking into Project Aries and trying to find out who worked on it. Once we have some names, Tate says you and I should go stateside and do some digging."

His brows shot up. "The captain actually thinks it's safe for us to go home?"

"The captain is tired of being on the run, and anxious to marry the love of his life," Nick replied dryly.

"And perfectly willing to risk *our* necks to make it happen, I see." The remark was only half-serious. He knew that Captain Robert Tate would gladly sacrifice his own life for his men, and Sebastian wholly returned the sentiment. Tate and Nick were the only friends he had in this godforsaken world.

"Okay, well, let me get back first and we'll figure out our next move from there," he said.

"Sounds good. Be careful, Seb."

"Always am, Nicky."

He disconnected the call and shoved the sat phone into his waterproof duffel, then slung the bag over his shoulder and headed for the open doorway of the unlit barn.

He was just crossing the threshold when the whir of helicopter rotors echoed in the air. Narrowing his eyes, Sebastian gazed up at the inky sky, and sure enough, glimpsed bluish lights winking amid the black backdrop. A second later, a military chopper whizzed overhead, followed by a second chopper, and then a third.

Huh. Well, *that* couldn't be good.

No sooner had the bleak thought entered his mind than the sound of car engines rumbled in the night air.

He didn't bother ducking out of sight; he was shrouded by shadows, so nobody would be able to spot him all the way from the road. Chewing on the inside of his cheek, he watched as half a dozen Jeeps sped along the one-lane dirt road. He couldn't make out individual passengers, but the sea of navy blue-and-gold uniforms said it all. San Marquez military.

"Now where are you hurrying off to, boys?" he murmured, eyeing the scene in interest.

Probably some skirmish with the ULF that needed to be handled, or at least that was what he guessed until he noticed three black medic vans sandwiched between the passing Jeeps. The vans were the equivalent of an American ambulance, yet the sirens weren't wailing, and the headlights were off.

Sebastian frowned. If the military was responding to an emergency, why go out of its way to make the ambulances *less* conspicuous? They should be plowing full speed ahead, lights flashing and sirens shrieking.

Unless the military didn't want anyone to know there was a medical emergency in progress…

As his shoulders stiffened, Sebastian moved away from the barn with purposeful strides. He took two steps in the direction of his Jeep before remembering that the damn thing was out of gas.

"Damn it," he muttered.

Because he knew for a fact that the priest didn't own a car, he had no way of following that military convoy. Not unless he did it on foot, which would be pointless. By the time he tracked the soldiers, whatever emergency they were racing toward could be yesterday's news.

Crap. He needed a vehicle. He scanned his brain, trying to remember if there were any cars at that farm he'd spotted five or six miles east of the church. Or he could always jog back to the Doctors International clinic and steal one of the pickups that had been parked out front, but the clinic was a good two hours away, so—

A loud snort interrupted his thoughts.

Sebastian glanced at the barn, his jaw tensing as he realized the solution to his problem was right beyond that door.

But… Crap. Would he be signing his own ticket to hell if he stole a horse from a priest?

A heavy sigh slipped out. Yeah, probably.

Not to mention that he hadn't been on horseback since…damn, since an eighth-grade trip to that dude ranch in Wyoming.

But, hey, like riding a bike, right?

Decision made, he strode into the barn and made a beeline for the first horse stall. Twenty minutes later, the healthier-looking of the two mares was saddled up and Sebastian was leading the spotted Appaloosa out of her stall.

He made sure to leave five-hundred American dollars on a bale of hay where the old priest would be sure to find it.

"I'm going with you," Lissa declared, her green eyes glittering with fortitude.

"You're staying here," Julia corrected. She shoved a spare flashlight into her backpack, along with an extra package of batteries.

"Jules—"

"Don't argue with me about this, Lis. Everyone else just got off a forty-eight-hour shift, and Kevin isn't here. With me gone, that leaves only Nadir and Marie-Thérèse to run the entire clinic by themselves tonight. They need you."

A frustrated breath flew out of Lissa's mouth. "Fine. But radio me the second you get there."

"I will," she promised.

She zipped up her bag and marched out of the supply room, with Lissa hot on her heels.

"Did Kev say what the emergency was?" Lissa asked.

"No. He didn't say much of anything." She pretended to adjust the straps of her bag, just so she wouldn't have to meet the nurse's eyes.

Don't come here.

Kevin's ominous warning continued to buzz in her mind like a persistent fly, and she couldn't seem to swat it away. She wanted to tell Lissa about what Kev had said, but she didn't want to raise a panic. Besides, the radio had been so static-riddled that she might have misheard him.

Don't come here. Ha. Fat chance. Did he honestly think he could say something like that and she'd actually abide by it? If her friend and colleague was in trouble, there was no chance of Julia staying away.

"I'll take one of the trucks," she said, swiping a set of keys from the bulletin board near the front door. "It'll get me there faster than my moped."

Lissa still looked unhappy as the two women stepped outside. "Drive carefully, love. And contact the clinic the moment you reach Esperanza."

"I will."

She slid into the cab of the pickup and stuck the key in the ignition. It took a few tries for the engine of the old truck to chug to life.

Poking her head out the open window, she waved at the redhead and managed a smile loaded with encouragement she certainly didn't feel. "I'll call you when I get there."

It was pitch-black out as Julia made her way to the

main road. The weak glow of the pickup's headlights didn't offer much help in lighting the way, but fortunately, she knew these roads like the back of her hand. For the past six months, she'd ridden her moped all over this region, but she still forced herself not to speed as she drove north. Hardly any of the locals who lived around here owned cars, but it wasn't uncommon for a herd of goats, or a stray cat or dog, to dart into the middle of the road.

Esperanza was about seventy miles northwest in the remote woodlands at the base of the mountain. During the day, the drive would take only an hour or so, but with the low visibility and reduced speed, Julia ended up nearing the little settlement almost two hours later.

Because she hadn't been able to see more than five feet in front of her during the entire drive, the sudden burst of light that came out of nowhere hurt her eyes.

Squinting, she gaped at the unexpected sight before her.

Military vehicles formed a barricade in the middle of the road, and upright floodlights had been set up in various spots to illuminate the area. Soldiers moved around with purpose, their murmured voices wafting into the open window of her truck. The uniforms identified the men as San Marquez military, but amid the blue and gold she also saw…green?

Her eyes widened as she realized precisely what she was looking at. Americans. Those were *American* soldiers.

And every single person wore a white surgical mask over his face.

"What the…" She trailed off, unable to tear her eyes off the confusing chaos up ahead.

Seeing as she couldn't exactly go straight, Julia pressed her foot on the brake and jerked the gearshift into Park, just as a shout rang out.

The next thing she knew, four soldiers were swarming her pickup like crazed fans surrounding a celebrity's limousine. The driver's door was thrown open, someone grabbed her arm, and her sneakers landed on the gravel with a thud.

"What are you— Let go of me!" she ordered when a strong male hand circled her upper arm and squeezed it hard. She shrugged the hand off and staggered backward.

"Who are you?" one of the soldiers demanded. She couldn't see his mouth beneath that surgical mask, but his blue eyes were as cold as an Arctic ice cap, and he'd spoken to her in English. "What are you doing here?"

"I'm Dr. Julia Davenport. A colleague of mine was supposed to—"

Her voice died abruptly as she suddenly noticed something up ahead in the distance.

She wrinkled her brow, trying to make sense of that head-scratching visual. Was that a big pile of garbage bags? What the hell were these soldiers doing with— Body bags. Oh, God. Those were *body bags*.

As horror whipped up her spine, Julia's gaze flew to the first person she saw. It happened to be a beefy African-American soldier with shuttered brown eyes and a thick black mustache poking out from the top of his mask.

"What's going on here?" she asked, her voice sounding far calmer than she felt.

The man didn't answer. Rather, he grabbed her arm

and forcibly moved her away from her truck. "Please come with us, ma'am," he said in a monotone voice.

Outrage slammed into her. "What? *No.* I'm not going anywhere until you tell me what's going on here."

Her protest was ignored. The grip on her arm tightened.

"I'm an American citizen!" she blurted out. "You can't just detain me for no reason! I haven't done anything wrong, damn it!"

She was still shouting out protests as the soldiers dragged her away.

Chapter 4

"What is your business here?"

Julia was grinding her teeth so hard that she was surprised the enamel hadn't yet filed away to dust. If they asked her that question one more time, she was absolutely going to scream.

For the past hour and a half, she'd been detained in a canvas tent, sitting on an uncomfortable metal chair in the middle of the dirt floor. The chair was the only piece of furniture in the tent, which lent the space a seriously ominous feel. She wasn't bound, she wasn't gagged, but the two guards at the entrance and the two soldiers looming over her made it clear that she was a prisoner here.

She had no frickin' clue what was going on, but it sure as hell wasn't good. Those body bags out there... Oh, God, and where was Kevin? Where were the people? As she'd been dragged through the village toward the tents set up near the tree line, all she'd seen were soldiers.

Esperanza was deserted. No signs of life. None.

"Answer the question, please."

Tightening her lips, she met the masked face of one of the soldiers, a tall man who carried himself with so much authority that she knew he must be the one in charge. The surgical masks everyone wore definitely indicated there was some sort of medical emergency in progress, but because nobody was wearing full hazmat suits, she deduced that the mysterious disease that had triggered these precautions probably wasn't airborne.

"I already answered your question," she said tersely. "My name is Julia Davenport. I'm a doctor and I run the clinic in Valero. I came here to check on my colleague, Dr. Kevin Carlisle."

"At this hour of the night?" Suspicion lined the man's tone. When he crossed his arms over his broad chest, her gaze was drawn to the four stars on the shoulders of his uniform.

She scanned her brain, trying to remember what that signified. Holy crap, he was a *general*.

Which spoke volumes about the importance of this interrogation.

Angrier than she'd ever been, Julia met her captor's eyes. "How many more times do I have to answer these same questions? I told you, Dr. Carlisle radioed me. It sounded like an emergency. I was worried. I drove up here to check on him. The end."

"Watch your tone," the second soldier ordered.

She shifted her gaze to him, noting that he looked younger than his counterpart and wore a uniform without any insignia. "Oh, gee, was I being rude? Are your other prisoners more polite and agreeable than I am?"

"You're not a prisoner," the general replied, sounding annoyed.

"Oh, no?" Arching a brow, she rose from her chair.

The two soldiers guarding the door instantly snapped the barrels of their assault rifles in her direction, their body language becoming menacing.

"That's what I thought," she said coolly, then sank back down.

The general's lips tightened. "Let's not play games, Dr. Davenport. I need to—"

"Games?" she interrupted. "Are you *kidding* me? This isn't a game, for Pete's sake! Where is my colleague? Why is the village overflowing with body bags?"

As expected, she didn't receive an answer. Just another question.

"Did you inform any of the staff at the Valero clinic that you were coming up here?"

"No."

The lie came out smoothly, and there'd been no hesitation on her part. Somehow, she'd known that answering yes to that would be the worst possible thing she could do. As it was, she'd only officially told Lissa about her plans, but the nurse had undoubtedly filled the others in after Julia had left. Maybe it was her paranoia talking, but she had the sinking feeling that these men would send a team of soldiers to the clinic if they thought she'd said anything to her coworkers.

"You left Valero without telling anyone?" The younger soldier looked unconvinced.

"I was alone in my tent when Dr. Carlisle's distress

call came in," she answered. "My colleagues had their hands full in the clinic with some potential malaria patients, so I just left. I planned on radioing them when I reached Esperanza."

The men exchanged a look, and then the general gave an imperceptible nod that made Julia's heart drop to the pit of her stomach. They knew she was lying. Crap.

She decided to distract them. "Why are you wearing masks?" she demanded.

"That is none of your concern," the general said stiffly.

"Are you kidding me?" she said again, as amazed as she was outraged. "I'm a doctor, and you're clearly worried that there's been an outbreak of something. Is it a bacterium? How is it transmitted?"

"Dr. Davenport, we are the ones asking the questions here. Now please tell us, who in Valero knows you came here?"

Disbelief spiraled through her. She shook her head a couple of times, wondering how any of this could possibly be happening, but the more she tried to make sense of the situation, the more afraid she became. Her palms dampened, her body growing cold. Something really, really bad was going on here.

God, Kevin, where are you?

"Dr. Davenport," the general snapped.

"No," she snapped back.

He faltered. "No, what?"

"I'm not answering any more questions until I speak to a lawyer." She scowled at him. "Or to someone who's willing to give me some answers of my own."

Then she shut her mouth, crossed her arms over her chest and glared at the two men hovering over her.

After a moment, the general spun on his heel and stalked toward the tent's entrance. The younger soldier quickly trailed after him.

Both men exited the tent, as did the two guards, but she didn't fool herself into believing that the latter had gone far. She suspected the guards were right outside those canvas flaps, ready to shoot her down if she tried to escape.

Escape.

What on earth was going *on?*

And why was she starting to suspect that the only way she was getting out of here would be in one of those body bags lying on the dirt?

Sebastian watched in growing alarm as more body bags were tossed into the back of the wide-load trucks parked at the entrance of the village. He'd counted thirty-five bags in the first truck, and another forty-one in the second. Had to be the villagers. Christ. More dead villagers.

The soldiers in charge of disposal efficiently carried out their task without comment or expression. Sebastian swallowed a rush of disgust, wondering how they justified it to themselves. Probably assured themselves they were good little soldiers simply following orders, and who were they to question *orders?*

His jaw tightened. Brought to mind all those soldiers in Nazi Germany—they hadn't questioned much either, had they?

Battling his rising fury, Sebastian crept deeper into the forest, moving through the shadows like a nocturnal predator. Being a black ops soldier meant he possessed the power of invisibility, the ability to sneak right underneath these men's noses, even slit their throats without anyone knowing he was ever there.

Through the trees, he espied a cluster of khaki-colored tents. The men in charge had set up a headquarters of some sort, and that was the place to be if he wanted answers. The strap of his M4 was slung over his shoulder, but he didn't reach for the rifle. Rather, he slipped a lethal hunting knife from the sheath on his hip and gripped the ox-bone handle with ease. If he had to eliminate a guard, he preferred to do it quietly.

He neared an opening in the brush and pressed himself up against the rotting bark of a rosewood tree. His position offered a line of sight to the entrance of a tent that two uniformed men had just emerged from. They were tailed by two heavily armed soldiers, and the uniforms marked all four as American. The entire village was crawling with both U.S. and San Marquez military, indisputable evidence that some sort of joint task force was in effect.

His stomach went rigid as he thought of those body bags. Task force? No, make that joint *cleanup crew.*

"She's lying."

The muffled voice drifted toward him, uttered by— holy hell, a United States Army general. Christ, they'd sent someone that high on the totem pole to handle this cleanup? This was bigger than he'd thought.

He inched closer, struggling to make out the conversation occurring twenty yards away.

"…to Valero. Question the staff, see what Carlisle told them."

"…necessary? And to contain that many people?"

"Easier if…"

Sebastian's gut swam with uneasiness. He needed to get closer.

Adjusting his grip on the knife, he moved without making a solitary sound, finding cover behind another tree, this one with low-hanging branches that allowed him to blend into the darkness.

"...the clinic will be handled."

The clinic? Waves of foreboding crawled up his spine, moving faster and gathering in intensity when the general uttered a very familiar name.

"Davenport needs to be handled, too."

Sebastian's shoulders became stiffer than a block of marble. Davenport? As in *Julia* Davenport? As in the woman he'd spoken to only hours ago?

"...won't be hard. Her death could be blamed on the virus."

The general seemed to mull it over. "Carlisle was checking on patients when he died."

"We'll say she was here, too. Making the rounds with Carlisle."

"The powers that be won't like this. Two dead American doctors? This won't look good." There was a savage curse. "But that's what they get for releasing Meridian this close to a damn international medical facility. Who was the genius who made *that* call?"

Meridian? Sebastian filed away the word as he watched the duo move away from the tent.

The general glanced at the soldiers manning the entrance. "If she tries to run, shoot her," he ordered.

Sebastian's body was strung tighter than a drum as the two men stalked off. If what he'd heard was accurate, then Julia Davenport was inside that tent. How the hell had *that* happened?

The colleague. Crap. She must have driven up here to check on her colleague, that Kevin guy she'd been worried about earlier.

Her death could be blamed on the virus.

His next breath came out ragged as a jolt of anger slammed into his gut. These bastards were planning to kill Julia and blame it on the virus.

No way.

No freaking way would he allow that to happen.

She's not your objective.

The nagging little voice only further pissed him off. He knew that rescuing the doctor wasn't his responsibility. Hell, all the mayhem and confusion of the past ten months was a direct result of his unit's attempt to rescue a *doctor.* But Harrison's death was no sweat off his back, not after they'd discovered the man was treating humans like lab rats.

But Julia Davenport? He'd be damned if he was going to let her become another casualty of that goddamn virus. So yes, he ought to be gathering more intel, listening in on more conversations, attempting to get a peek inside one of those body bags, but Sebastian was more than willing to give up any insight he'd find if it meant saving the smart, sassy woman who'd made his body burn today.

The soft hissing sound brought a frown to Julia's lips. She twisted around in the chair, trying to pinpoint where the noise had come from. She strained her ears, but the sound had stopped.

Tssssss.

Her forehead creased. Okay, what *was* that?

For a second she wondered if her captors had let

loose a poisonous snake in the tent or something. As her heartbeat quickened, she shot to her feet and examined the ground, but she didn't see a rattler crawling on the dirt.

Tssssss.

She spun around, gaping when she noticed a line slowly appearing in the tent wall.

Someone was cutting the canvas!

Fear and astonishment warred inside her, but the latter quickly overtook the former when a large hand poked through the slit in the tent and a familiar pair of silver eyes suddenly locked with hers.

Julia gasped. "Seba—" Her jaw snapped closed when he swiftly held his index finger to his lips.

A million questions ambushed her brain, but even if he hadn't ordered her to remain quiet, she suspected she wouldn't have been able to make her vocal cords work anymore. She was too dumbfounded.

The man who slipped into the tent like a ghost was not the same one she remembered from Valero. Gone were the casual pants and T-shirt. Now he wore a skin-tight black shirt that clung to the rippled muscles of his broad chest, and black cargo pants encased his long legs. He had black boots on his feet, and a nasty-looking rifle slung over one shoulder, though not as nasty as that blade he skillfully wielded in his hand.

Julia gulped as the sharp steel of the knife winked in the light from the electric lanterns illuminating the tent.

She was looking into the eyes of a warrior. The playful, sensual twinkle from before had vanished. Sebastian Stone was all business now, those gray eyes grim with fierce determination. Waves of strength and danger rolled off his powerful body, making her mouth go dry.

Without a word, he walked toward her and cupped her chin with one hand.

She jumped, then relaxed when she saw the unspoken question in his gaze.

Are you okay?

Julia managed a shaky nod. God, what was he doing here?

And why did she get the feeling that this man was the *furthest* thing from a freelance journalist?

Sebastian took her arm and led her to the slit he'd created in the tent. "Stay close," he murmured, his voice so low it was barely audible. "If I say move, move. If I say stop, stop. Do exactly what I tell you, do you understand?"

She stared at him, wide-eyed. And then her pulse took off.

Wait a minute—he was helping her *escape?*

"This entire village is crawling with soldiers," she whispered with a violent shake of her head. "They'll shoot us if we try to run."

"They'll kill you if you stay."

You. Not *us.* She didn't miss the distinction, and she suddenly grew queasy. There wasn't an ounce of confusion on Sebastian's rugged face, only focused intensity, which told her he must know a hell of a lot more about what was going on here than she did.

So maybe it would be prudent to listen to the man instead of arguing about his plans.

He reached behind him and pulled a black handgun from his waistband. "Do you know how to use one of these?"

She nodded.

He promptly shoved the weapon in her hands. "Good."

Her heart pounded a frantic beat in her chest as she watched Sebastian carefully part the canvas to peer out. He seemed satisfied by what he saw, because he ducked back in and shot her a firm look.

"Stay on my six, Doc. Do everything I say, and we'll both get out of this alive."

Julia had never been more terrified in her entire life as she followed Sebastian out of the makeshift escape route. Darkness immediately enveloped them, disorienting her for a moment. She breathed in the night air, a combination of earth and pine and decay, but then she caught a whiff of something else, something woodsy, musky. Sebastian. Despite the fact that she was scared for her life, that masculine scent actually made her heart skip a beat.

Go away, hormones, she ordered. *I'm trying not to die here.*

A hysterical laugh got stuck in her throat. Oh, God, how was any of this happening?

The back of the tent was perfectly positioned directly in front of the woods, and Julia stuck to Sebastian like glue as they crept toward the trees. For some inexplicable reason, she explicitly trusted the man leading the way. She had every intention of following him blindly and doing anything he asked without question, and that scared her almost as much as everything else that had happened thus far.

She kept her gaze on Sebastian, noticing how the strong muscles of his back flexed with each precise step he took. She was so focused on him, in fact, that she didn't notice the two bodies lying in the dirt until she'd almost tripped over them.

A squeak flew out, ending prematurely when Sebastian's warm hand clapped over her mouth to silence her. "Easy, Doc," he murmured.

Her heart began racing again, and now her palms were shaking. She immediately recognized the dead men—the two guards who'd been in the tent. She stared at their green uniforms, those lifeless eyes, the thin red lines slashing across their throats. Then her gaze shifted to the knife in Sebastian's hand.

Why hadn't she noticed before that the blade was stained red?

Oh, God. He'd *killed* these men.

He caught her eye, his expression grim. "Kill or be killed, Julia." Those soft words didn't alleviate her panic, only increased it.

It occurred to her that she knew absolutely nothing about the man she'd entrusted with her life, but when she looked into those silver eyes, she saw no malice. No threat. Only a glint of fortitude and unexpected concern.

Taking a breath, she tore her gaze from the motionless bodies on the dirt, but not before she spotted the plastic water bottle poking out from one of the soldier's pockets.

The water...maybe...don't know.

Kevin's words rushed into the forefront of her brain. The water, he'd said. Had he meant there was something in the water? Bacteria? A virus?

"We have to go back," she blurted out.

Sebastian's face filled with disbelief, and then he gave a stern shake of his head. "No way."

Ignoring him, Julia dashed toward the dead soldier. She grabbed the water bottle and twisted off the cap, promptly pouring out the remaining liquid on the ground. Sebastian stalked over, visibly aggravated.

"They'll have men swarming this entire mountain the second they realize you're gone," he said in a low voice. "We have to go, Doc. Now."

She stubbornly lifted her chin. "Not until I get some water."

"Oh, for the love of—"

"A water sample," she clarified. "We need a sample of the water. There's a well on the eastern edge of the village. That's where Esperanza's drinking supply comes from."

His brows furrowed, and then understanding dawned on his face. "You think there's something in the water."

"Kevin— Dr. Carlisle, my colleague, he said something about the water when he radioed." Frustration seized her body. "They'll try to cover this up, Sebastian. I can't let them do that. I *need* that water."

After a moment, he released a resigned breath, then snatched the bottle right out of her hand. "C'mere," he ordered, grabbing her arm and dragging her away.

"No," she protested. "I can't go until I get—"

"I'll get you the damn sample. Now, come here."

He led her to a thick cluster of tangled vegetation and practically threw her into it. "Stay out of sight. If I'm not back in five minutes, run."

He was gone before she could blink.

Julia crouched in the cramped space, gulping hard, trying to ease the terror clamped like an angry fist around her throat.

She couldn't believe Sebastian had gone back for a water sample. With those alpha-male vibes he was throwing off, she'd expected him to haul her over his shoulder and forcibly cart her away, yet he'd actually taken the time to listen to her. And now he was risking his life to carry out the task she'd been ready to do herself.

Her gaze kept darting to the watch strapped to her wrist. One minute passed. Two. Three.

If I'm not back in five minutes, run.

"Yeah, right," she muttered to herself.

If Sebastian didn't return in five minutes, she was going *back* for him. The man had risked his life to break her out of that camp, and he just expected her to abandon him? Fat chance.

When she heard a rustling sound, she shrank deeper into her hiding place and held her breath.

"It's me, Doc," came his raspy voice. "Time to go."

She slid out of the brush and joined him, eyeing the full bottle in his hand. "You went to the well?"

He nodded. "Is this enough of a sample, you think?"

"Should be more than enough."

"Good. Now let's get the hell out of here. They don't know you're gone yet, but those two guards I incapacitated will be missed soon."

"Incapacitated?" she echoed. "Is that what you like to call it? Because those men look more *dead* than incapacitated."

He didn't so much as flinch from the verbal jab. "What do we call saving your ass these days? Oh, right, *saving your ass,*" he said sarcastically, and then he took off walking.

Julia wasn't sure if she wanted to laugh or cry. There was no denying that this man had just saved her life.

But there was also no ignoring that he'd taken two other lives in the process.

Shoving aside the menacing reminder, she followed Sebastian, and they made their way through the forest. Their soft breathing and the crackle of twigs beneath their feet were the only sounds in the otherwise still air. At one point, Sebastian ordered her to stay put, disappeared in the shadows, and returned a moment later with a black duffel bag, which he must have stashed earlier, and then he slung the bag over his shoulder and signaled that they were resuming the trek. The temperature was dropping, making Julia grateful for the long-sleeved plaid shirt she'd worn over her tank top. She was glad for the sneakers, too, because they made walking in this mountainous terrain much easier.

But the longer they walked, the more concerned she got, until finally she couldn't hold her tongue any longer. "Where are we going?" she whispered.

Sebastian spared her a glance over his shoulder. "To meet our ride."

Bewilderment rippled through her, and it only got worse when they stepped into a rocky clearing ten minutes later and she laid eyes on the white-and-brown horse standing by a cluster of rosewood trees. The animal neighed at the newcomers' approach, then dipped its majestic head to munch on some blades of grass.

Julia stared at the horse for several long moments, then turned to look at Sebastian. "Okay. I'm sorry," she muttered, shaking her head repeatedly. "But before I go anywhere else with you, I need to ask this—who the hell *are* you?"

Chapter 5

"Really? We really need to do this now?" Sebastian suppressed a groan as Julia's sharp hazel eyes swept over him, up and down, side to side, inspecting every inch of his face and body as if he were an item she was considering purchasing. He knew she was confused by his presence, but he'd been hoping she'd save the interrogation for later.

"You're not a journalist, are you?"

He felt no remorse as he answered, "No, I'm not. And I'm happy to explain everything to you, Julia, I really am. Just *not right now.*"

There was no mistaking the urgency in his tone, and to his relief, she immediately backed off. "Okay, fine. I'll take a rain check on the in-depth explanation. But just…" She let out a shaky breath. "Just promise me I can trust you, Sebastian."

His chest squeezed. Crap. The vulnerability flashing in those big eyes of hers was completely uncharacteristic.

Of course, the observation was ironic, considering he didn't know Julia Davenport well enough to determine what was in or out of character for her. And yet he knew without a shred of doubt that revealing fear or insecurity was not something Dr. Davenport did often. If ever.

"You can trust me," he said quietly.

She visibly swallowed. "All right. Then let's go."

Sebastian's brows shot up as he watched her expertly mount the horse, swinging a denim-clad leg up and over and seating herself on the worn leather saddle. She noticed him gaping and smirked. "You coming, Sebastian?"

He resisted a grin and shoved his arms through his duffel's straps, heaving the bag on his back knapsack-style. He mounted the horse just as easily, settling in behind Julia and wrapping his arms around her slender frame as he reached for the reins.

When Julia leaned back into his chest, the top of her head tickled his chin. A heady scent filled his nostrils—orange blossoms and soap and something sweetly feminine.

"You comfortable?" he rasped.

"Yeah, I'm fine."

"Hold on. This might be a bumpy ride."

He directed the Appaloosa toward the rock-strewn slope from which they'd come, then gave her a sharp kick in the flank and a low demand to get moving. The mare instantly took off in a canter, then quickened her gait at his urging. The speed of the animal's gallop had surprised him on the ride north, and it surprised him again now.

Neither he nor Julia spoke. They rode as if their lives depended on it—not much of a stretch, seeing as their lives *did* depend on a speedy getaway. The steady clip-clop of the mare's hooves flying over the hard ground matched the steady beating of his heart. Even with the adrenaline still coursing through his blood, he felt calm, centered. He'd infiltrated that military camp without a single hitch. Killed two guards, rescued Julia, procured a water sample from the well and found the damn horse exactly where he'd left her.

All in all, a successful op.

The ride back to the road took them through the hills, and Sebastian paid close attention to their surroundings, eyes and ears open for any signs of trouble. But no sirens sounded. No helicopters flew overhead. No bullets whizzed past their heads. The soldiers in Esperanza must not have discovered that Julia was missing yet, and if they had, they were taking their sweet-ass time organizing a search party.

An hour later, they neared the town of Valero. He hated being out in the open like this, but at least it was the middle of the night, and with no lampposts or street traffic lighting the road, everything was pitch-black.

He slowed the horse to a trot. Now that he didn't have to focus on controlling the animal at a breakneck pace, he gradually became more and more aware of the warm, quiet woman sitting in front of him.

"You all right, Doc?"

"I'm fine. Perfectly fine." Her voice was subdued, but a slight tremor betrayed her assertion that she was "perfectly fine."

"Where did you learn to mount a horse like that?"

he asked, hoping to distract her from their precarious situation with small talk.

"I dated a cowboy once."

He was not expecting *that*. Before he could stop it, a chuckle slipped out. "Oh really?"

"Yep."

"Somehow I can't picture you with a cowboy."

"Well, it was more of a vacation fling, if I'm being honest."

She shifted, and the tantalizing scent of her once again filled his nostrils. His groin stirred, then tightened, making him suppress a groan. Crap. He actually had a hard-on. Why did Julia Davenport affect him this way?

Now *he* shifted, easing farther back in the saddle so she wouldn't feel the proof of his inappropriate arousal pressing into her ass.

"So you went on vacation, met a cowboy and did a little bit of riding?" He placed extra emphasis on the word *riding*.

He knew that if he could see Julia's face right now, she'd be blushing. The suggestiveness of that flirty question was probably as tasteless as the erection currently gracing his crotch, but he hadn't been able to help himself.

"Pretty much." She sounded slightly embarrassed. "It was during college. A few friends and I spent spring break in Texas, and yeah, I met a cowboy, he was cute, and I thought, why not?"

Sebastian laughed. "You don't strike me as the fling type."

"I'm not usually." There was a beat. "But every now

and then, I'm not averse to the idea of a no-strings affair."

Heat speared into him. Was that her way of saying she wouldn't mind a no-strings affair with *him?*

And wow, his thoughts were just getting more improper by the second, weren't they? He had to remind himself that he and Julia weren't taking this moonlit horseback ride because they were on a damn date— they'd just escaped a village where all the citizens happened to be in *body bags*. Christ. What was wrong with him?

Clearing his throat, he steered the conversation to their current predicament. "There's a farm about a mile and a half from here. I saw a couple of trucks in the driveway when I drove past earlier. We'll ditch the horse, take a truck and head straight for the harbor."

Her back stiffened. "I'm not going anywhere but the clinic."

"Sorry, Doc, but there's no way you're going back to the clinic. It's the first place those soldiers will look for you."

"I don't care." A stubborn note rang in her voice. "I have to warn everyone. Their lives are in danger now."

The clinic will be handled…

Remembering what he'd overheard, Sebastian stifled a sigh. Chances were, the situation had already been "handled," and as images of what most likely awaited them at the clinic flooded his mind, he struggled to come up with a way to talk her out of this. Short of knocking her unconscious and taking her to the harbor against her will, there wasn't much he could do. He knew with absolute certainty that Julia Davenport would be going to that clinic, with or without him.

"And I need to tell them about this possible outbreak of…Lord, of who knows what," Julia was muttering. "Kevin didn't give me any details over the— Oh, my God. *Kevin.* We didn't even look for him! What if he was being held in another tent?"

"He wasn't." Sebastian's voice came out grim.

"How do you know?"

Because tact wasn't his strongest suit, he took a beat to think about how to phrase it, how to tell Julia that her friend and colleague was—

"He's dead?" Julia's horrified inquiry interrupted his mental preparation. "He's dead, isn't he?"

Sebastian let out a breath. "Yes."

"You're sure?" she asked dully.

"I overheard the man in charge saying that Dr. Carlisle had died from the virus."

"I see."

No emotion in her voice. No tears. No expletives. Nothing.

If it weren't for the trembling of her slender shoulders, Sebastian would've thought Julia Davenport was made of ice.

After a moment of hesitation, he transferred both the reins into one hand and brought his free hand to Julia's arm, squeezing it gently. "I'm sorry about your friend, Doc."

She flinched from his touch, just for a second, before her back relaxed and her shoulders drooped. Leaning into his chest, she whispered, "So am I."

A brief silence fell until Sebastian cleared his throat again. "We'll approach the clinic from the hills. That'll give us a bird's-eye view, and if we see anything amiss, we get the hell out of here. Deal?"

He wasn't surprised when she protested. "I'm going inside."

"Not unless I determine it's safe." His tone brooked no argument. "Don't test me, Julia. If I say we go, then we go."

She twisted around, her hazel eyes flashing with resentment. "That alpha-male caveman crap doesn't scare me, Sebastian. If that's even your real name."

His lips twitched. "It is."

"Fine, great, I guess I'll just go ahead and believe you, same way I believed that you were a journalist writing an article about my organization!" Anger dripped from her every word. "Those people at the clinic? They're my *family* and I refuse to let any of them get hurt. Whatever went down in that village tonight, those soldiers want to cover it up. That's why the general kept asking whether I told anyone at the clinic where I was going. Cover-ups require shutting *people* up, which means that my colleagues are in danger, damn it!"

"I know."

"Oh, you *know?* And yet you're perfectly fine with abandoning those hardworking doctors and nurses and volunteers as long as it means you get out of this situation unscathed?"

He gritted his teeth. "First of all, keep your damn voice down. The way you're shouting, you may as well announce your location to anyone who might be looking for you. And second, I won't apologize for wanting to save my own skin above all others. I already risked my neck to save *you.* I can't save the whole damn world, Doc."

Without letting her respond, he dug the heel of his

boot into the mare's flank and urged her into a gallop. The wind blew in their faces, lifting Julia's braid and smacking the end of it into Sebastian's cheek. He grabbed hold of the silky plait and tucked it underneath the collar of Julia's shirt, then focused on leading the horse through the darkened foothills. There was a rise in elevation, the slope curving and climbing, and they followed the rocky trail to the outskirts of town.

When the Doctors International building came into view, Sebastian's spirits sank like a capsized raft.

"Oh, my God," Julia whispered.

There was no way to sugarcoat what was happening down below. No way to console the suddenly shivering woman in front of him. No way to reassure her that everything would be okay.

The clinic was engulfed in flames.

Great plumes of smoke rose from the wooden roof and were carried away by the late-night breeze. The orange flames were merciless, relentless, licking at the building, dancing around the wooden beams on the covered porch. Out front, two military Jeeps were parked on the dirt.

Soldiers in blue-and-gold San Marquez uniforms surrounded the burning building. Some simply stood by and watched the conflagration as if it were a fireworks display. The rest had weapons trained on the front door, and Sebastian suspected there were more soldiers positioned at the rear, manning all possible exits.

Making sure no human being made it out of that clinic alive.

Julia's slim frame shook even harder. Her soft sobs sent an arrow of pain to his heart. He wrapped his arms around her from behind and held her tight. "I'm sorry, Doc."

A strangled sound left her mouth. Another shudder wracked her body.

"Do you…do you think… Oh, God," she whispered, her voice thick with tears. "I hope they showed them mercy."

Sebastian's heart splintered in two. He was hoping for the same damn thing, because the thought of those doctors and nurses alive in there…burning alive… Christ. The memory of the teenage girl he'd met this morning embedded itself in his head, and agony sliced into his chest like a broadsword. Simone. Feisty Simone.

He found himself praying to a God he hadn't prayed to in years. Praying for the unthinkable, praying that those sadistic soldiers had at least had the courtesy of putting bullets into those people's heads before lighting that fateful match.

He and Julia watched the horror in complete silence. They sat astride the horse, shrouded in the darkness, Sebastian wishing he could take away the hot waves of pain rolling off Julia's body.

"What are they doing?" she asked suddenly.

Several soldiers were now taking spray cans to the vehicles littered in the courtyard. Sebastian's gaze followed the movement of their arms for a moment. He had to squint to make sense of what he was seeing. Once it registered, he clenched his teeth so hard that his jaw hurt.

"They're tagging the area," he hissed out, his vision becoming a red haze of fury and incredulity. "That's the ULF's symbol. The snake coiled around a machete.

Sons of bitches are laying the blame for the fire on the ULF's door."

The sheer audacity of it triggered the impulse to raise his rifle and shoot every last one of those bastards. They'd just burned down an entire medical facility full of innocent people, and now they were planning on passing it off as a rebel offense. Christ, once the U.S. caught wind of this... No, once the entire freaking world heard about this, the rebels would be hunted down and slaughtered for their "crimes" against these foreign relief workers.

But he couldn't dwell on the grisly implications for long, not when he realized that Julia was now shaking like a leaf in a tropical storm. Her breathing came out in unsteady pants, her slender torso rocking so hard he feared she'd topple right off the horse.

"Breathe, Doc," he murmured, gently stroking the sides of her arms "Breathe before you pass out."

He felt her deep inhale, heard her slow exhale. She repeated the breathing exercise, once, twice, three times, until finally her soft voice broke through the cool mountain air.

"Get me out of here," she choked out. "Please, Sebastian, just get me out of here."

Lissa. Simone. Marcus.

Dead.

Kevin. Marie-Thérèse. Kendra. Nadir.

Dead.

The names ran on a continuous loop in Julia's mind, flickering from one to the next like a slideshow of old family photos.

Lissa. Simone. Marcus.

Dead.

Enough!

The sharp internal voice penetrated her state of addled numbness. Julia suddenly became conscious of her surroundings. The water splashing against the hull of the fishing boat. The hiss of the wind as the vessel sliced through the waves. The dark sky overhead and the chill in the early morning air.

She was sitting on the splintered deck, huddled next to Sebastian, who'd slung a strong arm around her and urged her to get some sleep.

Sleep. Ha. Like she would ever fall asleep again. Every time she closed her eyes, she pictured the flames hungrily devouring the clinic. She pictured the bodies of her colleagues, her family. She pictured Marcus's teenaged daughter.

It's just death, Dr. Davenport. It's nothing new.

She almost laughed out loud. Right, just death.

Yet the reminder succeeded in providing some clarity to her muddled brain. Death *wasn't* anything new to her. During her residency in Boston General's emergency room, she'd dealt with death on almost a daily basis. Grown skilled at steeling herself against it.

That was what she had to do now. This wasn't the time to dwell on the loss. She needed to put the gruesome images out of her mind. She couldn't grieve now. Not if she wanted to stay alive.

Swallowing the pain, she stared at the light beginning to gather at the horizon line. Without a word, she watched the sun greet the dawn, wondering how such beauty could follow all the ugliness she'd witnessed tonight. The sunrise was gorgeous. Soft pinks and oranges and purples rippled in the sky, growing brighter, shinier, until an explosion of brilliant yellow lit up the horizon and the sun rose like a phoenix from the ashes.

"Pretty," Sebastian murmured.

Tears stung her eyes. "Beautiful," she whispered.

His strong arm tightened around her, and she found herself resting her head on his shoulder. Exhaustion settled over her, but she couldn't sleep. Couldn't close her eyes. Her gaze swept over the deck, landing on the pair of deckhands smoking cigarettes by the railing. The distinct flavor of sweet San Marquez tobacco floated in her and Sebastian's direction, and for the first time in years, she was gripped by an overpowering nicotine craving.

Stumbling to her feet, she caught the eye of one of the men. *"¿Usted tiene un cigarrillo adicional?"* she called.

A minute later, the deckhand was lighting a cigarette for her. Julia took a deep drag, drawing the smoke deep into her lungs before exhaling a cloud into the early morning air.

Sebastian stood up and joined her at the railing, his chiseled features revealing his surprise. "I didn't realize you were a smoker," he remarked.

"I'm not. Well, not anymore, anyway." She sucked down some more nicotine. "I quit three years ago."

Sebastian didn't make a smartass comment about her return to the dark side, which was damn fortunate for him, because had he lectured her, she might have ripped his head off. She was too angry at the moment. Too horrified. Too anesthetized. Too cold. Too everything.

She focused on the calm water for one long moment before shooting Sebastian a sidelong look. "The customs officials at the Ecuador port will detain me when I can't offer them any identification," she said flatly.

"We won't be going to the port."

Questioning that cryptic response would've taken too much effort, so she just moved on to the next issue at hand. "I won't be able to leave the country without my passport. Everything I own, all my ID and credit cards and belongings, it's all in my tent back at the clinic."

Her throat closed up as she thought of the clinic and pictured it being consumed by fire.

Grieve later, damn it!

"Your passport is useless now," Sebastian replied. "It's undoubtedly been flagged, which means if you tried to use it to board a flight, airport security will be all over you. Same with credit cards. If you paid for a bus, train or plane ticket using your credit card, they'll find you. You're officially a wanted woman, Doc."

A feeling of sheer helplessness climbed up the bumps of her spine. "Why? What the hell did those soldiers want from me?"

"You know exactly what they wanted—to shut you up."

"Because I caught them getting rid of those bodies." She heaved a weary breath. "But this is ridiculous. I can go to the American embassy for help. This conspiracy or whatever it is can't be government-sanctioned. Those men are obviously involved in something shady."

His answering laugh was dry. "And the government can't be shady? Wake up, Julia. Someone authorized that army general to initiate cleanup protocols. Someone dispatched all those soldiers."

"Who?"

He shrugged. "No clue."

She raised the cigarette to her lips and took another frustrated pull. "I don't understand this. Any of this!

What am I supposed to do now? If I can't go to the embassy, how do I get home? How do I get back to Boston?"

"You don't. And you shouldn't," he said in a deadly voice. "Your life is at risk now. You know that the villagers in Esperanza were killed by a virus that was intentionally released by the American government, or the San Marquez government, or both. Chances are, the people in charge will sweep this under the rug, but if it does make the news, they'll probably blame it on a malaria outbreak or a rebel massacre, like they did in Corazón."

"Corazón? Wait, wasn't that the village that Hector Cruz burned to the ground?"

Sebastian released a harsh laugh. "That's what they want you to think. But the rebels didn't murder the people in Corazón. They died of a virus, just like the folks in Esperanza."

Skepticism grabbed hold of her. "So you're saying that this virus is actually being tested on unsuspecting people in remote San Marquez villages?"

"That's what the evidence seems to suggest."

She studied Sebastian's face, noting the hard set of his jaw. You'd think he'd look tired and disheveled after a long night of breaking into military camps and riding horses and bribing a fishing captain for a ride, but the man was utterly alert and put-together. His gray eyes were sharp, he didn't have so much as a smudge on his all-black getup, and the dark blond stubble covering his face only made him appear even more handsome.

After taking one last drag of her cigarette, Julia flicked the butt into the water and turned to meet Sebastian's eyes. "I think I want that explanation now."

Chapter 6

"Who are you, Sebastian?" Julia pressed when he didn't utter a word in response.

Leaning forward, he rested his elbows on the rusted steel railing and fixed those deep gray eyes on the calm waves beyond the boat. "I'm a soldier. Special Forces."

Her eyes narrowed. "Active duty?"

"I was until my own government decided they preferred me dead."

Julia battled another burst of skepticism. "Someone is trying to kill you?"

"Yup. The first attempt was right after my unit was recalled back to the States ten months ago. Couple days after our debriefing, I was nearly hit by a car in front of my apartment."

"Are you sure it wasn't an accident?"

He snorted. "The driver was gunning for me, Doc. Cops didn't believe me either, but trust me, I know a threat when I see one. You develop a sixth sense working black ops. Someone wanted me dead that day, and they tried again two months later. I was on my bike when the brakes just up and failed—two days after my mechanic replaced them. I spun out on the interstate, nearly got decapitated by a damn eighteen-wheeler."

Her eyes widened. "Did the police believe you this time?"

"Nope. My mechanic said the brake lines were clearly cut. Cops enlisted their own man to verify, and he insisted it was a brake malfunction." Sebastian's voice dripped with contempt. "I didn't stick around long enough to argue. I hooked up with Tate and Prescott, and got the hell out."

"Tate and Prescott?" she echoed.

"The last two members of my unit. Everyone else is dead." His tone thickened with grief. "Tate—he was our commanding officer —well, his brother Will died in Corazón during that last op. But the others were killed after we got home, and all of them died from bogus causes—mugging, cancer, drunk driving accident. It was total BS and we all knew it. Then someone tried to blow Tate's brains out, supposedly a gang-related drive-by, but he knew better. He suggested we get the hell out of the country before we wound up dead."

"So you, and Tate, and—Prescott?" When he nodded, she went on. "So you're all hiding out now? In Ecuador?"

"We've been moving around the past eight months. Our last safe house was an old fortress in Mexico, but Tate's fiancée insisted we switch to more civilized accommodations." He rolled his eyes. "Eva maintains that just because we're on the run doesn't mean we have to live like hobos. So we're holed up in a beach house on the coast now."

Julia's eyebrows soared. "Your commanding officer brought his fiancée on the run with him?"

"He met her on the run," Sebastian corrected. "Tate wanted her to go back to the States and wait there until he found a way out of this mess, but she refused." He shrugged. "I think you'll like her. She's got a little sass in her, just like you, Doc."

A frazzled breath left her mouth. She didn't feel at all sassy at the moment. Just bone-tired and unbelievably sad. "So you're taking me to your hideout?"

He nodded. "It's the safest place for you at the moment."

"You really think the general sent people to find me?"

"No doubt about it." Sebastian curled his fingers over the metal railing and gazed out at the water. "You're on somebody's hit list now. The same somebody who tried to shut up the men in my unit."

She absorbed that terrifying truth, let it settle, gave herself a few seconds to indulge in an internal freak-out, but just as the panic tried to seize her body, she quickly forced it out. She couldn't allow herself to surrender to the fear. She needed a distraction, damn it. For her, the best distraction had always been to bury herself in her work, and so she hastily snapped her brain into doctor mode.

"What do you know about this virus?" she asked Sebastian.

"Not much, I'm afraid." He drifted away from the railing and walked over to his duffel bag.

Julia trailed after him, watching as he unzipped the

bag. He'd stashed his rifle in there, along with the gun he'd given her in the woods, but he still wore his hunting knife in a sheath at his hip. And from the bulge beneath his black shirt, she knew he must have another pistol tucked in his waistband.

Sebastian removed the water bottle they'd brought with them from the village, his silvery gaze fixed on the clear liquid swishing inside the plastic container.

"You think something in this water killed those people, huh?"

She nodded. "A strain of bacteria makes the most sense. Do you know what kinds of symptoms the villagers were exhibiting?"

"Not really. One source said there were some visible nosebleeds and foaming at the mouth. What did your colleague tell you over the radio?"

"Not much. I think I heard him coughing, and he sounded confused, disoriented even. But he mentioned the water, so I figured there might be a connection there." She chewed on her bottom lip. "I have no idea what this disease could be. Cholera, typhoid, *E. coli*... and those are just bacterial infections. It could be protozoal, parasitic, viral—"

"The general and his man definitely used the word *virus,*" Sebastian interrupted.

"A waterborne virus..." She searched for her mental databases. "SARS, hep A, polio... I think those are the most common in terms of water transmission, but I don't recall nosebleeds and foaming at the mouth being signs of any of those."

"This disease was most likely engineered in a lab, Doc. It probably won't have the classic symptoms of any one illness. The virus could be mutated as hell."

"Good point."

In the distance, land became visible, lush green and earthy brown, but rather than stay on course, the boat began to veer to the left. Julia craned her neck to glance up at the pilothouse, where their captain stood at the helm, slowing the engine as he steered away from the awaiting harbor. The captain was in his early sixties, with a head of long gray hair, tanned leathery skin and a bushy beard that seemed to consume his entire face. He also wore a permanent scowl, which made Julia wonder what Sebastian had offered the man to convince him to give them passage.

The closer they got to land, the more uneasy Julia became. The fishing vessel chugged its way into a narrow inlet bordered by a lush forest. She had no idea where they were going, but Sebastian didn't look concerned. Earlier this morning at the marina, he'd left her hidden in the shadows while he went to arrange transport, and when he returned, he mentioned that he'd made a call on his satellite phone and secured a "pickup" for them. She wasn't sure what that meant, but she trusted that Sebastian knew what he was doing.

Much to her chagrin, she couldn't curb this unfailing faith she seemed to have in the man. Instead of demanding more answers, she was infuriatingly content to take his lead, and she had a feeling that she wouldn't last five minutes without Sebastian. For a woman who'd always been able to take care of herself, relying on a man and placing her survival in his hands was more than a little maddening. And yet she was doing exactly that. Without a single complaint.

Jeez. What was wrong with her?

"All right. This is where we get out," Sebastian announced.

Julia gaped at him. The boat was nowhere near the shore—the muddy bank was at least twenty yards away.

He slanted his head, studying her face. "You *can* swim, can't you?"

"Yes, but…"

"This is as close as we can get. The water's too shallow and there're some nasty jagged rocks down there. They'll rip the keel apart if our captain gets any closer."

Although that made perfect sense to her, it didn't make her any more enthusiastic to jump overboard.

Sebastian shoved the water bottle in the duffel and zipped up the waterproof bag before slinging the straps over his shoulder. He glanced up at the captain and nodded his thanks, then did the same with the deckhands, who were watching Julia with unrestrained amusement.

It was the laughter in their eyes that gave her the kick in the butt she needed.

She followed Sebastian to the railing, then hesitated. "So you just want me to jump?"

Humor twinkled in his eyes. "I could throw you in, if you'd prefer."

"Jumping it is."

With a sigh, she carefully climbed the rail until she was balancing atop it in her sneakers. It was a good seven-foot drop to the water, and in the back of her mind she couldn't help but think about those "nasty" rocks Sebastian had mentioned. Wouldn't it be just her luck? Escaping from the scene of a—for lack of a better word—*massacre,* only to meet her maker while leaping off a barnacle-covered fishing boat into shallow water.

"Any day now," came Sebastian's sarcastic voice.

Julia stared at the calm blue-green water for a few more seconds, then took a deep breath, closed her eyes and jumped.

The water was warmer than she'd anticipated. It completely engulfed her, soaking her clothes, her hair, her tired, grief-stricken bones. She kicked her feet, propelling herself to the surface, and squeaked in surprise when she noticed Sebastian's wet head right beside hers.

"You all right, Doc?"

She spat water from her mouth. "I'm good."

"Let's head in."

They swam side by side, Sebastian's duffel floating beside him as they made their way to shore. Julia felt like a drowned rat by the time she heaved herself onto the muddy, pebble-strewn bank. She wrung out her braid, then the tails of her plaid shirt.

"Ugh. There's nothing worse than wet denim," she griped, wiping her hands on the front of her damp jeans.

"Don't worry, you won't be wearing it for long. Eva will lend you a change of clothes when we reach the safe house."

"And how exactly are we getting to this safe house of yours?" Her suspicious gaze drifted to the trees. "Please don't tell me we're hiking again. In wet clothes."

"Our pickup is only a mile away," he assured her. "We'll get there in no time."

Her next complaint died on her lips when Sebastian peeled off his wet long-sleeve shirt. He wore a tight black wifebeater underneath, and the fabric was molded to a chest so ripped, so perfectly sculpted, that Julia's entire body began to tingle with awareness. And his arms…roped with muscle, dusted with light blond hair, rippling with strength. Wow. Just…wow.

A knowing gleam lit those sexy gray eyes. "Are you okay?"

"I'm fine," she muttered, wrenching her gaze away. "Let's just get this hike over with."

Sebastian's soft chuckle confirmed that her appreciation over his delectable form was still written all over her face.

As the heat of embarrassment stained her cheeks, she followed him into the thick vegetation, cursing under her breath the entire time. Water oozed out of her sneakers at her every step, and her jeans were plastered to her legs, making it difficult to walk. They'd been marching through the forest for only five minutes when she had to call out for a break.

Gritting her teeth, she unbuttoned her plaid shirt and shrugged out of the wet sleeves. Her white tank top was soaked, too, but at least the material wasn't as heavy and stifling as the plaid. She quickly tied the shirt around her waist and said, "Okay, I'm ready."

Sebastian cleared his throat. "Um. For the sake of full disclosure here, you should know that I can see... well, *everything*."

Julia hastily looked down at her chest, and her cheeks grew even hotter. Crap. She'd forgotten that she was wearing a thin, white bra beneath that thin, white tank. Sure enough, she could make out the dusky outline of her areolae, and there was no mistaking the hard points of her nipples poking through both sets of fabric.

When her gaze collided with Sebastian's, another rush of awareness flooded her belly. Those magnetic gray eyes smoldered with unmistakable desire. He wanted her. This gorgeous, powerful warrior actually wanted her.

Of course he does. You're standing practically top-less in front of him.

Swallowing, Julia broke the eye contact. "Thanks for letting me know," she said awkwardly. "But how about we both pretend you *can't* see through my shirt so that way I can maintain some illusion of modesty?"

His lips quirked. "Sure."

As they set out again, she had to wonder how Sebastian always seemed to know exactly where they were. Either the man was a walking GPS, or else he was very familiar with this particular "pickup" point.

"It's right through these trees," he said twenty minutes later.

When they abruptly stumbled onto an honest-to-God road, Julia was startled. Well, it was more of a trail, if anything, unpaved and bordered by towering trees on each side, but it was definitely wide enough to accommodate the beat-up Jeep parked ten yards away.

Sebastian took her arm. "Come on, Nick's waiting."

His strides suddenly became hurried and she had to struggle to keep up with him. When they reached the olive-green vehicle, the man in the driver's seat hopped out and made a beeline for Sebastian. The two men joined in one of those manly man side-hug/back-slap type of embraces, while Julia hung back and warily watched the exchange.

"Julia, this is Nick Prescott," Sebastian introduced. "Nick, this is Julia Davenport, the doctor I told you about."

Nick extended a hand. "Nice to meet you, Dr. Davenport."

She returned the handshake, a tad surprised by the warmth that radiated from Nick's amber-colored eyes.

He was around the same height as Sebastian, boasting a head of shaggy brown hair and an attractive face, and though he wasn't as blatantly masculine as Sebastian, he possessed his own version of sex appeal—the sweet, boyish kind that so many women foolishly overlooked.

Sebastian tossed his duffel in the back of the Jeep. "We should go," he announced. "None of us can afford to be out in the open like this."

His matter-of-fact observation was an unwanted reminder that her life was officially in shambles. Twenty-four hours ago, she'd been doing rounds at the clinic, checking on potential malaria patients and awaiting the arrival of the journalist who'd requested an interview with her.

Now the clinic had been reduced to ashes, her patients and coworkers were dead and the journalist turned out to be a Special Forces operative who was living on the run.

And now *she* was on the run.

God, how was any of this happening?

"You should try to get some sleep during the drive." Sebastian's voice was gentle as he opened the door for her. "I know it sucks being in those wet jeans, but I'll find you a change of clothes soon."

Julia climbed into the vehicle and settled on the tattered backseat. "I doubt I can sleep. Every time I close my eyes I see…"

Lissa. Simone. Marcus.

White-hot agony streaked through her chest. She blinked rapidly, trying to control the tears threatening to spill over.

"I know, Doc. I know how hard this is," Sebastian said gruffly. "But it's only gonna get harder, so you might as well get some rest before the next catastrophe strikes."

She croaked out a laugh. "Gee, how reassuring. You should become a motivational speaker."

He shot her a crooked grin. "I won't apologize for being a realist."

"More like a pessimist," Nick piped up as he slid into the driver's seat. "Stone over here always expects the worst, Doc. His glass is forever empty. Bone-dry, even, not a single drop of moisture in there."

Julia glanced over at Sebastian to hear his rebuttal, but he didn't deny any of it. For some reason, that caused a wave of sadness to swell inside her. Despite the pain and heartache she'd suffered in her life, despite the death and destruction she witnessed on a daily basis, she'd somehow managed to cling to hope. Hope that life would get better, hope that her efforts would actually make a difference. If that made her naive, then so be it. But no matter how bad things got, she couldn't bring herself to let go of that hope.

Nick started the engine and sped off, raising a cloud of dirt behind them. In the front seat, the two men spoke in muted voices, but after a while, Julia quit trying to follow the conversation. Her eyelids had begun to droop, her head so heavy her neck could no longer support it. She'd claimed that she'd never sleep again, yet as the wind hissed past her head and the scenery flashed in her peripheral vision, she surrendered to the fatigue.

She didn't know how long she slept, but it must have been hours because when her eyes opened again, the sun was high in the sky, hinting that it was early afternoon.

She lifted her head from the edge of Sebastian's duf-

fel, which she'd been using as a pillow, and tried to figure out where the heck they were. The winding dirt road
seemed to be smack in the middle of the wilderness.
Low-lying branches and palm fronds slapped the sides
of the Jeep, and the scent of salt permeated the air. The
ocean must be nearby, yet she couldn't orient herself
no matter how hard she tried.

Eventually, she gave up and instead studied Sebastian's rugged profile. His dirty-blond hair was mussed
up, his chin covered with thick beard growth. He was
staring straight ahead, and neither he nor Nick had spoken since she'd awakened. Then, as if sensing her eyes
on him, he swiftly turned around.

"You're awake."

"Am I? Because I still feel like I'm in a nightmare."

His expression softened. "I'm sorry."

It didn't escape her that he'd made no attempt to
correct her, that he hadn't offered any assurances. *I'm
sorry.* That was it. On one hand, she appreciated that
he wasn't patronizing her by downplaying the severity
of their predicament.

On the other hand, would it kill the man to be a little
less gloom-and-doom?

The trees thinned out, revealing a small house up
ahead. It had a white stucco exterior and a flat tin roof,
nothing fancy, but bigger than she'd expected and incredibly isolated. Another Jeep was parked on the gravel
clearing out front, along with a couple of dirt bikes
and—inexplicably—a child's red tricycle. A dusty path
at the side of the house sloped down to the white sand
ten yards away, where the waves lapped against the
shore.

Craning her neck, Julia spotted a long wooden dock

extending out at least thirty feet, and a white speedboat bobbing in the water at the end of the pier.

Sebastian helped her out of the Jeep, his warm, callused hand settling on her arm and eliciting an unexpected shiver.

"Cold?"

"A little," she lied.

"Come on, let's go in and find you some clo—"

The rear door of the beach house flew open before he could finish and Julia flinched when a man with dark hair and piercing green eyes appeared on the rickety back porch. Wearing camo pants, a white T-shirt and black boots, he was a seriously imposing picture, and the deep scowl on his face only upped his deadliness factor.

She knew this must be Tate, Sebastian's commanding officer, and *commanding* was a very apt description.

As he stalked toward them, Julia glanced at Sebastian with wariness. "Your friend doesn't look happy," she murmured.

He didn't have a chance to answer, because the friend in question had reached them and those moss-green eyes were piercing Julia's face like an angry blade.

"You've got to be kidding me," Tate muttered in lieu of a greeting. Then he shifted those furious eyes at Sebastian. "What the *hell* compelled you to bring her here?"

Chapter 7

Sebastian had been forewarned that Tate wasn't happy he was bringing Julia to the beach house, but just like he hadn't apologized over the phone to Nick, he wasn't apologizing to Tate now. Rather, he matched the captain's steely expression and said, "Dr. Davenport is no threat to us. If anything, she's an asset."

Tate's gaze took in Julia's unkempt braid, damp clothing and fatigue-lined eyes. "An asset," he echoed, sounding unconvinced.

Other women might have recoiled under that harsh glare, but Julia squared her shoulders and glared right back. "If it helps, I don't particularly want to be here either. Sebastian didn't give me much of a choice."

Her frosty tone brought another flash of displeasure to Tate's green eyes.

Sebastian quickly spoke before the captain could. "Julia was being held in Esperanza. A United

States Army general was interrogating her. I got her out."

"Did you search her for wires?"

Julia snorted. "Oh, for Pete's sake, we all know you can see right through my shirt. Does it *look* like I'm wearing a wire?"

"And if it weren't for her," Sebastian went on, pretending neither one of them had spoken, "we wouldn't have a potential lead on this virus. Julia was the one who figured out it might be in the water."

Tate's features sharpened. "It's waterborne?"

"We don't know, but I secured a water sample from the village. We need to get it tested ASAP."

"I think I know someone who can help," Julia said helpfully. "He—"

"That won't be necessary," Tate interrupted. "We'll get our own people to handle this."

She let out a sardonic laugh, then glanced at Sebastian. "You didn't tell me I'd be receiving such a warm welcome."

Before he could attempt to defuse the bomb of hostility in the air, the front door flew open again and Eva Dolce waltzed out. The woman looked gorgeous as usual, her Spanish, Italian and American heritage responsible for her unusual combination of silky black hair, vivid blue eyes and smooth olive complexion. A thin green sundress clung to her centerfold curves, her brown sandals clicking as she marched toward the group.

Eva took one look at Julia's bedraggled appearance, then turned to frown at her fiancé. "Seriously, Tate, you couldn't let the poor woman change out of those wet clothes before you started in on the cross-examination?" Her gaze shifted. "Hey, Sebastian. Welcome back."

He nodded at her. "Hey, Eva. This is Dr. Julia Davenport. She worked at the clinic in Valero when she ran into a wee bit of trouble."

Without hesitation, Eva wrapped an arm around Julia and began leading her away. The two women were about the same height, yet Eva was a force to be reckoned with, and Julia shot Sebastian a panicked look over her shoulder.

"Don't mind Tate," Eva was assuring her. "He's kind of a jerk until you get to know him. And he's naturally suspicious, so…"

As the women drifted toward the front door, the three men stayed outside. Tate still looked unhappy, while Nick, who was leaning against the Jeep, seemed amused.

"I like the doctor," Nick said. "She's got a backbone on her."

"She's got guts, too." His voice sounded raspier than usual, so he cleared his throat. "After we left the camp, she was willing to risk her neck and go back for a water sample. If I'd refused to do it, I have no doubt she would've found a way to do it herself."

"What else do we know, aside from the possibility of water transmission?" Tate asked as they headed for the house. "Did you see any of the bodies?"

Sebastian shook his head. "They were all bagged up. But we can add coughing and/or disorientation to the symptoms we already know about. Oh, and the general said the name *Meridian* in reference to the virus."

"Meridian?" Tate echoed quizzically.

"Could be what they're calling it. Also, this is definitely a cooperative effort between the U.S. and San Marquez, but taking into account that the American general was leading Julia's interrogation, I think our government's calling the shots here."

They reached the front porch, but Sebastian hesitated before opening the screen door. "The deaths in Esperanza weren't an accident. The general said in no uncertain terms that the virus had been intentionally released in the area. He was unhappy about it because the village wasn't far from the Doctors International clinic."

"So our government really is testing a biological weapon on foreign soil," Nick said, shaking his head in disbelief.

"Seems so." Sebastian leveled a stern look in Tate's direction. "And, Captain? Try to tone down the death glares around the doc, all right? She lost a lot of people she cared about last night."

"Nick said the soldiers torched the clinic?" Tate's tone was grudging, as if he didn't want to feel any sympathy for Julia but couldn't help himself.

"With dozens of innocent people inside it. Julia's coworkers, her friends, her patients." A rush of fury entered his bloodstream, tensing every muscle in his body. "They're going to blame the fire on the ULF, same way they blamed the rebels for the dead villagers in Corazón."

"We need to find out who's green-lighting the testing of the virus, damn it."

Tate sounded frustrated beyond belief, and Sebastian didn't blame him. He was sick and tired of hitting brick wall after brick wall in his quest for answers. The other members of his unit had been killed to cover up the events of Corazón, which meant that someone wanted to keep the virus a secret. So who had authorized this biological weapons project? The president? The Department of Defense? Someone on a lower rung of the ladder who was operating without official consent?

Rubbing his temples, Sebastian strode into the house. Female voices wafted from the direction of the bedrooms, and he hoped that Eva wasn't grilling Julia too hard about everything that had happened. He couldn't stop thinking about that haunted look in Julia's hazel eyes, the way she'd sat on the deck of the fishing boat, silent, unblinking, thinking about her loss.

Other women might've fallen apart. Sobbed. Screamed. Collapsed from grief. But not Julia. The woman exuded quiet strength. Even when overcome with anguish, she managed to keep it together, which he appreciated. The last thing he'd wanted to do last night was comfort a hysterical female.

And the last thing he wanted to do right now was rack his brain trying to make sense of this whole mess. He hadn't slept in more than twenty-four hours, for chrissake.

"I need a shower. And some shut-eye," he announced. "Can we finish this later?"

The others nodded. "We're frying up some fish for dinner," Nick told him. "I'll wake you before we eat."

"Sounds good."

He walked toward the narrow hallway leading to the bedrooms, bypassing the room he was bunking in and heading for Tate and Eva's room instead. Although the beach house's three bedrooms were tiny, the place was a million times more habitable than the crumbling stone fortress they'd been holed up in two months ago.

He knocked on the door, waited for the okay, then

entered the room to find Julia sitting at the edge of the double bed with Eva's three-year-old son, Rafe. Loose waves of brown hair fell over Julia's slender shoulder as she bent to examine the inside of the little boy's forearm. Eva was looming over them, biting her lip in worry.

"'Bastian!" Rafe shouted happily. The second the kid caught sight of him, he shot off the bed and launched himself into Sebastian's legs.

"Hey, kiddo," he said gruffly, scooping the excited child in his arms.

"Don't worry," Julia told Eva. "It's just a minor heat rash. It'll probably go away on its own, but you can keep applying that mild cortisone cream. Loose clothing helps, too, and so does staying hydrated."

Sebastian chuckled, then rolled his eyes at Eva. "She's not here on a house call, for Pete's sake."

"Who's Pete?" Rafe demanded.

The boy was wiggling up a storm in Sebastian's arms, so he finally set him down, wondering how Eva managed to keep up with that overenergetic kid without having a nervous breakdown. On the other hand, Rafe was pretty darn cute, which made it impossible not to love him. Sebastian hadn't been thrilled about Eva bringing her kid along, but the woman turned into a ferocious mama bear when anyone raised the suggestion of sending Rafe to stay with his grandparents. She refused to leave Tate, and she refused to send Rafe away, which meant that the kid wasn't going anywhere.

But Rafe had grown on him. Sebastian still tried to keep his distance, and he definitely didn't like being alone with the rug rat, but having him around wasn't as horrible as he'd thought it would be.

His gaze shifted to Julia, who'd changed out of her damp clothes and into a blue print dress that swirled around her ankles. The garment was a little loose on the top, one strap repeatedly falling off her shoulder, but that didn't surprise him. Julia was rail-thin compared to Eva's curvaceous form.

Sighing, he met her eyes. "Did Eva offer you any lunch, or did she just whisk you in here and demand you diagnose the rash on Rafe's arm?"

"She offered to feed me. I turned her down." Julia swallowed. "I still don't have an appetite."

"Well, I'm crashing for a few hours. You should probably do the same." He edged toward the door. "We'll all talk later, okay?"

Her face donned an indecipherable expression. "Okay."

"You can sleep in here if you want," Eva said gently. "Rafe and I will make ourselves scarce, and I'll come get you before dinner."

"Fishies!" Rafe exclaimed, clapping his hands together in glee.

Julia arched a brow and waited for a translation.

"Tate took him fishing this morning, so we're frying up their catch tonight," Eva explained with a grin.

After Eva and Rafe left the room, Sebastian took a step toward Julia. Before he could stop himself, he cupped her angular jaw with both hands and studied her face. Her breath hitched in surprise, those hazel eyes flickering with uneasiness.

"Are you okay, Doc? *Really* okay?" He couldn't control the husky note in his voice.

Rather than shy away, she leaned into his touch. "I'm

hurting," she murmured. "I'm hurting bad. But I'll be fine."

Her honesty floored him, as did her resilience. His gaze landed on her lips, noting the slightly fuller bottom one. With her brown hair free of its braid and cascading over one shoulder, she looked younger, prettier, softer. As his pulse kicked up a notch, he swept his thumbs across her silky-smooth cheeks, his mouth tingling with the urge to kiss her.

But he reined in the impulse, knowing now was not the time.

When his hands dropped from her jaw, Sebastian could have sworn he saw a glimmer of disappointment on her face.

He took a step backward, suddenly feeling awkward, edgy. "I'll be right next door if you need me, Doc."

"Thank you."

They stared at each other for a moment, and then he cleared his throat, forced himself to break eye contact and slid out the door before he did something foolish.

Like kiss her senseless.

Several hours later, Julia helped Eva clear the table while the three men and Eva's son remained on the wooden oceanfront deck. Throughout dinner, she'd been trying to get a sense of these people and how they fit together, and she was now confident she had everyone figured out.

Although none of the men were officially part of the military anymore, Tate still stood out as their leader. There was no mistaking his authority, and Sebastian and Nick constantly looked to him for the final word on any given matter.

Nick, on the other hand, was clearly at the bottom of the pack. At twenty-seven, he was the youngest, and he lacked that lethal air both Sebastian and Tate radiated in spades. His tall, muscular body left no doubt that he could kick some serious ass, but Julia didn't get a killer instinct vibe from the man.

As for Eva and her little boy, Julia's confusion about their presence had evaporated after five minutes of being in the same room as Tate and Eva. It was obvious the couple loved each other fiercely, and they were not only protective of each other, but of Rafe as well. Because the boy didn't refer to Tate as "Daddy," Julia had deduced that he was Eva's son from a past relationship, but Rafe clearly adored the intense soldier, and Tate was surprisingly sweet around the boy.

And then there was Sebastian. As alpha and intense as Tate, yet there was something more…*sexual* about him. He exuded raw masculinity, potent sex appeal, and every time she looked in his direction, her entire body grew hot and tingly.

Earlier in the bedroom, she'd truly thought he was going to kiss her. The heat in his eyes had been unmistakable, the brush of his fingers on her cheek utterly seductive. When he'd walked away, she hadn't been able to fight the disappointment that erupted inside her. And how insane was that? She wasn't supposed to be thinking about silly things like kissing—not after everything she'd lost.

"Hey, sweetheart, get out here," Tate called from the patio. "We need you."

Rolling her eyes, Eva dropped a stack of dirty plates in the sink. "Damn man never says please," she told Julia. "And then he gets pissy when Rafe doesn't mind *his* p's and q's, and refuses to admit that he's the one setting the bad example."

Julia grinned. She actually really liked Eva, though it had taken a while to get past those stunning looks. The woman belonged on the cover of a magazine, making Julia feel frumpy and hideous in comparison. But Eva had turned out to be as smart as she was beautiful, and a little sassy, just like Sebastian had said.

"Sorry, *sweetheart*," the raven-haired woman called to her fiancé. "I didn't quite hear you."

Tate raised his voice. "I said get out here."

"What was that?"

"Get out here." A beat. "Please."

Eva broke out in a grin. "Be right there!"

As Julia was about to turn on the faucet and tackle the dishes in the sink, the other woman swatted at her hand. "Leave them, Doc. We have more pressing concerns."

With a lack of enthusiasm, Julia followed the other woman back outside. During dinner, they hadn't spoken about what had happened in Esperanza and Valero, and she wasn't quite ready to talk about it yet. She knew decisions needed to be made, knew a plan had to be formulated, but she simply didn't have the stomach for any of it at the moment.

Nevertheless, she sank into the chair next to Sebastian, grateful that at least they were choosing to include her in the discussion. She knew Tate still didn't trust her, but frankly, she didn't care. She had nothing to prove to the man.

"We need to find a reputable lab that can test the water sample Stone brought," Tate told his fiancée after she sat down. "Preferably one that employs a lab tech who's looking to score some extra cash. There can't be a record of this."

Eva nodded in agreement. "I'll see what I can find."

"Or you can let me take the sample back to Boston," Julia spoke up, her jaw tight. "I tried to tell you this earlier, but I know someone who can help, and he'll do it without asking any questions."

Tate's lips curled in distrust. "Forgive me if I don't take that at face value, Dr. Davenport."

It amazed her that he was still able to look so damn menacing even with a sleeping toddler draped across his chest.

"Who's this friend?" Sebastian asked, his tone far more encouraging than his commanding officer's.

She shot Tate a quick scowl before turning away from him. "Frank Matheson. He's a microbiologist and a professor at Harvard. He works out of a lab on campus, mostly does research, development, taking on the occasional government contract." When all three men stiffened at the word *government,* she quickly reassured them. "He's discreet, and he would never, ever betray me. He thinks of me as a daughter."

"We'll find a lab here," Tate said firmly.

Julia rolled her eyes. "Right, you're going to bribe a lab technician to test the sample and trust that the person you paid off keeps the results to himself. Sounds like a *much* better plan."

"She has a point," Nick said cautiously, reaching for the beer bottle on the table.

"Frank can be trusted," she insisted. "And he'd be helping out of a sense of loyalty, not greed. Your lab tech will sell you out the second someone offers him more money."

As a short silence hung over the table, Julia stared at the dark ocean twenty yards away, then up at the crescent moon shining in the inky-black sky. It was a warm night, the water calm, the breeze balmy. She inhaled the fresh, salty air, realizing this was the first time in a long time she wasn't running around in a stressed-out daze.

And yet she missed the commotion of the clinic. She missed her patients. Her coworkers.

Her throat clogged, and she swallowed the lump of sorrow that formed there. They were all gone. The clinic was gone. And for what? So the military could cover up whatever inhumane tests they were conducting on unsuspecting people?

"I think we should let Julia contact her friend in Boston," Sebastian finally said, his tone resigned. "We can ship him the sample—"

"No way," Tate cut in. "We're not letting that sample out of our sight. If it's going to Boston to be tested, then one of us is going with it."

"I'm the one who has to go," Julia said. "Frank won't agree to help unless I'm there to ask for it in person. He won't trust any of you, even if you drop my name."

Tate didn't look the slightest bit pleased about the idea of sending her to Boston alone. Neither did Sebastian, who turned to her with a frown. "You're not going anywhere without backup, Doc." He glanced at Tate. "If she goes, I go with her."

"And while they take care of the lab part, I'll keep digging about Project Aries," Eva spoke up.

"Project Aries?" Julia echoed.

Sebastian nodded. "Remember I told you my unit was sent to Corazón? Well, we were ordered to extract a man by the name of Richard Harrison, an American doctor who was supposedly being held hostage by the ULF. Long story short, Harrison was already dead when we arrived. Turns out he worked for a private research facility that specializes in biological weapons development. He was in charge of something called Project Aries, which we think has to do with the virus he was testing in Corazón."

"I've been looking into it, trying to find out more details, but it's slow-going. Some of these databases are impossible to hack into," Eva said, running a frustrated hand through her black hair.

Julia was taken aback. "Wait—you're a hacker?"

"A damn good one," Nick piped up.

"I'm working with a friend to crack this," Eva admitted, "but we keep striking out at every turn. We need to find out who else worked on Project Aries, what the objective was, what this virus actually *is*."

"Well, Frank can help us with that last part," Julia answered. "The man's a genius."

"Then it's settled," Sebastian said. "The doc and I will head to Boston while you guys stay here and do what you can to shed some light on Project Aries."

Although Tate didn't look particularly happy about this latest development, the man didn't object.

"We'll need to secure some papers for Julia," Sebastian added. "How fast can Fernando get them done?"

"Less than twenty-four hours if we email him the photos." Nick was already scraping back his chair. "I'll grab the digital camera."

The next thing Julia knew, she was being ushered inside and forced to pose for several photographs in front of the white wall in the cozy living room of the beach house. Nick even asked her to tie her hair up for some shots, for "authenticity," whatever that meant. The photo shoot didn't last long, and when it ended, she drifted outside again and made her way down to the water's edge.

Tate, Eva and Rafe had disappeared into their bedroom, and Nick had stayed in the living room, hunched over a table laden with laptops and monitors. She'd noticed the computers earlier, as well as the fact that the men were armed at all times. Eva didn't seem to mind it, but for Julia, it was an obtrusive reminder of the danger they faced. These men had been forced to leave their homes and flee to another continent.

And now she was in the same awful boat.

She hugged her chest, gazing at the silent ocean. A part of her was still in denial about everything. She wasn't *really* in jeopardy, right? Those soldiers who'd detained her hadn't *really* planned on killing her, had they? But even though she wanted so desperately to believe that this was nothing more than a messed-up misunderstanding, the memory of the clinic being devoured by red-and-orange flames rendered that impossible.

Her colleagues and patients had been murdered.

She would have been murdered if Sebastian Stone hadn't come to her rescue.

"You're too damn skinny."

Speak of the devil. At the sound of Sebastian's rough voice, Julia turned around.

She watched him approach, her gaze drawn to the rippled six-pack beneath his white T-shirt. His long cargo shorts revealed a pair of muscular legs dusted with golden hair, and as he got closer, she noticed that he still hadn't shaved. Dark blond stubble coated his powerful jaw, and her fingers itched with the urge to stroke that prickly growth.

Distracted by his sheer sexiness, she tried to remember what he'd just said, then frowned when it sunk in. "It's hard to find time to eat when I'm working," she said defensively.

But he was right—the fact that she was nearly drowning in Eva's dress told her that she'd lost more weight than she'd thought. Eva was definitely packing more curves than Julia in her chest and butt regions, but she was still a slender woman, which meant that Julia was indeed skinnier than she ought to be.

"But if it makes you happy, I'll eat more," she said grudgingly.

Sebastian came up beside her, chuckling softly. "Wow, that was easy."

She edged closer to the waves, her bare toes sinking into the warm, wet sand. Sebastian was also barefoot, and he followed her right into the water, not even complaining when his ankles got splashed.

She bunched up the hem of Eva's filmy blue dress and brought it up to her thighs so the fabric wouldn't get wet. The lukewarm water lapped at her shins, the ebb-and-flow motion oddly comforting.

"Eva's really nice," she murmured. "I'm surprised she ended up with someone as grumpy as Tate."

Sebastian laughed. "Me, too."

"He *is* sweet to that boy, though," Julia had to concede. "He loses some of those sharp edges when he's talking to Rafe."

"That was another surprise. Tate's not much of a kid person, but he warmed up to Eva's son fast."

"Who's…" She hesitated.

Sebastian read her mind. "Who's Rafe's father?"

She nodded.

"You wouldn't believe me if I told you."

She was instantly struck with curiosity. "Well, now you *have* to tell me."

"Hector Cruz."

Julia's mouth fell open. "Are you serious?"

"As a heart attack."

"Eva had a child with the former leader of the United Liberty Fighters?"

"Yes."

She shook her head a couple of times, trying to make sense of that. Hector Cruz had been at the ULF helm for more than a decade before he was killed in a military raid two months ago. Julia had watched the coverage on the news, and she didn't remember hearing anything about Cruz leaving behind a son. There hadn't been mention of a wife or girlfriend either.

But that wasn't even the perplexing part. After spending an entire evening with Eva Dolce, Julia couldn't fathom how that intelligent, caring woman had gotten tangled up with a group of revolutionaries.

"Eva was young and idealistic when she met Cruz," Sebastian said, yet again decoding her thoughts. "It didn't take long before she realized what a tyrant he was, but by then, she was knocked up and at his mercy." He shrugged. "She's been living on the run, too, ever since the kid was born."

"She must have been relieved when Cruz was killed during that ambush."

Sebastian's laugh was long and husky. "She *orchestrated* the ambush, Doc."

"I'm confused again. The news reports said that an

elite San Marquez military unit located Cruz's hideout and eliminated him."

Now he snorted. "Elite is right. Me, Tate and Eva were the ones who infiltrated Cruz's base camp, and we're the ones who blew it all to hell."

"And you killed Cruz?"

"Tate did."

When she winced, Sebastian's gray eyes softened. "Don't look at me like that, Doc. Remember what I said in Esperanza?"

She swallowed. "Kill or be killed."

"Exactly." He released a breath. "This is a dangerous world we live in. It's inhabited by a lot of greedy, selfish, sadistic people who will trample over you to achieve their goals. Cruz stole from the people he claimed to be protecting. He and his men murdered and raped and pillaged, and he would've killed Tate if Tate hadn't killed him first. Same with those guards standing outside your tent—who do you think would've pulled the trigger when the general gave the order for you to die? Those men, Julia."

"I know." She spoke in a tortured whisper. "But it's difficult for me to think in those terms. I took an oath to save lives, not take them."

"You're saving your own life. That's equally important."

"I guess."

She moved away from the water and let the flowing skirt fall down her legs. Sand clung to her wet feet, but she didn't bend over to brush it off just yet. She wasn't ready to go in, and apparently Sebastian was in no hurry either.

As she fixed her gaze on the waves again, she became aware of how just how close they were standing. His muscular arm brushed her shoulder, and that appealing woodsy scent filled her nostrils and made her light-headed. She couldn't help but remember their flirty exchange at the clinic, how badly she'd wanted to kiss him. So much had changed in such a short amount of time, and yet one thing hadn't changed at all: she *still* wanted to kiss him.

No matter how inappropriate it might be, no matter how much her heart ached at the moment, she still wanted to discover what Sebastian Stone's lips would feel like pressed against her own.

So find out.

Julia wasn't sure if it was confidence or insanity that fueled her next move, but either way, grabbing Sebastian by his collar and bringing his head down for an impulsive kiss was completely out of character for her.

She felt his big body stiffen for a moment, but he recovered quickly, returning the kiss with such passion she nearly keeled over. Her knees wobbled, pulse raced, palms dampened. Sebastian's lips were firm, his mouth warm as he slanted it over hers and deepened the kiss.

When his tongue slid into her mouth in one sensual glide, she was helpless to stop him. The skill with which he kissed her stole the breath from her lungs. He licked, swirled, explored, his mouth hot and insistent as it met hers in blistering kisses that made her entire body burn with uncontrollable arousal.

As her hands came up to rest on his broad shoulders, his slid down to stroke the small of her back. They were both breathing hard, panting each time they broke apart for air, groaning each time their mouths reconnected.

She'd never felt this way before. Hot, needy, desperate. She bit Sebastian's lower lip, then sucked on it, eliciting a growl from deep in his chest.

"Holy hell, baby, that's hot," he muttered, and then he did the same damn thing to her, making her moan with abandon.

She had no clue how long they stood there, bare feet sinking in the sand, arms wrapped around each other, mouths and tongues dueling, but when they finally pulled apart again, her lips were swollen and her hair was a tangled mess from Sebastian's fingers running through it.

"I... Wow." She gulped, then sucked in a steadying breath. "I don't know what came over me."

His gray eyes smoldered with residual passion. "I'm not complaining."

Julia offered a faint smile. "So...what now?"

She wasn't sure what she'd expected him to say. Maybe "now we make out some more." Or maybe "now I take you inside and rock your world." She would've been just fine with any response, really.

Except the one he gave her.

"Now we pretend that didn't happen." All the humor had left his eyes, and now his expression was somber.

She raised her brows. "Are you joking?"

Sebastian shook his head. "We can't sleep together, Julia. Especially tonight. You watched the clinic burn to the ground yesterday, for chrissake, and we've been on the move ever since. You're afraid and upset and the adrenaline high is still—"

"Oh, for the love of God," she interrupted. "Would you quit telling me how I'm feeling? Why do men always do that?"

"You're telling me you're *not* upset, then?"

"No, of course I'm upset," she said irritably. "But you know what would make me *less* upset? Some forget-your-problems sex."

Another glimmer of heat flared in his gray eyes, but it burned out fast. "Maybe so, but it's still not a good idea, Doc. Right now I can't focus on anything other than getting out of this mess. I'm tired of hiding out, I'm tired of looking over my shoulder. I want this situation over and done with, and until that happens, I can't get involved with anyone."

A sigh slipped out of her throat. Crap. How was she supposed to fault him for that? She'd been running for only one day. He'd been doing it for months and months. *Of course* he had more urgent concerns at the moment than sex.

"I understand," she said quietly.

Relief flooded his handsome face. "Thank you. And look… You're a beautiful woman, Doc. I'm attracted to you, no denying that. But—" He shrugged awkwardly before taking a step away. "Sex just isn't on my mind right now. It's not a priority." Another step. "Anyway, let's go inside. I want to see if Nick heard from our contact."

With a nod, Julia trailed after him, happy he couldn't see her face because she knew she was blushing from embarrassment, not to mention the lingering desire coursing through her blood.

Now we pretend that didn't happen.

Ha. Fat chance, she thought as she followed Sebastian back to the house.

Chapter 8

At noon the next day, Sebastian, Julia and Nick left the beach house and drove to a small town two hours north of the coast to pick up identification papers for Julia. The men's contact had shipped the documents to a UPS office that seemed bizarrely out of place in the one-horse town of Poca Colina, which translated to "little hill." Now, as Sebastian tore open the envelope and studied their man's handiwork, he couldn't help but be impressed.

"Fernando did good," he remarked before extending the American passport, Massachusetts driver's license and birth certificate in Julia's direction.

Their fingers brushed, and his groin instantly tightened at the feel of her warm, delicate fingers. He hadn't been able to look her in the eye all morning, and in the rare instances when their gazes had connected, he'd been barraged with the memory of last night's makeout session. Christ, those kisses. He couldn't remember the last time his body had burned so hot, the last time his heart had pounded that hard.

In that moment, he'd needed Julia Davenport more than he'd needed his next breath. He'd been ready to rip that dress off her slender body, throw her down on the sand and screw her until they both couldn't move for days.

But he'd restrained himself at the last second, miraculously finding the strength to not only end that explosive kiss, but to make it clear that he couldn't get involved with her.

He'd lied to her, though, when he'd told her that sex wasn't on his mind. Yeah freaking right. Sex had been on his mind from the moment he'd met Julia at the clinic in Valero. The only problem was, she didn't seem like the type who'd be interested in a casual affair. When she'd told him about the cowboy she'd met on spring break, she'd claimed to be open to a no-strings affair, but he was still hesitant to take her up on the offer. You didn't mess around with women like Julia—smart, kind, respectable. She deserved more than a fling, but unfortunately, that was all he'd ever be able to give her.

"These are flawless." Julia's amazed voice broke through his thoughts. She was examining the documents he'd just handed her. "I'm afraid to ask how much it cost."

"Don't worry, we can afford it," Nick answered with a shrug.

The shrewd glint in her hazel eyes said she wanted to know more, but Nick didn't give her the chance to question him. He moved away from the plate-glass window of the courier office and strode toward the Jeep.

"Are we going to the airport now?" Julia asked.

"Yep." Sebastian checked his watch. "Our flight leaves in an hour."

"I'm surprised you're okay with this. I mean, you haven't been back on American soil since the attempts on your life. I know you're traveling under a different name, but aren't you afraid someone will recognize you at the airport?"

He burst out laughing. "Wait, do you think we're flying commercial?"

Her brows puckered. "Aren't we?"

"Hey, Nick, the doc thinks we're flying commercial," he told his fellow soldier.

Nick laughed. "Come on, Davenport, you're not *that* naive, are ya?" he said good-naturedly.

Her cheeks turned an appealing shade of pink. "I didn't think I was, but hell, I guess I am," she muttered.

Still chuckling, Sebastian waited until Julia hopped into the back of the Jeep before he slid into the passenger seat.

"We're catching a ride with a cargo jet at a private airfield," he explained as Nick started the engine and pulled away from the dusty sidewalk. "It'll take us all the way to upstate New York. After that, we'll rent a car and make our way to Cambridge."

Julia accepted their itinerary without a single protest, which he appreciated. He was discovering that absolutely nothing fazed the woman. She took everything in stride, and though she had no problem speaking her mind, she was also quick to follow orders. She trusted him to make decisions, so long as they were directly related to her safety, and he appreciated that above all else.

And yet the irony of it didn't escape him, because he was the *last* person she ought to be trusting with her life.

The airfield wasn't far from Poca Colina. They'd dealt with the man in charge only twice, once when Nick went to investigate a cholera outbreak in San Marquez, another time when Tate needed to rendezvous with one of their many contacts. The members of the spec ops community looked out for one another. Weapons, ammo, papers, transport, information—it was only a phone call away, no questions asked.

Nick followed the red dirt path toward a large metal gate. The runways in the distance were actually paved, a drastic difference from previous airfields they'd utilized. The airstrip housed three large hangars, and the selection of planes littering the tarmac was quite impressive. Mostly twin-engine Cessnas, but Sebastian also spotted a Boeing cargo aircraft that seemed out of place in such primitive surroundings.

Driving toward the area near the main hangar, Nick put the Jeep in Park and said, "Make sure you check in the second you get stateside, Seb."

"Will do." He hopped out of the vehicle, helped Julia out, then grabbed his go bag from the back.

"It was nice meeting you." Julia offered Nick a warm, albeit wry, smile. "I wish it had been under different circumstances, though."

"Me, too, Doc. Me, too." Nick lifted his hand in a quick wave. "Be safe, guys."

A minute later, the Jeep was going out the way it came in, leaving Sebastian and Julia alone for the first time all day.

She was wearing her jeans again, as well as that white tank top that had been responsible for keeping him awake half the night. Every time he'd closed his eyes he'd pictured that see-through fabric…Julia's small, puckered nipples poking right through her paper-thin white bra….

His mouth watered just thinking about it, and he had to wrench his eyes away. "C'mon, our pilot's waiting."

They walked through the open door of the hangar. As Sebastian's boots thudded against the waxed floor, several men in dark blue jumpsuits glanced over suspiciously.

"I'm looking for Ricardo," he called, his voice bouncing off the hangar walls.

One of the workers jabbed a finger at the cargo jet Sebastian had been admiring before. With a nod of thanks, he kept walking, Julia sticking close to his side, and as they crossed the cavernous space, he noticed several more men gathered a few yards away. All three stopped to leer at Julia as if they hadn't seen a woman in years.

Setting his jaw, Sebastian rested a possessive hand on Julia's slender arm.

Her head swiveled in surprise, and then a knowing smirk curved her lips.

"What?" he mumbled.

She raised a brow and lifted one shoulder. "Nothing."

Ignoring that strange rush of protectiveness, he quickened the pace and practically dragged her toward the cargo jet. The large door at the rear of the plane was wide open, revealing dozens of wooden crates and burlap sacks filling every inch of the cargo hold. Two dark-skinned men chattering in loud Spanish were securing a pallet of crates to the wall, strapping mesh netting over it to keep it in place.

Metal rattled as a thin man with dark skin and bushy facial hair descended the set of steps at the side of the jet. "Stone?" he called.

Sebastian nodded. "Ricardo?"

The man nodded back. He spared Julia a brief look before stalking over to shake hands with Sebastian. According to Tate, Ricardo was reputed to be one of the best pilots in the world, having served in an elite fighter unit within the Colombian Air Force. The man ran this cargo airline now, which was apparently his only legitimate business. His other enterprises were rumored to be far more nefarious.

"We're all set for takeoff," Ricardo said in surprisingly good English. "Time to get you strapped in."

Julia looked alarmed. "Strapped in?" she hissed as they followed Ricardo to the back of the plane.

After they climbed the ramp leading into the cargo hold, Ricardo led them to a narrow metal bench spanning the wall adjacent to the cockpit. "Buckle up. Flight duration will be six hours or so." That was all the man said before he marched off and left them to their own devices.

Sebastian stowed his duffel bag underneath the bench, then sat down and strapped himself in with the crisscross belts affixed to the wall behind him. As he clicked the belts into place, he eyed Julia expectantly. "Better buckle up, Doc."

Shaking her head, she sat beside him and secured herself. "This can't be safe," she said in dismay.

"Safer than flying commercial," he replied with a shrug.

A whirring noise whined in the air, followed by the rumble of the jet's engines roaring to life. The cargo hold began to rattle, the crates and bags on board shaking from the vibrations. It was easy to guess the contents of the cargo—along with the smell of gasoline and oil hanging in the air, Sebastian made out the rich aroma of coffee beans, which had him craving a cup of coffee.

It was too damn noisy to hold a conversation without shouting, so he and Julia stayed quiet during takeoff. He noticed her white-knuckling the edge of the bench, and her face was pale as the plane took flight and the wheels retracted with a loud metallic screech.

Before he could stop himself, he covered one of her hands with his own and dragged his palm over her tense knuckles. Julia's gaze flew to him in surprise.

"Relax," he told her, a teasing note in his voice. "Ricardo has flown this route hundreds of times. The coffee always reaches its destination, safe and sound. We'll be fine."

Her fingers relaxed slightly. "You're right. I'm being silly, aren't I?"

"You're allowed to be." He tipped his head to the side. "I think this is the first time you've shown any fear since we met, and a lot of pretty terrifying things have happened since then."

She sighed. "I'm still trying to decide if I hallucinated half of it."

"You didn't." He stroked her knuckles again. "I'm sorry you got dragged into this."

"So am I. God, and to think, if Kevin hadn't contacted me over the radio I never would've known about this virus or that someone is treating human beings like guinea pigs." She smiled sardonically. "I never thought I'd say this, but a part of me wishes I was still living in ignorance."

"Me, too."

A staticky sound crackled in the cargo hold, followed by Ricardo's muffled voice. "We've reached the necessary altitude. You can unbuckle your belts now and take it easy. I'll let you know if we hit turbulence."

As he unsnapped his belt, Sebastian noticed the bemused expression on Julia's face. "What is it?" he asked.

"I'm just wondering how you have all these contacts. You got perfect identity papers done in less than twenty-four hours. You have a pilot willing to sneak you into the States. You seem to have an endless supply of weapons, computers, a safe house. How do you have so many connections?"

"The black ops community looks after its own."

"For free?" She sounded incredibly dubious.

He laughed. "For a hefty price," he corrected. "But after the three of us left town, Tate and I found out that our little Nicky was holding out on us. Turns out Prescott is filthy rich. We all cleaned out our bank accounts before we took off, and his cashout was in the seven-figure range. He's pretty much been bankrolling everything since we went into hiding."

"Is it family money? Or was he some entrepreneur superstar before he joined the army?"

"No clue. Nick doesn't talk about it, and we don't ask. I assume it's family money, though."

Julia shifted around so she was facing him. "What about you? What's your family like?"

His stomach clenched as pain swelled inside it. "Dead."

"You have no family at all?"

"Nope. My dad died in combat when I was fifteen

years old—he was a marine. Mom died of cancer about ten years ago."

And Tommy. Greg. Lynn.

His heart squeezed so hard he thought it might burst. Christ, he wasn't allowed to think about them. It still hurt so damn bad, even after all these years.

"No grandparents, aunts?" Julia prompted.

"All four of my grandparents died a long time ago, and my parents were only children, so I've got no uncles or aunts or cousins scattered about." He was suddenly eager to change the subject before she pushed for any more details. "What about you?"

"Parents divorced when I was ten," Julia replied. "My sister and I lived with my mother, who isn't the easiest woman to get along with. She's very controlling, very old-fashioned. My dad actually fought for custody of us and lost. He was a doctor, too, a surgeon at Boston General."

"Is that why you went into medicine, because of your father?"

She nodded. "I wanted to follow in his footsteps." Sorrow washed over her face. "He died a few weeks before I graduated from medical school."

"Ah hell, Doc. I'm sorry." He stroked her hand again, marveling at how smooth her skin was. "I bet he was real proud of you, though."

"He was." She smiled, a faraway look entering her eyes. "But I'm not sure how he would've felt about my going to work for Doctors International. He wanted me to work at the hospital with him."

"Why *did* you decide to work abroad?"

She focused her gaze on the coffee crates on the opposite wall. "Just wanted to make a difference, I guess."

There was clearly a lot more to the story, but Julia didn't continue and he didn't push. He did, however, regret his change of topic the moment his next question flew out of his mouth. "Why is it that you don't have a boyfriend?"

She arched a brow. "Why is that you don't have a girlfriend?"

"Fair enough." Sebastian grinned. "You first."

Julia stretched out her legs and leaned her head on the wall behind her. "I've dated two men over the past three years, and neither one could handle the traveling I do for work. I'm gone nine out of twelve months of the year—I'm pretty confident I'll never meet a man who's on board with that. Nobody wants an absentee partner."

"You could always find a man who wants to travel *with* you," he pointed out.

"True."

"Maybe a colleague? A relief worker you meet abroad?"

"I don't date colleagues. Ever. It's a rule of mine. I've seen too many relationships between coworkers blow up in their faces. And I haven't met anyone overseas who's sparked my interest." She shot him a pointed look. "Except for you."

Damned if that didn't make his groin stir. Crap. He couldn't believe she'd brought it up, yet at the same time, he wasn't surprised. Julia struck him as a woman who always spoke her mind, regardless of any discomfort it might cause.

"Anyway," she said with a dismissive wave of her hand, "your turn. Why aren't you with anyone?"

"Other than the fact that I'm hiding out from my own government? I'm a commitment-phobe," he said gruffly.

She laughed.

"I'm serious. I don't do permanent. I don't *want* permanent." He offered a rueful smile. "I'm not cut out for relationships, Doc. I bore easily."

"I see."

He doubted that—because every word he'd just said was a big fat lie. But he'd perfected that line of reasoning over the years, feeding it to the females who attempted to make sense of his love-'em-and-leave-'em ways.

Beside him, Julia suddenly narrowed her eyes, looking far too astute for his liking. "Wait a minute—do you think *I* want permanent? Is that why you scurried away like a skittish kitten last night?"

"Skittish kitten? I don't recall it going down that way. In fact, I'm fairly positive that I didn't *scurry*."

"You may as well have." A defiant gleam lit her eyes. "I think you lied to me yesterday when you said sex wasn't on your mind. I think you *totally* want to have sex with me."

A laugh popped out before he could stop it. "I'm digging the confidence, Doc. Really."

"Am I wrong?" she challenged.

He supposed he could've lied, but Julia was so damn up-front about everything that he felt he owed her the same courtesy.

"No, you're not wrong," he admitted.

"But you're worried I won't be satisfied with temporary, huh?" She released a self-deprecating breath. "It's the doctor thing, right? Men always assume that because I'm a doctor, I'm superserious and therefore looking for a serious relationship. But that's bullcrap, you know. I can do a casual fling. If anything, that's *all* I can do right now."

He couldn't control the anticipation that rose inside him. He studied her pretty face, trying to assess if she was for real. In his experience, women often said they were fully down for casual, while at the same time secretly plotting how to turn casual into *forever*. But Julia's guileless expression and tone of voice seemed sincere.

"You can be satisfied with temporary, huh?" he said slowly.

"Yes."

"You sure about that?"

The hot air in the cargo hold grew even muggier, thickening with promise. Sebastian's gaze lowered to those small, perky breasts of hers, perfectly outlined by her white tank top. Her nipples hardened right before his eyes, flooding his mouth with saliva and making his fingers itch with the urge to play with those pebbled buds.

He brought his eyes back north, watching the flush rising in her cheeks, the way she moistened her bottom lip with her tongue.

"Well?" he asked.

A tiny smile lifted the corners of her generous mouth. "I'm sure."

"Okay, then."

Before she could blink, he thrust his hand in her hair and yanked her in for a kiss.

He swallowed her surprised gasp with his lips, loving the way she melted into him, rubbing her breasts against his chest like a contented cat, opening her mouth to grant his tongue access. He'd intended for it to be a quick kiss, a sealing of the deal, a hint of everything he'd do to her when they got near a bed, but Julia clearly had other ideas. She broke the kiss, grabbed the bottom of her tank top and whipped the garment over her head, leaving her in that flimsy white bra that didn't hide a damn thing.

Sebastian's mouth went dry as a bone, his pulse taking off to another dimension. "What are you doing?" he rasped.

She rolled her eyes, then stood up and unbuttoned her jeans. "What do you think I'm doing?"

It took every ounce of willpower to channel his inner gentleman. "We...can't do this here."

"Says who?"

She wiggled out of her jeans and kicked them away.

Holy hell.

She was standing in front of him in nothing but her white bra and teeny pink panties, a picture of pure temptation. His gaze roamed her body—those little round breasts, the tiny tucked-in waist, her long slender legs. Her wavy brown hair cascaded down her back, her cheeks were pink with arousal and her hazel eyes gleamed with challenge.

Never in a million years would he have guessed Julia Davenport capable of stripping to her underwear in the back of a cargo jet.

"You're just full of surprises," he murmured.

"And you're just full of excuses. Come on, Stone, I don't have all day. Take off your clothes."

"Aren't you bossy."

"I'm a doctor. I'm used to giving orders."

Any hesitation he'd had floated away in the coffee-scented air of the fuselage. Sebastian wasted no time peeling off his T-shirt, kicking off his boots and shucking his pants. His erection strained against the front of his black boxer briefs, and Julia's gaze instantly zeroed in on the telltale evidence of his arousal.

She took a step toward him, her blatant appreciation bringing a jolt of pure male satisfaction. "You like my body?" he said gruffly.

"Mmm-hmm."

Those hazel eyes devoured his bare chest, his abdomen, his crotch, his legs. Everywhere she looked, his skin burned. Desire built in his groin, thick and relentless. With a growl, he tugged her into his arms again and kissed her roughly, loving the way she moaned against his lips.

Excitement pounded in his blood and skated over his flesh. "Wrap your legs around me," he ordered, then cupped Julia's surprisingly plump ass and lifted her up.

She hooked her legs around his waist and dug her bare feet into his ass, kissing him with fervor as he carried her over to a nearby pile of burlap sacks. It was as close to a bed as they were going to get, and the scratchy burlap sure as hell beat the dirty, oil-streaked floor.

He laid her down on the makeshift bed, then stood over her for a moment, admiring the view. "Christ, Doc, you're beautiful."

She blushed. "I thought I was too skinny."

"Doesn't mean you're not beautiful." Sweeping his tongue over his bottom lip, he gestured to her chest. "Unhook the bra."

Her fingers flicked the front clasp and parted the two cups, revealing a pair of small, lily-white breasts tipped by dusky pink nipples.

His mouth watered again. "Now take off the panties."

Her throat bobbed as she swallowed. Gripping the elastic of her pink panties, she dragged the fabric down her legs.

Sebastian focused on the narrow strip of brown curls at the juncture of her thighs. His heartbeat took off again. Wrestling his gaze away from all that female splendor was damn near impossible, but he forced his legs to transport him back to the bench, where he plucked a condom from the zippered medical kit in his duffel.

When he returned to Julia, he was already sheathed and more than ready to lose himself in this woman.

A tad impatient, he lowered his body over hers and captured her mouth again, making her moan with the hungry demands of his tongue. Her short fingernails gouged his bare back, and she began rocking beneath him, murmuring nonsensical words that made him chuckle.

It wasn't until he positioned himself at her entrance that she seemed to regain her senses. "Be gentle," she blurted out. "It's been a while for me."

He couldn't fight his curiosity. "What's a while?"

Julia hesitated before answering. "Two years."

"Almost a year for me," he confessed.

"Really?"

He nodded.

Her sweet smile had his heart doing a strange little flip. "So apparently you need this as much as I do," she murmured.

He pushed a teasing inch into her wet heat, and they both released soft groans.

"I need it bad," he agreed in a hoarse voice, so unbelievably aroused he feared he might be a little too quick on the trigger.

Knowing release was dangerously close, he focused on Julia's pleasure rather than his own. He kissed her neck, eliciting a breathy sigh from her lips. Gently cupped her breasts, and listened to her breath hitch. Teased her clit with his thumb, making her eyes go hazy with arousal.

"How do you... You're..." She trailed off, then moaned when he feathered his thumb over her swollen nub at the same time he drove his cock in deep.

"How do I what?" he prompted, absolutely loving the look of exquisite pleasure on her face.

"Know exactly how to make me feel good," she choked out.

"I'm just listening to your body, baby."

He nibbled on her earlobe, doing his best to ignore the throbbing erection that was demanding he quicken his tempo. He refused to let go until Julia toppled over the edge, and luckily, that didn't take long at all. As he felt her inner muscles clench around him, he picked up the pace, continuing to rub her clit as he thrust into her with long, smooth strokes. The moment Julia cried out in release, he squeezed his eyes shut and gave himself over to his own climax, stunned by the shock waves of pure bliss that rocked his body.

Gasping for air, he collapsed on top of her. Pleasure continued to course through his blood, heating his body and fogging his brain. He could feel Julia's heartbeat hammering against his chest. Knew she was equally affected and bowled over by the encounter, because her eyes were full of wonder when he peered down at her.

"Wow," she said, her voice tinged with awe. "That was... Wow."

Raising himself up on his elbows so he wouldn't crush her, he brushed his lips over hers before withdrawing from the tight clasp of her body.

"Ugh, I'm totally going to have a rash on my butt," Julia groaned as she sat up. "That burlap is itchy."

Remorse washed over him. "I'm sorry. Maybe we shouldn't have—"

She held up her hand to silence him. "Don't you dare apologize. I loved every second of what just happened. It was... Wow."

He laughed. "You know, for a doctor, you sure have an abysmal vocabulary."

"Do you have a better word to describe what just happened?"

Sebastian searched his brain. "It was..." Resignation fluttered through him. "It was *wow.*"

Grinning, Julia hopped to her feet with surprising agility. It wasn't until she'd gathered up her discarded undergarments and began getting dressed that her expression sobered.

In a pained voice, she slowly met his eyes and said, "Does it make me a terrible person that for a second there I completely forgot about everything that's happened?"

He yanked his boxer briefs up to his hips, then approached Julia and gently drew her into his arms. "You're not a terrible person. You're allowed to put away the bad for a while and focus on the good."

"But now the bad is back."

"Yep," he said grimly.

She swallowed. "And I have a really strong suspicion that it's only going to get worse."

He didn't offer any reassurances. Like Julia, he was thinking the same thing.

Chapter 9

They didn't reach Cambridge until two o'clock in the morning. Julia was thoroughly exhausted as she climbed into the queen-size bed of their hotel room, yet while Sebastian passed out the second his head hit the pillow, she couldn't seem to sleep no matter how hard she tried. It had been an action-packed day and her brain refused to shut off.

Earlier, they'd landed at a small airport near Albany that catered to cargo airlines, then took a cab to a car rental agency to secure a vehicle. She'd rented the car under her new name—Julie Francis—and the clerk at the desk hadn't batted an eye when Julia handed over her fake driver's license. Three hours later, she and Sebastian had checked into this hotel, and now here she was, wide awake, staring up at the ceiling and wondering what horrors tomorrow would bring.

The events of the last couple of days continued to

run through her mind like reruns of a bad sitcom. The clinic was a pile of ashes. Her friends were dead. Her life was in danger. And in between those gruesome images were snippets of actual joy—making love to Sebastian on the plane, their easy conversation, the surprisingly entertaining drive to Cambridge.

But it was the lovemaking part that hogged most of her thoughts. She still couldn't believe *she'd* instigated that incredible encounter. Stripping, challenging him to give in to the attraction between them. And what followed had been the most intense, amazing, thrilling sex of her life. She'd given Sebastian complete control over her body, a realization that continued to astound her. She *never* relinquished control, not in her professional life and not in the bedroom, and yet she'd let Sebastian take charge earlier.

And he'd shocked her by knowing exactly how to bring her pleasure without her having to direct him the way she'd done with previous lovers.

Rolling over on her side, she studied Sebastian's sleeping face. His features were more peaceful than she'd ever seen, his sensual mouth relaxed. She was tempted to run her fingers along the defined line of his jaw, stroke the stubble growing there, trace the outline of his sexy lips, but she didn't want to wake him. Instead, she closed her eyes, eventually falling into fitful slumber.

When she opened her eyes the next morning, the sun was streaming in through the gauzy white curtains across the room. Sebastian's side of the bed was empty. Yawning, Julia sat up and glanced at the bathroom door, which was ajar. The shower was running, wisps of steam rolling out from the crack in the door.

Her heart somersaulted as she imagined Sebastian standing naked under the spray, water coursing down his muscular body, sliding over his golden skin and perfectly defined muscles. She was tempted to join him in the shower, but a glance at the alarm clock showed it was almost nine o'clock, and she knew they needed to get going as soon as possible.

A few minutes later, the water shut off and Sebastian appeared in the doorway wearing nothing but a white towel that hung low on his trim hips.

A jolt of heat seared right through her clothes and made her skin tingle.

"Morning," he said, his gray eyes meeting hers.

"Morning." She slid out of bed and headed for the bathroom. "Do I have time to take a quick shower, too?"

"Of course." The corners of his mouth curved. "I would've asked you to join me, but you looked so damn peaceful and I didn't want to wake you."

"I'm glad you didn't. I was tossing and turning all night."

"By the way, I drove into town while you were sleeping and picked you up a few things," he told her. "Toothbrush, hairbrush, clothes. I had to guess at your size, so hopefully it all fits. I left everything in the bathroom."

Julia was touched. "Thank you. You didn't have to do that."

"I figured you were probably getting tired of wearing that same see-through shirt all the time." Those gray eyes smoldered with desire. "Not that I'm complaining. I *love* that shirt."

"Of course you do." Rolling her eyes, she walked into the bathroom and shut the door behind her.

Because she wasn't the type of woman who spent an

inordinate amount of time on her appearance, she was ready to go in less than thirty minutes. She'd put on one of the outfits Sebastian had bought her, pleased to find that the jeans fit perfectly. She paired them with a V-neck black T-shirt, ankle socks and the new pair of running shoes she discovered at the bottom of the shopping bag. She braided her hair in her usual no-nonsense style and grabbed the sunglasses she'd also found among Sebastian's purchases. The man had thought of everything.

The sunglasses came in handy once she and Sebastian walked out of the hotel lobby and stepped outside. It was a beautiful, sunny day, much hotter than usual for mid-May in Massachusetts. As they strode to the hotel parking lot toward their rental, she noticed Sebastian examining his surroundings as if he couldn't quite understand what he was seeing.

"What's wrong?" she demanded.

He seemed distracted, his silvery eyes focused on the lampposts lining the sidewalk running parallel to the lot. "What? Oh, nothing's wrong. The return to civilization is jarring, I guess. I couldn't fully appreciate it last night because I was so damn tired, but now..." He shook his head. "It's weird being back."

"Are you from Massachusetts?" she asked, realizing he'd never actually told her where he was from.

"Nah, I was raised in Virginia Beach. Haven't been back there in years, though. When the unit wasn't on assignment, I was living in an apartment in Richmond."

He started the car and drove out of the lot, shooting her a sidelong look. "So this guy's lab is directly on campus?"

Julia nodded. "It's right past the natural history museum, on Oxford Street. I'll tell you where to go once we get closer."

As they set out toward Harvard's Cambridge campus, she toyed with the end of her braid, praying that Frank wouldn't ask too many questions when she showed up at his lab with a potentially deadly water sample. She didn't have to worry about Frank not being there— using Sebastian's "secure" smartphone, she'd spoken to a receptionist in the biology department who'd confirmed that Dr. Matheson was on campus and would be all week.

"We need to be careful today." Sebastian's voice hardened as he uttered the warning. "How close are you with this guy?"

"Close enough. Why?"

He didn't look happy about that. "Okay, listen up, Doc. At this point, we have to assume that the general in charge of the Esperanza cleanup has contacted his superiors. They know you escaped, and they probably assume you're hiding out somewhere in San Marquez. With that said, these people aren't stupid. They'll have placed tails on everyone you know in the States, and tapped their phones, just in case you make contact. So, I repeat, how close are you and the professor?"

"We're good friends. I have lunch with him whenever I come home." A tremor of fear traveled along her spine. "Do you really think they'll be watching Frank in hopes that I come to him for help?"

"Good chance. Which is why we need to take certain precautions." His tone became dry. "And just so I don't come off like a moron when we meet this man, maybe you can tell me exactly what it is a microbiologist does?"

She cracked a smile, knowing he was trying to take her mind off the scary scenarios he'd just painted. "Well, Frank's expertise actually lies in virology, which is a subfield of microbiology," she explained. "Basically, he studies viruses."

"How viruses work, how they spread—that type of stuff?"

"Pretty much, except it's more complex than that. He also focuses on the virus's evolution, the way it interacts with the host organisms, the way it reproduces. And along with that, he tries to develop more efficient ways to isolate a virus and culture it so it can be studied." She laughed. "Most of it is way over my head, too, so trust me, you won't be the only one feeling like a moron. And Frank tends to get very lecturey when he's passionate about something, so be prepared."

"Lecturey?" Sebastian echoed with a grin. "Do all doctors just arbitrarily make up words like that?"

"Yup. Oh, turn left up there," she ordered.

He slowed down as they navigated the campus. Thanks to the great weather, students had flocked outdoors, littering the school's manicured lawns, milling outside the gorgeous ivy-covered buildings. Julia fixed her gaze out the window, watching as people hurried by, carting textbooks or chatting on cell phones as if they had no care in the world. Sebastian was right— it *was* weird being back home. After living in Valero for six months, Julia now felt disoriented as she stared at the beautiful historical buildings and happy young faces and modern conveniences like phones and laptops and tablets.

Sebastian didn't stop right away—he did three passes around the block before his rigid shoulders finally relaxed. She'd noticed his hawk-eyed gaze doing a thorough sweep, though she had no clue what he was looking for.

"Parking!" she exclaimed when she spotted a black Honda beginning to move away from the curb. "Take the spot. You don't understand how miraculous this is. You won't find anything closer and we can walk the rest of the way."

"Yes, ma'am." Sebastian pulled into the space without question.

His vigilance only intensified as they got out of the car. When he popped a pair of aviator sunglasses on the bridge of his nose, Julia couldn't see his eyes anymore, but she had no doubt he was still inspecting every inch of their surroundings. And she knew he could probably whip out his gun in a nanosecond; she'd seen him tuck the black Beretta under the waistband of his snug jeans before they left the hotel. He'd offered her a weapon, too, but she'd declined—she was a decent shot, but guns made her nervous.

Five minutes later, they climbed the steps of the building that housed Frank Matheson's lab. Julia was hit by a wave of nostalgia as they entered the familiar lobby. She suddenly flashed back to her college days, remembering how eager she was to finish medical school, how excited she'd been for her residency at Boston General. She would've worked in the same hospital as her father if that heart attack hadn't taken him from her. And then, only two years later, Mia was gone, too.

Her heart ached as she pictured her sister's face. God, she still missed her. She wondered if her mother thought about Mia as often as Julia did. Probably not. Darlene

Davenport didn't do emotions. The woman was carved from a block of ice.

Julia led the way to the stairwell. Frank's lab was in the basement of the building, and the fluorescent-lit corridor was empty as she and Sebastian headed down it. They reached a pair of double doors, one bearing a bronze nameplate with Frank's name and field.

She entered the lab without knocking, same way she'd done when she was a student here and Frank Matheson was the biology professor who'd taken her under his wing. They'd become close friends over the years, Frank treating her like the daughter he'd never been able to have. He'd once confessed over drinks that he was sterile thanks to a bad case of the mumps he'd had as a child. His wife had left him as a result and rather than remarry, he'd thrown himself into his work.

"Jules?" Frank was agape when he spotted her in the doorway.

She smiled sheepishly. "Hey, Frank."

From the corner of her eye, she noticed Sebastian's observant gaze doing another sweep, and his shoulders stiffened when Frank Matheson made a beeline for Julia. He took a protective step toward her, ready to come to her rescue if need be.

But Julia wasn't scared of the man dashing toward her. Frank looked every bit the mad scientist: a head of gray hair sticking up in all directions, wild brown eyes and a beard that seemed to devour his face. Rather than a white coat, he wore brown corduroy pants and a blue button-down with the tails sticking out.

"What are you doing here?" he exclaimed after he'd hugged her so tightly her lungs pleaded for oxygen. "When did you get back from San Marquez?"

"Late last night."

Frank narrowed his eyes as he glanced at Sebastian. "And you brought a friend."

She knew her former professor didn't like having strangers in his lab, so she quickly introduced Sebastian, finishing with, "I'm sorry we just showed up like this, but we really need your help, Frank."

His bushy gray eyebrows furrowed. "Should I be worried?"

Never one to sugarcoat, Julia let out a sigh. "Yes. Can we sit down?"

With visible concern, he gestured for them to follow him to the other end of the spacious laboratory. Several long tables filled the space, covered with every piece of equipment known to man—microscopes of various sizes, centrifuges, rows and rows of test tubes. Large refrigerated cabinets housed an array of vials containing samples in an assortment of colors, and the stark overhead lighting was nearly blinding.

Frank led them to the only table in the lab that wasn't overloaded with stacks of paper or equipment. He sat on one of the tall metal stools, while Julia and Sebastian settled across from him.

Without a word, Sebastian placed the water sample from Esperanza in the center of the table. They'd transferred it into a durable plastic vial, and Sebastian had been keeping it on his person since they'd left San Marquez. A second sample had been left behind with Tate, just in case something happened to this one.

Frank cocked a brow at the vial. "What's this?"

"That's what we were hoping you'd tell us," Julia said flatly.

"I'm confused here, Jules. I thought you weren't

coming home for another three months. Why aren't you at the clinic?"

"First, I need to know, has anyone come around asking about me?" she asked, shooting him a grave look. "Cops, military, government officials?"

"What? No." Amazement trickled from his voice. "*Should* I be expecting someone?"

"Maybe," she admitted. "People might be looking for me, Frank. And if anyone comes by, you can't tell them I was here."

"All right. Now I'm worried. What's going on, Jules?"

With a heavy breath, she gave him the short version of the story. He interrupted more than once, and several times his eyes widened or his mouth fell open. She knew how farfetched it all sounded, yet to Frank's credit, he kept his skepticism to a minimum.

"Are you sure those people died from a virus, Jules? You said so yourself, you never saw the bodies."

Sebastian spoke up. "The men in charge made several references to a virus. And like Julia mentioned, this wasn't an isolated incident. The same virus, or one similar to it, was released ten months ago in another village."

Frank was looking increasingly alarmed. "And there's nothing more you can tell me about it? Modes of transmission? Incubation period? The ways in which it manifests?"

"We don't know much." Lines bracketed the corners of her mouth. "Potential symptoms are nosebleeds, foaming at the mouth, coughing maybe. We really don't know. That's why we came to you. We need to find out everything we can about this thing."

Her former professor rubbed his chin, those brown

eyes growing distant as he gave it some thought. "I don't like this," he finally said. "You should go to the police. If those villagers really were murdered, not to mention everyone at the clinic, you need to inform the authorities."

"We can't." She shook her head in frustration. "Those soldiers were discussing the idea of killing me and blaming it on a virus! We can't involve the police in this. The people in charge will just swoop in and orchestrate another cover-up."

Frank shifted on his stool, looking extremely reluctant.

Sebastian, who hadn't said much during the discussion, leaned forward and rested his elbows on the tabletop. "Look, Dr. Matheson, I understand where you're coming from. Normally when people wind up dead, you call the cops, they investigate, catch the bad guys and case closed. But whatever's going on here, it's bigger than that. Someone is going to great lengths to keep the testing of this virus on the down low, and now that Julia knows the truth about what happened in the village, she's a target. Do you understand?"

Worry erupted in the older man's eyes. Julia had to hand it to Sebastian—he'd homed in on Frank's weakness: the affection he felt for his surrogate daughter.

"Are you really in danger, Jules?" Frank asked quietly.

She nodded.

He reached for the vial and turned it over in his hand. "This won't be easy," he confessed. "There might not be enough of a sample here. When viruses are present in water, it's typically in very low numbers. It's far easier to detect a bacterium, or a parasite, as opposed to a virus."

Her heart dropped. "But you can do it, right?"

"I can try." He stroked his salt-and-pepper beard in a contemplative pose. "I suppose you want this done as soon as possible?"

"As fast as humanly possible," she said ruefully. "And when I say this is life or death, I really frickin' mean it."

Both men chuckled, and then Frank grew serious again. "I'll do my best, but if you'd paid any attention in my class, you'd know that detection using cell cultures takes time."

"How much time?" Sebastian asked sharply.

"A few days, a few weeks." The scientist shrugged. "The cells must be observed for signs of cellular destruction, and some viruses need as long as two weeks of growth before I can reach any conclusive results."

Sebastian looked as frustrated as Julia felt. "Is there any way to speed up the process, Doc?"

For a second she thought he was talking to her, until she noticed those intense gray eyes focused on Frank. She experienced an odd spark of disappointment at the realization that Sebastian was so quick to assign the same nickname to someone else.

Call her pathetic, but she'd enjoyed feeling special.

"I can combine the culture with molecular detection," Frank said thoughtfully. "Molecular methods often produce results in only twenty-four hours. What I can do is use reverse transcriptase-polymerase chain reaction—"

"And you lost me," Sebastian interrupted with a laugh.

Julia grinned at her old friend. "Just skip the explanation and give us the bottom line—will this combination of methods produce definitive results?"

"It should." Frank sounded confident. "Let me get
started on this right now. I can keep you apprised of
any progress I make—do you still have the same cell
number?"

She swallowed a lump of sadness, deciding not to
mention that her cell phone, along with all her belongings and all her friends, had burned right along with the
clinic. She quickly banished the heartbreaking memory.

"No, but you can call Sebastian's phone." She
glanced at Sebastian, who quickly supplied the number.

"Do you need to write that down?" he asked when
Frank didn't reach for the notepad and ballpoint pen
next to his arm.

"I have a head for numbers, young man. Don't worry,
I'll remember it." To illustrate, Frank recited the phone
number without a single error.

Sebastian stood up and reached into his back pocket.
He pulled out a slender black flip phone and handed it
to Frank. "Use this phone when you contact us. It's a
disposable, and it can't be traced."

The professor slid off his stool, his expression taking on that glint of focused intensity Julia had seen so
many times before.

Knowing he was two seconds from entering "science
world," she rounded the table and gave him a quick hug,
overcome with a rush of gratitude. "Thanks, Frank. I
owe you one."

He planted a kiss on her forehead. "You know I'll do
anything for you. Now skedaddle. Give me some time
to work on this."

She took a step away, then halted. "I don't need to tell you to keep this quiet, do I? Discretion is key."

"Don't you worry, Jules. My lips are sealed."

Two days later, Julia paced the carpeted floor of the hotel room, biting on her bottom lip and trying hard not to panic. It had been eight hours since Frank's last call and she was getting worried. She and Sebastian had been twiddling their thumbs in this room for what was beginning to feel like an eternity.

"Why hasn't he called again?" she demanded.

Sebastian was lying in the center of the bed with his arms propped behind his head, wearing nothing but a pair of gray sweatpants the same dark shade as his eyes. His bare chest gleamed beneath the dim ceiling lamp, but not even his deliciously tight six-pack could ease her distress. Last time Frank checked in, he'd sounded incredibly distracted, and she'd also picked up on a quiver of fear in his voice.

"I'm sure he's just running some more tests," Sebastian answered. "Yesterday he said he was following up on a hunch, remember?"

"I remember." She gnawed on the inside of her cheek. "He's scared, Sebastian. I heard it in his voice today. It must be about the results."

Sinking down on the edge of the mattress, she studied Sebastian's unruffled expression and shook her head in dismay. "Why don't you look worried?"

"Because worrying achieves nothing. I don't operate on what-ifs. I focus on facts, on what's right in front of me. And right now, we don't know much of anything." He held out one muscular arm. "C'mere. Let me distract you for a bit."

Immediately, a rush of warmth flooded her body. It was official—she was addicted to this man's touch.

When he yanked her against him, she melted into him like butter on a hot pan, wondering why she transformed into a completely different woman when she was in Sebastian's arms. He brought out a sensual, uninhibited side she never knew she possessed.

"You taste like chocolate and strawberries," he murmured as he slanted his mouth over hers in a deep kiss.

"That's because you made me eat an excessive amount of both for lunch," she reminded him.

"Just trying to fatten you up a bit." He said it teasingly, then cupped her breasts over her shirt.

Julia shivered, feeling utterly wanton as she rubbed her hardening nipples into his palms. She loved the way he touched her. Loved the mind-shattering sensations he evoked in her, the new and unfamiliar responses he summoned from her body.

He shoved his hands underneath her butt and lifted her onto his lap. The ridge of his erection pressed into her mound, making her moan. He was always so hard, so ready. It was liable to give her an ego, how turned on he got whenever she was around.

With heavy-lidded gray eyes, he peeled off her T-shirt and tossed it aside, then tackled her bra. "I need to taste you, baby."

Baby. He only called her that when they were in bed, and she found herself eagerly anticipating the moments when those two rough syllables exited his sexy mouth. But nothing was as thrilling as the wet suction of that mouth as it closed around her nipple.

Sighing with pleasure, she closed her eyes and gave herself over to his erotic ministrations. His tongue came out to lick her nipple, flicking against the puckered bud before he sucked it hard, bringing a jolt of heat and a sting of pain. Sebastian slid one hand between her legs and stroked her over the thin material of her leggings, his tongue continuing to tease and torture her aching breasts.

As her muscles tightened and her sex quivered, it occurred to her that she'd had more orgasms in the past two days than in the past five years combined. And when Sebastian dipped a hand into her leggings, pushed aside the crotch of her panties and stroked her damp folds with skilled fingers, yet another orgasm blew through her, making her sag into his broad chest as she shuddered with pleasure.

How did he always manage to make her come apart without warning like that?

She stared at him in wonder, about to ask him that very question, but then she glimpsed the expression on his face and her breath hitched. Raw, hungry lust. Taut features. Glittering gray eyes. He wanted her, and a part of her still couldn't fathom how a gorgeous warrior like this would be drawn to a scrawny, frizzy-haired workaholic like her.

Rolling onto her side, she cupped the bulge in his sweatpants, eliciting a low groan from him. "I'm really enjoying this fling," she murmured, running her hand up and down his hard length.

"Me, too." His eyelids grew heavy as he thrust his erection into her hand.

She stroked him for several lazy moments before tugging on his waistband to pull down his pants. With her body still loose and relaxed from her climax, she didn't feel the urgency to have him inside her. She was in the mood to explore now, to tease him the way he liked to tease her, to torment him the way he tormented her.

He wasn't wearing anything beneath his pants, and his erection sprang up to greet her, long and thick and weeping with desire. Smiling, Julia crawled between his legs and encircled his shaft with one hand, giving it a firm squeeze.

Sebastian groaned.

Pleased with his reaction, she decided to drive him crazier—she lowered her head and wrapped her lips around his engorged tip.

He jerked off the bed, a hoarse curse leaving his lips.

"Baby, you're going to kill me," he muttered, one hand coming down to slide into her hair. She'd left it unbraided, and he twined several long strands around his finger before cupping the back of her head to bring her closer.

Julia took him deep, loving the husky noises he made, the way he moved his hips to the rhythm of her strokes. She used her mouth and tongue and hands to send him over the edge.

Sebastian was struggling for breath by the time she released him. "C'mere," he said roughly.

Julia clambered up his strong body and kissed him, laughing when he flipped her on her back and hovered over her, his gray eyes glimmering with hunger. "That was incredible, Doc." He dipped his head to nibble on her ear. "Now give me five minutes of recovery time, and then I'm going to—"

A ringing cell phone interrupted him.

"Answer the phone," he finished wryly.

He jumped off the bed and swiped his phone from

the chest of drawers on the other side of the room. "It's Frank," he announced.

Julia shot off the bed, all playfulness and desire flying out the window to make room for the dread that filled the air. She listened to Sebastian's side of the conversation, all two words of it, then frowned once he hung up. "What did he say?" she demanded.

"He wants us to meet him at the lab."

Sebastian swiftly reached for his Beretta and unloaded the clip to check his ammo, while Julia stuck her feet into her sneakers and grabbed the messenger bag she'd bought at the campus bookstore yesterday. Her new IDs were stashed in there, along with the gun Sebastian had demanded she carry.

"Did he say anything about the sample?" she asked as they hurried out the door.

Sebastian's jaw was tight. "All he said was for us to get there ASAP."

It was hard not to freak out after hearing *that*. She'd been friends with Frank long enough to know that he didn't throw around orders like ASAP unless absolutely necessary. The man must be in a real panic.

Julia was doing some panicking herself on the way to Harvard. She nervously tapped her fingernails on her thighs, wishing Frank had provided a few more details over the phone. Whatever he'd discovered, it couldn't be good.

Sure enough, when she and Sebastian flew into the lab twenty minutes later, the frantic look in her former professor's brown eyes was impossible to miss. This afternoon he'd opted to wear his white coat, and to Julia's alarm, she glimpsed a reddish stain under his right breast pocket.

Was that *blood?*

"Thanks for getting here so fast," Frank said somberly, leading them toward the back of the laboratory.

Julia felt the color drain from her face as they approached a table with half a dozen cages on it. The cages were small and covered with protective plastic wrap, and each one contained wood chips, a plastic wheel, and a dead mouse.

Or at least she thought the mice were dead. Those white motionless lumps could be sleeping for all she knew.

But Frank's forbidding expression said otherwise.

"It's bad, isn't it?" she said bleakly.

"Bad?" Frank shook his head, looking both astounded and horrified. "Let me put it this way—if this virus found its way into a major water supply? The results wouldn't be bad. They would be *catastrophic.*"

Chapter 10

Science had never been Sebastian's favorite subject in school. Actually, anything academic hadn't been his style—he much preferred being active, which was probably why he'd finished with an A in phys ed and a D in biology. Now, as he listened to Frank Matheson spit out the most technical-sounding explanation on the planet, he had to hold up his hand to interrupt the man.

"English, Doc," he pleaded. "I have no idea what you're saying."

Matheson ran his fingers over his bushy gray beard, still looking frazzled. "I'm sorry. I often forget to speak in layman's terms." He gestured at the microscope to his left. "As I was saying, the culture showed results in an alarmingly short amount of time. Within twenty-four hours, the host cell displayed signs of the virus, and it was replicating at a disturbing rate. Healthy cells began to degenerate within hours of viral detection."

Sebastian's gaze strayed to the cages on the other table. From his vantage point, it was clear that the mice inside those cages weren't moving. Unease swam in his gut, growing stronger when Frank noticed where his attention had drifted.

"Dead," the microbiologist confirmed. "They're all dead."

"You tested the virus on the mice?" Next to him, Julia's face was pale, but her expression was sharp and inquisitive. She stepped closer and peered inside one of the cages, furrowing her eyebrows.

"That's why I took an extra day," Matheson replied. "The accelerated reproduction cycle of this virus is unlike anything I've ever seen. I wanted to see how it reacted to a living organism."

Sebastian met the other man's eyes. "And?"

"And it's deadly. Like I said before, after twenty-four hours of infection the subject begins to exhibit symptoms. From what I was able to gather, this virus targets the central nervous system, but its manifestation was slightly odd. After about an hour or so, the test subjects exhibited some bleeding of the eyes, nose and ears, along with a high temperature and sluggish behavior. Two hours after that, the seizures began, and several of the mice showed signs of paralysis. By the four-hour mark, they were all dead."

A sickening feeling churned in his stomach. "Would human beings be affected in the same way as the mice?"

"Most likely, yes."

Looking extremely troubled, Julia sat on a nearby stool and started playing with the bottom of her braid, a habit Sebastian had come to associate with both distress and deep contemplation. "It sounds a bit like polio," she remarked.

Matheson nodded. "That was my thought as well. The poliovirus is quite similar. It also attacks the nervous system, infecting the brain, spine and surrounding tissues. In rare cases, polio can cause encephalitis, which is what I believe the test subjects ultimately died of."

Julia's head lifted sharply. "You autopsied the mice?"

"Only two of them, and I found evidence of infected brain tissue." The man rubbed his beard again. "This virus is similar enough to polio that I wouldn't be surprised if it's simply a mutated strain of it. But its incubation period is shorter, the replication rate is faster, and I don't believe there's any possibility for survival. I hypothesize that whoever becomes infected with this virus will die approximately twenty-eight hours after ingestion, barring the administration of an antidote." He cocked his head. "Is there an antidote?"

Sebastian's mouth tensed. "We have no idea. And you're certain this thing was manufactured?"

Matheson nodded fervently. "You won't find this disease in nature. It was engineered in a lab, and I must emphasize again—if a water supply becomes contaminated, the outcome will not be desirable. This virus is incredibly fast-acting. It can wipe out an entire population in a *day*."

And it had been designed for that very purpose, Sebastian thought grimly. The development of biological agents was nothing new—he wouldn't be surprised if every nation in the world dabbled in bio warfare, experimenting with potential weapons and coming up with defenses against them. Yet this current administration had spoken publicly and repeatedly about the president's stance on biological warfare. Defense, not development. President Howard had always been firm on that.

Question was, was someone going behind the president's back to develop this new weapon, or was the man in charge aware of the project?

"So what do we do now?" Julia asked.

It took him a moment to realize she was talking to him, but with those big, hazel eyes focused on him, he couldn't even remember what she'd asked. Her mere proximity was a huge distraction, and for the past forty-eight hours, he hadn't been able to get enough of Julia Davenport. The woman continued to surprise him, not just with the sensuality and enthusiasm she displayed between the sheets, but with her strength, her intelligence, her ability to accept this messed-up situation and seek out solutions rather than whine.

He knew she hadn't enjoyed being cooped up in the hotel room for two days—even though he'd tried his damnedest to distract her—but the woman hadn't complained once, which only made him like her even more.

But he didn't like a damn thing about this latest development. He'd known this virus couldn't be good, but he hadn't expected it to be *this* bad. For the life of him, he had no freaking idea what their next move should be.

Letting out a breath, Sebastian finally offered a helpless shrug. "I guess now we check in with Tate and hope that Eva found some new information about Project Aries."

"That's it?" Julia didn't sound at all satisfied. "And if she struck out again, then what? We sit around and wait?"

"I don't see what other choice we have."

"You can contact the CDC," Matheson suggested. "In fact, I highly recommend you do. They need to be made aware of this virus." He glanced at Julia. "This is a deadly biological agent, Jules. We can't just store the sample in my lab. It needs to be locked up in a government facility."

Her teeth dug into her lower lip and then she made a frustrated noise. "We have no idea who in the government we can even trust. We could be handing the sample over to the very person who authorized the creation of it."

"And then you'd be announcing your location to the people who most likely want you dead," Sebastian added, resting a protective hand on her shoulder.

"So would you," she replied. "They want me dead for knowing the truth about Esperanza. They want you dead for knowing the truth about Corazón. I'm scared that if we contact the CDC or Pentagon or whichever defense agency, they'll just detain us the way they detained me at the village, and…"

He finished the words she couldn't seem to get out.

"And this time we won't come out of it alive."

"I need coffee." With a weary exhalation, Julia buckled her seat belt and glanced over at Sebastian, whose discontented demeanor most certainly matched her own.

She hadn't gleaned an ounce of comfort from Frank's findings. This virus was even more dangerous than she could've ever dreamed. Cell degeneration within twenty-four hours of infection? Death after twenty-eight hours? It was downright petrifying, especially if human subjects were to be affected in the same way as the mice, which Frank believed was more than likely.

"Should we hit that coffee shop on the other side of campus?" Sebastian suggested in response to her declaration.

"Please," she said gratefully.

A few minutes later, he parked in front of the bustling café, illegally and without apology.

"I'll risk the ticket as long as I get a caffeine fix," he explained when he saw Julia's amused look. "And food. I could definitely go for some food."

They strode into the café, and Julia inhaled the intoxicating aroma of ground coffee beans, baked goods and fresh fruit. The loud whirring of a blender cut through the chatter in the room as the barista prepared a fruit smoothie for a waiting customer.

"What can I get you?" the harried-looking young woman asked as she slapped a lid on the smoothie and handed it to the shaggy-haired student at the counter.

They ordered two turkey clubs, a tray of banana muffins and two large coffees, then drifted to the end of the counter so Julia could dump a couple of sugars and a splash of milk into her tall foam cup.

As they waited for their food, she absentmindedly glanced at the television mounted on the wall in front of her. It was turned on to CNN, and a news report on the rising global oil prices blared out of the speakers. Indifferent, she was about to turn away when a very familiar image suddenly appeared on the screen.

"Sebastian," she hissed, but she didn't need to alert him—his gaze was focused on the same thing.

A photograph of the Doctors International clinic in Valero filled the screen, before it split off to show a reporter standing live in front of the burned ruins of the building.

"…believed to be the actions of a South American revolutionary group," the woman was reporting. "The United Liberty Fighters have been responsible for countless fires, robberies and terrorist attacks over the past decade. Recently, the group lost its leader in a military ambush that devastated one of the ULF's base camps. A new leader has since taken the helm, Javier Luego, who has denied the ULF's involvement in this latest attack."

Julia clenched her teeth. Of course Luego denied it—he *wasn't* responsible for the fire and murders of her coworkers. Sebastian had been right, though. The military was blaming everything on the rebels.

"…among the victims, two American doctors. Dr. Marcus Freeman—" a photo of the African-American surgeon flashed on the screen "—and Dr. Julia Davenport."

She sucked in a breath as her own face gazed back at her.

"Freeman and Davenport were identified using dental records, due to the state of the remains—"

"Your sandwiches are ready!" the guy at the counter called.

Before she could blink, Sebastian had grabbed the bag containing their food and was practically dragging her to the door. "Get in the car," he said briskly.

Julia slid into the passenger seat without question, gripping her coffee cup with both hands because she desperately needed something to hold on to. Shock continued to course through her veins, making it difficult to formulate any coherent thoughts.

"They're saying they found my *remains,*" she blurted out, shaking her head in astonishment. "They're saying I'm dead."

Sebastian's profile revealed his calm, unfazed features. "It's to their advantage, Doc. That way, when they track you down and kill you, they won't need to conjure up some BS story because everyone already thinks you died in a fire."

She swallowed her rising anger. "This is *insane*. How can these people just—" A thought struck her. "My mother! Oh, God, they probably contacted my mother and told her about the fire. I have to call her and—"

"You can't," he interrupted. "That's what they're hoping you'll do. Mark my words, Julia, your mother is being watched. Her phones are tapped, her internet and financial activities are being monitored. They're waiting for you to make contact."

"Do you think they know I'm in the States?"

"I'm thinking no, but we can't rule anything out. That's why we need to lay low. Now that your picture is all over the news, you can't risk being out in the open." His strong jaw went rigid. "Christ. We really need to figure out our next move, Doc."

She wholeheartedly agreed, but each time she tried to think of what the next logical step ought to be, her mind drew a blank. They couldn't involve anyone in the government, not until they determined who could be trusted. They couldn't involve the military for the same reason.

"What about the media?" she suggested. "We can tell them everything, and if the people after us try to make us look like a bunch of nut jobs, we give every last member of the press a sample of the virus."

"That's a possibility, except I don't know how I feel about letting this water sample out of our hands. If the wrong person gets a hold of it…"

"You're right." She pursed her lips. "But I still say we blow this conspiracy right open. If we make enough noise, our pursuers will have a hell of a time trying to shut us up. And if we wind up dead, they'll only be proving us right."

"If we raise a fuss about this, they won't kill us,"

Sebastian agreed. He laughed dryly. "But they'll lock us up, either in prison or at some sanitarium, claiming we're criminals or psychotic. And remember, these people have the clout to do that."

Strands of frustration tangled in her insides, congealing into hard knots that made her stomach hurt. By the time they got back to the hotel and strode into their room, her appetite was nonexistent and the smell of food wafting from their takeout bag made her nauseous.

She joined Sebastian at the small table under the window and flopped down on one of the cushioned chairs, but when he handed her the turkey sandwich, she simply shook her head. "I can't eat right now." When he frowned, she had to smile. "I'll eat it later, I promise."

Sebastian, on the other hand, seemed to have no problems with his appetite. He polished off his sandwich in a matter of minutes, then devoured three muffins before calling it quits and reaching for his coffee. She tracked the movements of his strong, callused hands as he wiped the corner of his mouth with a napkin, as he brought his cup to his sensual lips, as his corded throat worked to swallow his coffee.

He was so unbelievably attractive. So masculine. So magnetic. Everything about this man intrigued her— his messy dark blond hair, his seductive gray eyes, his perpetual five o'clock. She could look at that sexy, rugged face for hours.

Catching her staring, Sebastian's lips quirked in a grin. "Everything all right?"

"Just thinking about how sexy you are," she admitted, feeling her cheeks go hot. "And I'm also wondering why nothing seems to faze you."

"I'm very easygoing," he said with a shrug.

Something about his tone brought a tug of suspicion. "Are you? Are you really easygoing, Sebastian, or…or are you just really good at pretending nothing bothers you?"

For one brief second he looked startled, but then he offered another shrug accompanied by a careless chuckle. "I'm not that good of an actor, Doc."

Yes, you are.

For the first time since they'd met, Julia glimpsed a chink in his laidback armor. It was a facade. A pretense. Sebastian Stone was hiding a whole lot of pain inside that big, powerful body of his.

"Why did you enlist in the army?" she heard herself ask.

He looked surprised by the swift change of subject. "For the same reason you became a doctor—to follow in my dad's footsteps and make him proud."

"That's not the only reason I went into medicine. I also wanted to save lives, to make a difference."

"So did I." A faraway note entered his deep voice. "And I wanted to be a hero. Just once, I wanted to feel like I had something worthwhile to offer people."

An internal alarm dinged in her head. "What made you think you didn't?"

His expression instantly grew shuttered. "I just never felt very heroic growing up. My dad, he died a hero. Died serving his country. He was a hero in the military community, well-liked, respected. You should have seen the people who showed up for his funeral—he had friends in high places, that's for sure."

"Aside from being a hero, what was he like?"

"Strict. Cold at times. Demanded excellence. No tolerance for error. If you didn't do something right the first time, he got pissed, which was ironic because one of his favorite phrases was 'practice makes perfect' yet requiring practice implies that you *won't* knock a task out of the park the very first try. So then why get mad when he takes me shooting for the first time and I can't hit the damn target right away?" Sebastian shook his head, mystified. "The man was hard to understand sometimes."

"Parents usually are." Julia sighed. "I still don't get my mother, and I've had thirty years to try and figure her out."

Much to her disappointment, the conversation came to an end when Sebastian's phone rang. That he put the call on speakerphone spoke volumes about his trust in her, and warmth suffused Julia's body.

"What's up, Tate?" Sebastian asked without delay.

"Are you near a TV?"

"Yeah, and I think I know what you're going to say. We already saw it on CNN. They're blaming the fire on the rebels, just like we—"

"This isn't about the fire," Tate interrupted. "Turn on the television. Any frickin' channel. Call me back after."

Julia and Sebastian exchanged baffled looks. An eddy of uneasiness swirled in her belly as Sebastian grabbed the remote and pointed it at the TV. The screen came to life a moment later, and like Tate had said, it didn't matter which channel they chose—seemed like every regularly scheduled program had been preempted for this late-breaking live coverage.

The aerial shot showed unfamiliar streets littered with dozens of ambulances, police cruisers and fire trucks, but it wasn't until Julia glimpsed a van bearing the logo of the Centers for Disease Control and Prevention that she truly understood what had happened. People in full hazmat suits swarmed the area, while the journalist reporting from a helicopter hypothesized about what was occurring down below.

At the bottom of the screen, a stream of text moved in a horizontal scroll. With wide eyes, Julia read the words as they flashed by, unable to believe what she was reading.

More than seven hundred dead. Outbreak in Dixie, New York. Small town's entire population discovered dead mere hours ago.

Gaping, she turned to Sebastian. "Oh, my God. Are you seeing this?"

He looked as nauseous as she felt. "I'm seeing it." Then he changed the channel, seeking out more details.

Dixie was a tiny town in upstate New York with a population of eleven hundred citizens. Seven hundred or so of those citizens were now dead—some had been discovered in their homes, some had suffered seizures and collapses outside or in public, some had managed to get to a hospital before succumbing to their illness. The whole town had been quarantined, and it seemed like every agency known to man had sent agents to Dixie.

"At the moment, we have no idea whether this disease is contagious or if it is airborne," a male reporter said urgently. "As you can see, protective gear is being utilized, which indicates that whatever killed the citizens of Dixie can potentially spread through the air." The Asian man suddenly touched his earpiece. "Wait a minute, folks, we're receiving an update. Thirty-eight more deaths have been reported. And at current count, there are one hundred and sixty-four people presently *un*affected by the illness."

The shot cut back to the studio, where a pair of concerned-looking anchors sat behind a bright blue desk. "Bill, can you tell us anything more about this disease?"

"We don't know much else, Marie. Attempts have been made to contact the CDC, as well as the World Health Organization, but they haven't released any more details."

Julia's entire body felt numb. Cold. Winded. More than seven hundred people dead. Just like those lab mice.

"We have to turn ourselves in," she blurted out.

Sebastian's head jerked over in shock. "What are you talking about, Doc?"

"They don't know anything about this virus, Sebastian. But *we* do. We know exactly what it does, exactly how it's transmitted. We have to contact the CDC, just like Frank said."

Indecision flickered in his gray eyes. "We need to think about this. We can't just—"

The blond news anchor on the screen interrupted Sebastian. "There has been a new development!" she announced. "A terrorist group has just taken responsibility for the death toll in Dixie, New York! This is a terrorist attack! I repeat, the unprecedented events we have been reporting on for the last hour is a result of a *terrorist attack*."

Chapter 11

Julia's mouth fell open. After one speechless moment, she grabbed the remote from Sebastian's hand and turned up the volume.

"The network just received a video from the United Liberty Fighters, a revolutionary group based in the South American island nation of San Marquez," the blond reporter continued. "Just minutes ago, this network as well as several others received a video from what is believed to be a militant faction of the ULF. They claim to have splintered from their counterparts and are taking full responsibility for the deaths in Dixie, New York."

"What the *hell* is going on?" Sebastian burst out, raking a hand through his hair. "How did any member of the freaking ULF get their hands on this virus?"

Julia had no answer for that. She was glued to the screen, growing more and more alarmed by the second.

"The tape is currently being edited by our producers, as it contains content that may not be suitable for all audiences," the anchor was saying.

Sebastian quickly changed the channel, flipping until he found a network that was speedier with the airing of that tape. A man's fuming, red face filled the screen, his swarthy skin tone hinting at South American descent. He was ranting and raving, spittle flying into the lens as he spoke so fast that it was hard to keep up. A minute in, the anchors identified him as Raoul Escobar, the unofficial leader of the splinter group. His anti-American spiel lasted for several minutes before he finally got to the heart of the matter.

"We know what you've been doing in our country and we do not approve of your unspeakable treatment of our people." Escobar's accented voice trembled with fury. "You enjoy killing our people with your disease? We will take that disease and kill *your* people with it."

Horror smashed into Julia's chest like a baseball bat.

"Christ," Sebastian muttered. "They know the virus was engineered in the States."

"And now they're using it against us," she breathed.

Shock, fear and terror vied for her attention, each one coursing through her bloodstream until her entire body felt weak and her head grew foggy. The television continued to blare out bits and pieces of the terrorist tape, while updates buzzed along the bottom of the screen.

"We do not ask for much," Escobar was saying, bitterness oozing from his tone. "Our fellow soldiers have been attempting to achieve this for many years, but we are not pleased with Luego's slow-moving efforts. We have decided to speed up the process."

Julia grew sick to her stomach as she waited for Escobar to go on, but the terrorist leader had decided to pause for dramatic effect. His bushy black mustache twitched as a frown pinched his lips, and those dark furious eyes continued to blaze.

"Your little town of Dixie was a warning shot," he announced. A despicable smirk lifted his mouth. "Your government wiped out two of our villages. We were generous—we wiped out only *one* of yours. Now it is time to show your gratitude."

He went quiet again, making Julia want to hit something. "Come on, you psycho, tell us what you want," she snapped.

Escobar cleared his throat. The quality of the digital tape was surprisingly excellent, showing every hard line in his angular face as he revealed his intentions.

"We have one demand: remove all American influence from our country—social, economic, military, *all influences*. Remove your troops from our capital city of Merido and its surrounding areas, as well as the doctors and aid workers who take it upon themselves to poison our people. Our nation does not want your interference. We do not welcome *any* foreign interfercnce. All foreign-born citizens will be expelled from San Marquez when we come to power. Our nation will be purified, once and for all."

Julia's jaw dropped. The whole purification speech sounded a lot like the mentality of Nazi Germany, bringing another rush of horror to her body.

"Holy hell, these people are *nuts*," she said.

Sebastian's features hardened. "Not nuts. Just extreme nationalists with unrealistic expectations."

Unrealistic proved to be prophetic when Escobar

fixed a deadly look at the lens and said, "You have one week to remove your presence from our country."

"One *week?*" Julia exclaimed. "That's impossible. They can't possibly hope to remove all traces of America from the economy. Our countries are heavily involved in trade."

"As a sign of acceptance to this agreement, you have seventy-two hours to remove your military forces from San Marquez," Escobar finished. "If you do not, we will release the Meridian virus into the water supply of a major U.S. city."

"Meridian virus?" she echoed. "Isn't that what the general in Esperanza called it, too?"

"I guess it does have a nice ring to it," Sebastian said sarcastically. "But whatever they're calling it, they just informed the CDC that the virus is waterborne."

On the TV, Escobar was replaced by the open-mouthed, pale face of the sole male news anchor, who attempted to recap everything they'd just seen on the tape. But the man could barely contain the quaver of panic in his voice, and soon after, the screen cut to the live coverage still occurring in Dixie.

When Sebastian's phone rang again, Julia actually welcomed the distraction. She felt as if she'd just ridden a roller coaster for the past twenty minutes. Her brain felt battered and bruised from all the information that had been fed into it, and she couldn't control the shaking of her hands. A major U.S. city. These people were willing to kill thousands and thousands of people, millions even, to get their demands met.

"Did you see all that?" Tate's voice barked out of the phone speaker.

Sebastian muted the TV. "Yep. I guess Luego wasn't

cutting it in the eyes of his followers." There was scorn in his voice when he said the name of the ULF leader. "And as if one rebel group wasn't enough, now the ULF has split into two. Rebels and terrorists."

"My question is, how the hell did Escobar and his group get their hands on the virus?" Tate demanded. "Project Aries was hush-hush."

"Whoever's in charge had to have informed someone in the San Marquez administration," Julia spoke up. "That was a joint task force in Esperanza, which means that at least some people in San Marquez know about the project."

"Yeah, but I can't imagine the U.S. giving anyone else the virus," Sebastian said slowly. "They didn't recruit any San Marquez scientists to run the tests. They sent Richard Harrison, an American, to oversee the project."

Tate concurred. "Stone's right, there's no way they're placing a deadly biological agent in the hands of anyone who could use it against them. They may be testing it on foreign soil, but make no mistake, they consider this an American weapon."

"So then how did Escobar get the virus?" Sebastian repeated.

"Best bet? Someone involved in the project sold out his country."

Julia's eyebrows shot up. "You think one of the scientists who worked on Project Aries sold the virus to terrorists?"

"Scientist, military member, politician—it could be anyone who has knowledge of Project Aries. But Eva's focusing on scientists first. She's still digging into Harrison's background and trying to find more details about his lab, which we believe engineered the thing. I'll keep you posted on what she finds."

"In the meantime, we need to contact the CDC, or someone in the government," Julia said firmly.

There was a short silence on the other end of the line. "Seb?" Tate finally said.

"She's right. We can't just sit on what we know. A terrorist group has its hands on a biological weapon, Captain. At the moment, we're probably the only people other than the scientists who created the virus who know a damn thing about it."

"Frank has two days' worth of research logs," Julia said. "He has video of the lab mice's reaction to the virus, observations, notes—all this needs to go to the CDC. They need to know what they're dealing with, and the second they have a sample in their hands, they can start working on a potential antidote."

Tate's low curse emerged from the speaker. "You're right. It needs to be done." A pause. "How're you going to do this, Sergeant? We still have that list of army names we came up with, the one of officers we might be able to trust."

Sebastian leaned back in his chair and absently rubbed the stubble coating his jaw. "I don't know, I'd like to stay away from the usual military channels. But there might be someone at the Department of Defense that I can contact. A friend of my father." He released a breath. "It would help if I knew what our status is in the military community—are we considered deserters? Are they saying we're dead?"

"No clue. Eva can't access our files. They're beyond classified. Look, I trust your gut, so whoever you decide to take this to, I'll back you on it."

After they hung up with Tate, Sebastian rose from his chair, walked over to Julia and helped her to her feet. "C'mere," he said gruffly.

The next thing she knew, she was enveloped in his strong embrace. His arms came around her waist, sliding up the bumps of her spine and stroking the center of her back.

"What's this?" she murmured as she buried her face in the crook of his neck. She breathed in the woodsy scent of him, wondering why he always managed to smell so great.

"You were paler than snow," he answered. "You looked scared, and I figured you might need a hug."

Despite the fact that she was still reeling with shock, she laughed softly and looped her arms around his broad shoulders. "I don't think a hug is going to erase this panicky feeling, but it does help."

"Good." He brushed his lips over hers, just a soft, reassuring kiss before he released her and plopped down on the bed.

She sat next to him and reached for his hand. "So who's this man you think we can trust?"

"Brent Davidson. Last time I spoke to him, he was working in the deputy secretary's office as some sort of liaison. He's pretty high up on the DoD ladder."

"Wow. Your father really did have friends in high places. Were he and Davidson close?"

Sebastian nodded, carelessly rubbing the center of her palm. The calluses on the pads of his fingers tickled her flesh. "They were very close. Brent and his wife would come over for dinner once a month, and he and my dad went on yearly hunting trips."

"Did you and your mother keep in touch with him after your dad died?"

"We did. Even kept up the monthly dinners. But Mom died about five years after Dad, and once I enlisted, I didn't see as much of Brent anymore. We had lunch whenever I was in town, and I know he kept tabs on me when I was in the army. If there's anyone I'd trust in the government, it's him."

"Then we go to him," Julia said simply.

She scooted closer and rested her head on his shoulder. Without hesitation, he slung his arm around her and brought her closer. They sat there in silence for several minutes, while the news reports ran over and over again in Julia's head. One thousand people dead. More deaths to come if the terrorists' demands weren't met.

The memory of those body bags in Esperanza crossed her mind, making her shiver. What if the virus really *was* released in a major city? How many body bags would be required this time?

"It's a nine- or ten-hour drive to Virginia." Sebastian's voice interrupted her grisly thoughts. "If we leave now, we'll get there around ten tonight. I'll contact Brent once we're there."

"Shouldn't we contact him before we commit to a nine-hour drive?" she pointed out. "What if he's on vacation or something?"

Sebastian responded with a firm shake of the head. "I don't want to give him any time to put together a team or—"

"A team?"

"To apprehend us. We don't know how my former commander explained away our absence. When three black ops soldiers go AWOL, there's bound to be some fallout. If Commander Hahn declared us traitors, Brent won't be very happy to see me." Sebastian shrugged. "If he's on vacation, we pick someone else at the DoD we might be able to trust."

"Makes sense."

Hopping to his feet, he took a purposeful step toward the duffel bag across the room. "Gather your gear, Doc. It's time to hit the road."

As they neared the seven-hour mark of their drive, it occurred to Sebastian that this was the most time he'd spent with one woman in years. The realization was so startling that he took his eyes off the windshield to swivel his head at Julia, who was eating a bag of potato chips in the passenger seat.

"What?" she said when she caught him staring. "Do I have crumbs all over my face or something?"

"Nope. I'm just glad to see your appetite has returned," he said lightly.

Shifting his gaze back to the road, he tried not to dwell on the confusing emotions fluttering through him, but it was impossible not to. He really was happy that her appetite had returned. And he was happy that her cheeks had regained their rosy color again. Happy that the fear and worry had left her eyes.

Above all, he was happy that she was sitting here beside him. He wouldn't have wanted to be in this car with anyone else, and that startled him more than anything.

He liked Julia Davenport. He liked her a helluva lot, and even more, he wanted to know everything about her. What she did in her spare time, her favorite food, what kind of music she preferred. He wanted to hear about her travels and the patients she'd treated over the years and the places she still wanted to visit.

And not only did he like her, but he *worried* about her. He consistently found himself wanting to make sure she was okay. That she was well-fed. That she had enough to drink. That she wasn't too tired.

What the hell was up with that? He wasn't that guy anymore, the one who worried about the people in his life, the one who tried to protect the people he loved. Nowadays, he didn't love *anyone.* It was the only way to ensure nobody else got hurt.

"You're being scarily quiet." Julia's voice held a note of intrigue. "What's on your mind, Stone?"

"You," he admitted.

"Oh, really?"

He kept his tone casual. "I was wondering what your favorite kind of music is."

"Easy. Classic rock."

Grinning, he shot her a sideways glance. "I don't believe you."

"Then don't believe me," she scoffed. "But it's true. I'm all about the rock icons. Zeppelin, the Stones, Supertramp, ZZ Top." She cocked her head. "What are *you* into?"

"Same thing. With the occasional hip-hop track thrown in for good measure."

"Ooooh, a gangsta," she teased.

He rolled his eyes. "Yeah, that's me. Gangster to the core. I haven't picked which gang I want to join yet, but I'm leaning toward the Bloods."

She laughed, and the melodic sound sent a jolt of heat shimmying up his spine. If someone had told him that he'd become addicted to this woman, he probably would've been dubious as hell. With those big doe eyes, small breasts and fragile body, she was definitely not his type, at least not the kind of woman he'd been gravitating toward in the last ten years. Once upon a time, though, he definitely would've been drawn to Julia. Her features lent her that air of vulnerability that would've appealed to his protector nature.

Protector. Ha, what a joke. Even now, he still tried to delude himself into thinking he was capable of taking care of the people in his life, when all the evidence pointed otherwise. He'd lost everyone he'd ever loved, and the only reason the cycle of heartache had ground to a halt this past decade was because he'd shut himself down. His heart was immune now, locked up tight, and nobody was ever going to penetrate that sucker.

Still, it wouldn't hurt to raise his guard a few more notches. Julia was getting too close. Her razor-sharp intelligence, the wanton sensuality she wasn't even aware she exuded, her nerves of steel and abundance of courage...he liked everything about the woman, which meant it was time to remind them both of the very temporary nature of their relationship.

"Hey, we made great time," Julia exclaimed as the sign for Arlington whizzed past the passenger side.

She was right. They'd made the drive in eight and a half hours, and he hadn't even been speeding. Because he couldn't draw any undue attention to him and Julia, he'd followed every last traffic law, no matter how badly he'd wanted to rev the damn engine of this sedan and floor it all the way to Virginia.

Flicking the turning signal, he changed lanes, then drove smoothly off the interstate exit ramp. After about a mile, he glimpsed a motel on the side of the road and turned into the parking lot.

"Wait here. I'll get us a room," he told her.

A bell dinged over the door of the motel office, but the young male behind the counter didn't even look up when Sebastian walked in. His gaze was glued to the television in the corner of the ceiling, which was playing clips from the video Raoul Escobar had released to the press.

"Didja see this?" the clerk demanded, sounding awed. "This is some crazy stuff right there."

"Crazy," Sebastian agreed. He dropped a fifty-dollar bill on the countertop. "I need a room."

Without wrenching his eyes from the TV, the clerk slid over a clipboard. "Fill this out."

Scribbling a fake name, address and credit card number, he slid the clipboard back to the kid, and received a big red key in return.

"Towels in the bathroom. Wi-Fi password is the motel name and your room number. Check out time is 10:00 a.m." The kid recited the facts without once looking at Sebastian. As Escobar's angry eyes flashed on the screen, the clerk shook his head. "Frickin' terrorists! Think they can mess with us? You're in for a rude awakening, ass munch!"

Trying not to roll his eyes, Sebastian left the office, got back in the car and drove to the spot in front of their designated room. The interior ended up being nicer—and cleaner—than he'd expected. Queen-size bed in the center of the room, a chest of drawers, a small kitchenette area and a bathroom equipped with a handful of fluffy white towels.

He removed his Beretta from his waistband and

dropped it on the kitchen table, then bent down to unzip his duffel. He found one of the prepaid cell phones, then pulled out his own to search for Brent Davidson's number in the contact list. He punched the number into the other phone, and as he waited, he glanced at Julia, who had plopped down at the foot of the bed and was worrying her bottom lip with her teeth.

"Davidson," a brusque male voice answered.

"Brent. It's Sebastian. Sebastian Stone."

Silence.

"Brent, you there?" he asked curtly.

"Yes. Yes, I'm here." Disbelief hung from the other man's voice. "Sebastian! I can honestly say I didn't expect to hear from you."

His guard instantly shot up. "And why is that?"

"Hahn said you were living it up in Brazil."

An incredulous laugh lodged in Sebastian's throat. Was that the official story? That he'd moved to South America to, what, work on his freaking suntan? Yet he didn't pick up on a single note of mistruth or insincerity in Brent's voice. Christ. Maybe that really *was* how the army had justified his absence.

"Yeah. Yeah, I guess I was," he said noncommittally.

"Well, it's good to have you back. We'll have to catch up over dinner. When are you—"

"I need to see you, Brent. Tonight."

There was a beat, followed by a loud bark of a laugh. "Sebastian, that's impossible. I took your call because it came from an unfamiliar number and I thought it might be related to this pandemonium bomb I'm trying to defuse. I'm in the middle of a national crisis at the moment. In case you haven't seen the news, there was a *terrorist attack* on U.S. soil today—"

"Why do you think I'm calling?" he interrupted.

Another beat. "You're saying you have information about the attack?"

"That's exactly what I'm saying."

"Where are you?" Brent demanded. "I'll send a car to bring you to the Pentagon and—"

"No." His tone was so harsh that Julia flinched from her perch on the bed.

"What do you mean, *no?* Stone, if you have any information pertaining to this attack, you'd damn well better tell me or I'll charge you with obstruction—"

"I have every intention of sharing what I know, Brent. But only with you. And only if you come to me. Alone."

"What the hell is going on?"

"Come alone and I'll tell you."

A resigned breath floated over the extension. "When and where?"

"Thirty minutes. At the place where we last saw each other."

Brent paused, as if trying to remember where that place had been. "All right. Fine."

"And if you bring backup, I'll know, Brent. I'll know, and I'll disappear, so don't even think about bringing one of your bodyguards."

There was another pause, followed by a chuckle. "I wouldn't dream of it."

A click sounded in his ear, indicating the other man had hung up. The second he disconnected the call, Sebastian broke the flip phone in half, then tossed it on the frayed carpet and gave it a few good stomps with the sole of his heavy black boot.

Julia's lips twitched. "Isn't that overkill?"

"No such thing." He gathered up the pieces of the disposable phone and tossed them in the wastebasket, then extended a hand at Julia.

She rose without question and walked right into his arms, the top of her head tickling his chin. He was a full head taller than her, which never ceased to amaze him because the woman often seemed larger than life. He remembered the day they'd met at the clinic, how self-assured she'd been, how confident her gait was as they strode side by side down that hallway. Inside that skinny, delicate exterior, she was a force to be reckoned with.

"Is it wishful thinking on my part if I think you'll agree to stay in this motel room while I meet with Davidson?" he asked, cupping her angular jaw with both hands.

A stubborn gleam entered her eyes. "Definitely."

"You'll definitely stay behind?"

She snorted. "It's definitely wishful thinking on your part."

"Figured I'd try." He dropped a quick kiss on her sassy mouth before pulling away. "Come on, let's go. I want to scope out the area before we expose ourselves."

"What area? Where exactly are we meeting this guy?"

"The last place I want to be."

Fifteen minutes later, as Sebastian drove through the gates of the Arlington National Cemetery, Julia instantly reached for his hand and clasped it tightly. Her hazel eyes shone with sympathy. "Oh, Seb, I'm sorry."

Seb.

He couldn't control the rush of warmth that flooded

his chest. It was the first time she'd used the nickname, and he enjoyed hearing it far more than he should.

"This is where your dad's buried?" she prompted.

He swallowed the lump in his throat. "Yeah."

His gaze landed on the endless rows of white headstones. Veterans, soldiers who'd died in combat, military families…all the graves blurred past the window as he drove deeper into the shadow-cloaked grounds. He kept his eyes and ears open, his senses on alert, seeking out any hints of danger. His internal threat meter wasn't going off, but he still made sure to park the car as far away as he could from their actual destination.

A few minutes later, he and Julia set out on foot, his boots and her sneakers barely making a sound as they crossed the manicured lawn.

"So many of them," she murmured, a note of sorrow in her voice.

"Too many," he said hoarsely.

As they got closer to the section where his father was buried, he withdrew his gun from his waistband and held it at his side. He searched the darkened lawn, but his threat readings remained low.

He led the way through the rows and rows of headstones, choking on another lump of sadness. He had to force himself to focus. To sweep his gaze over his surroundings, to stay alert, to stick close to Julia.

When a tall oak tree with low-lying branches came into view, Sebastian headed toward it and came to a stop. Sticking close to the shelter offered by the tree, he pulled Julia to his side and said, "Now we wait."

They didn't have to wait long. Only minutes later, the sound of a car engine echoed in the cemetery and a pair of headlights emitted a pale yellow glow in the distance. Narrowing his eyes, Sebastian readjusted his grip on the Beretta and eyed the sleek black BMW, which didn't slow down as it drove right past their section. But Brent Davidson had always driven Beemers, for as long as Sebastian had known him.

"Is that him?" Julia murmured.

"I think so."

Several more minutes passed, but the BMW didn't make another appearance, and neither did Brent. Sebastian was just beginning to wonder if they'd been stood up when he heard a rustling sound. His back stiffened, and then the nape of his neck began to tingle and his internal alarm system began to shriek.

"Son of a—"

He didn't get a chance to finish. The cold steel of a gun barrel pressed into the back of his head, and then a deep male voice growled, "Don't move."

Chapter 12

Sebastian snapped into action, spinning around and locking the male wrist with both hands. The charcoal-gray Glock fell out of his would-be assailant's grasp and clattered to the grass. As adrenaline raced through his blood, Sebastian kicked the weapon away and tackled the other man to the ground in two seconds flat.

Grunting, he straddled Brent Davidson and dug his elbow into the man's windpipe. "What the hell was *that?*" he snapped.

Davidson began wheezing for air. He batted at Sebastian's thighs with his fists, but to no avail. The man might have sneaked up on them like a freaking ninja, but now Sebastian had the upper hand and he didn't intend on giving it up.

"What the *hell* kind of move was that with the gun?" he demanded, sinking his elbow deeper.

Julia's sarcastic voice filled the night air. "Do you

honestly expect him to answer any questions when you're crushing his trachea?"

Good point.

As the adrenaline sizzling in his veins began to dissipate, he lifted his arm and let the other man breathe. Red-faced, Brent began to cough, sucking oxygen into his lungs so fast it was a miracle he didn't pass out.

Sebastian took the time to examine the man, noting that Davidson had barely aged since he'd last seen him five years ago. There were some new wrinkles around his eyes and mouth, but his hair was still as black as night, with only a few strands of silver threaded through it. His blue eyes were sharper than ever, and the body beneath his black suit was surprisingly trim for a man in his sixties who rode a desk all day.

But Brent's peak physical condition didn't surprise Sebastian; Brent was a legend in the spec ops community, a former supersoldier who'd kicked more ass and taken more names than Sebastian could only dream of. Brent was probably the only man capable of sneaking up on him like that, and he couldn't help but feel a spark of grudging admiration that the man had succeeded in catching him unawares. A rare feat, that was for sure.

Still, didn't mean he was letting this stunt slide.

"Next time you point a gun to my head, be prepared to pull the trigger," he muttered before easing his weight off Davidson's chest and standing up.

"Next time you order me to *come alone,* I expect you to do the same," Brent shot back.

Julia offered a sheepish look. "He has a valid point," she said.

Brent staggered to his feet, adjusting his striped red-

and-black tie before reaching up to rub his neck, which was red and beginning to swell.

Experiencing a tug of guilt, Sebastian fixed an apologetic look at his father's old friend. "I'm sorry. I promise I didn't summon you here to tackle you to the ground and nearly strangle you to death." He had to grin. "But you should know better than to sneak up on a fellow Special Forces alum."

"Also a valid point." Brent finally cracked a smile. "It's good to see you, Stone."

"You, too, Brent."

The two men embraced, and then Brent slapped Sebastian on the shoulder and cocked his head at Julia. "Who's she?"

"Dr. Julia Davenport."

A wrinkle appeared in Brent's forehead. "Why does that name sound so familiar?"

"Because I'm supposedly one of the American casualties in the fire that burned down a foreign aid clinic in Valero," she said dryly.

Recognition dawned in the man's eyes. "That's it. Yes, your picture landed on my desk earlier this morning before the Dixie attack." Now those blue eyes darkened with suspicion. "What the hell is going on here?"

The trio stepped out from the shadows of the tree, each man putting away his weapon. They walked over to the wrought-iron bench five yards away and sat down. Sebastian kept Julia close to his side, keeping a protective hand on her thigh.

"So Hahn said I'm living in Brazil, huh?"

Brent nodded. "Apparently as of nine months ago. Your former CO claims you chose not to re-up. I checked your file after I heard that and it lists you as receiving an honorable discharge last August."

"So you thought I really skipped town without saying goodbye?"

"Goodbyes were never really your style. I figured you'd get in touch with me eventually. But you weren't in Brazil, were you?"

"Nope. I've been hiding out for the last eight months."

"What do you mean 'hiding out'?"

"Someone tried to kill me. Twice." He clenched his teeth, trying to quell the escalating fury. "First time, they sent someone to run me down with a car. Second time, they cut the brakes of my Ducati."

"'They,'" Brent echoed warily. "Who's they?"

"You tell me."

A short silence fell, and then Brent's astonished laughter echoed in the night breeze. "You think I had something to do with the attempts on your life?"

"No, but you must have heard something about it," he countered. "And it wasn't just me. Five members of my unit turned up dead once we got stateside after our last gig. They all died of bogus causes, Brent. And then my captain nearly got his head blown off in a drive-by and I almost got splattered all over the pavement. Someone was deliberately trying to eliminate every last man on our team."

The older man finally displayed a glimmer of worry. "What did your last op entail?"

Secrecy and security clearance be damned, Sebastian outlined that final mission—the deployment to San Marquez, the attempt to save the doctor from the rebels, discovering the village up in flames.

"Cruz and his soldiers didn't kill those people," Sebastian said. "They burned the bodies because they feared the virus was contagious."

"And you're certain it's the same virus? This Meridian thing Escobar mentioned in his video?"

"Fairly certain."

He quickly went on to explain what happened in Esperanza, and Julia piped in with her own play-by-play. Each word she uttered dug a deeper groove into Brent's forehead.

"So you're saying that a U.S. military unit was in charge of an op to cover up the testing of a biological weapon on foreign soil?"

Sebastian studied the older man's face for any sign that they were being played, but those blue eyes reflected nothing but shock and horror. Either the man was a phenomenal liar, or he truly hadn't known about any of this.

"So *you're* saying the Department of Defense knew nothing about this?" Sebastian countered.

"*I* sure as hell didn't. I have no clue whether the deputy secretary or the damn secretary himself is aware of it, but if they are, they've kept me in the dark." Brent rubbed his temples as if warding off an oncoming migraine. "The first time I heard about this so-called Meridian virus was earlier today. I've been with the deputy secretary at the Pentagon all day, and he was as shocked as I was by the terrorist attack."

"Of course he's shocked," Julia muttered. "I'm sure whoever authorized this project didn't intend for the virus to be released *here*. Apparently it's okay to treat foreigners as guinea pigs, but God forbid any innocent Americans get hurt."

Brent let out a breath. "I understand your anger, Dr.

Davenport. And I appreciate the effort you've expended to learn what you can about the virus. Did you bring the sample with you?"

Sebastian noticed Julia's hand tightening over the strap of the canvas messenger bag on her shoulder. The bag contained the sample and Matheson's research notes, but he could tell she wasn't anxious to part with it just yet.

He didn't blame her. Although he believed that Brent hadn't been aware of Project Aries, he still didn't fully trust the man, and that mistrust only deepened when Brent turned to him and said, "You need to come in officially."

"No way," he said emphatically.

"I promise you, I will protect you. We'll take your story to the secretary of defense himself. Barrett—"

"—might be behind this entire mess," Sebastian finished. "For all we know, Secretary Barrett green-lighted Project Aries."

"Then we contact the Bureau, place you and Dr. Davenport in protective custody." Immediately after the words left his mouth, Brent chuckled ruefully. "Don't bother answering—we both know you'll reject the offer."

Sebastian just shrugged.

"How do we handle this, then? I don't have the authority to negotiate with you, Stone, and I don't have the time to sit here and chat. In less than forty-eight hours, Escobar and his troop of crazies plan to release a virus that will kill who knows how many innocent people." Anger colored the man's tone. "So if you have any useful information about this Meridian virus, hand it over now. Otherwise I'll have no choice but to place you under arrest for obstruction of justice."

"Relax, Brent, we have every intention of sharing what we know." Sebastian took the bag from Julia and held it out. "We contacted a microbiologist to test the sample we got from the well in Esperanza. All his research notes are in here, too."

As the bag exchanged hands, he quickly gave Brent a rundown of Matheson's findings, making sure to keep Frank's name out of it. When he finished, Brent's face was devoid of color. "It's that bad?" he said flatly.

Sebastian and Julia nodded.

"Shit." Jaw tense, Brent abruptly stood up. "I have to head back to the Pentagon. My superiors need to be briefed about this."

"I'd appreciate it if you could keep our names out of it," Sebastian said. "No one can know that Dr. Davenport and I are in the States."

"It'll be a lot easier if you just come in with me."

"I can't. Not until I know who authorized the killing of my unit."

"I'll do what I can to look into that," Brent promised. Then he hesitated. "And I'll also keep your names out of this virus inquiry, but with that said, I want your word that you'll leave the investigating to us from this point on. We can take it from here." He took a step. "How do I get in touch with you?"

"You don't." Taking Julia's hand, Sebastian helped her to her feet and glanced at Davidson in gratitude. "Thanks for meeting us, Brent. Please don't make me regret this."

"I'll do my best. Stay in touch, Sebastian."

"I'll do my best," he mimicked.

Brent headed off, making it five yards before he stopped to face them again. "And don't think I didn't notice that you never gave me your word," he called.

"You know I don't make promises I can't keep," Sebastian called back.

The sound of soft laughter carried in the air, and then Brent disappeared into the shadows.

After Brent was gone, Sebastian drifted toward one of the white headstones ten feet away and stood there for a moment, gazing at the inscription. A moment later, Julia's quiet footsteps crunched on the crisp grass and she came up beside him. "Are you okay?" she asked gently.

He fixed his gaze on the grave. James Marvin Stone. Colonel. U.S. Marine Corps.

"He would've wanted me to go with Brent, to turn myself in," Sebastian murmured.

Julia sounded taken aback. "You really think so?"

"My dad was very by-the-book. He followed the rules, to the extreme almost, and he had a terrifying amount of faith in our democratic system. He would have believed Commander Hahn when Hahn said he didn't have a target on his back. He would have trusted his commanding officer. And he would have died."

"Seb…"

Swallowing hard, he turned away from his father's headstone. "Whatever. He's dead anyway, so there's no point in talking about what he would or wouldn't have done."

He jumped when he felt Julia's hand on his arm. Her touch was gentle, warm and comforting. She glided her hand up to his face and ran her fingertips over the stubble coating his jaw.

"You're right. It doesn't matter what your father

would've done. It matters what *you're* doing." She traced the line of his jaw, bringing a shiver to his body. "And you're doing the right thing, Sebastian. Right now, we can't afford to trust blindly."

He was oddly touched by the reassurance. He leaned into her touch, enjoying the way she rubbed his prickly beard growth with her palm. "We should go," he said, his voice coming out rough. "I have a feeling tomorrow will be another long day."

A knowing smile lifted her lips. "We're totally going to keep investigating, right?"

"No doubt about it, Doc."

Julia was wiggling out of her jeans before they even entered their motel room half an hour later. She felt disheveled and grimy from that eight-hour drive, followed by the trek through the cemetery, and the only place she wanted to be at the moment was in the shower. Kicking away the jeans, she slid her black cardigan off her shoulders, then whipped her T-shirt over her head and walked toward the bathroom in her bra and panties.

A wolf whistle sounded from behind.

Rolling her eyes, she looked at Sebastian over her shoulder. "I feel like I just walked past a construction site."

"Baby, if you ever walked by a construction site wearing *that*—" he indicated her skimpy red panties and matching bra "—you'd cause so many workplace accidents there'd be no one left alive."

She laughed, then caught her breath when Sebastian started stripping right before her eyes. "I take it you're joining me in the shower?" she murmured, unable to tear her eyes off his incredible body.

Each piece of clothing he removed provided her with a new delicious body part to focus on. The tanned expanse of his chest, dusted with hair and sculpted with muscle. His trim waist, ripped thighs, long legs. In the unforgiving motel room light, the handful of scars marring his body were more visible. A white one beneath his left pectoral, a puckered one over his right hip. When she'd asked about the scars, he'd simply shrugged and described them as "a couple of teeny battle wounds," but her doctor's eyes saw right through that line of bull.

The line under his pec? Definitely caused by a blade of some sort. And the puckered scar? Clearly a bullet wound, and not a through-and-through either, seeing as there was no exit scar.

But apparently knife and bullet wounds were no biggie to a tough guy like Sebastian Stone.

"Jeez, Doc, quit ogling me," he said mockingly. "It's my job to ogle *you,* remember?"

They headed for the bathroom, where Julia stared at the miniscule shower stall before turning to the naked man beside her. "Both of us won't fit in here."

"Sure we will. We'll just have to stand real close…" He wagged his eyebrows. "And our bodies will be all wet and slippery as they bump into each other. I can't freaking wait."

Another laugh flew out. God, the more time she spent with this man, the more she liked him. He was so magnetic, so sexy, so entertaining.

And he kept showing her new facets of his personality that she wouldn't have ever expected to find. Like the tenderness with which he touched her—a man that big and powerful wasn't supposed to be so gentle. And his tendency to go all Mother Hen on her—*eat, drink, get some rest.* Normally she'd be incredibly annoyed being fussed over like that, but with Sebastian, she didn't feel pressured, or as though he had no confidence in her ability to take care of herself. She knew he thought her capable—he'd said it time and time again—but that didn't stop him from being so protective of her.

As Sebastian leaned into the stall to turn on the water, Julia's gaze landed on his spectacular bare butt. Her mouth actually watered, and she had to forcibly snap herself out of her lust-filled haze before she gave in to the urge to pinch that taut bottom.

She unhooked her bra and stepped out of her panties, then joined Sebastian in the shower. Hot water rushed out of the showerhead with a surprising degree of pressure, quickly filling the stall with a cloud of steam. Julia dunked her head under the spray and let the water soak her body before stepping aside to let Sebastian have a turn.

He was right—their bodies were slick, colliding and rubbing as they maneuvered around in the tiny glass stall. All that slippery contact succeeded in turning her on beyond belief, and a glance at Sebastian's lower body confirmed that he was getting as worked up as she was.

Grabbing a bar of soap, Sebastian caught her by the waist and then his husky voice cut into the rushing water. "This is the best shower I've ever had, Doc."

Her laughter bounced off the tiled walls.

With a sexy grin, he brought the soap to her body and proceeded to lather her into a whole new state of turned on. He dragged the soap over her aching breasts, letting the suds cover her nipples before he tweaked those erect buds with his fingers. His hands danced and explored, gliding over every inch of her body, and then he was suddenly on his knees, dropping the soap and letting it clatter to the shower floor.

Julia squeaked as those rough-skinned hands parted her thighs. Her gaze flew south in time to see Sebastian pressing his mouth to her core. Shock waves of pleasure hit her hard. She nearly keeled over, but he quickly planted a hand on her waist to steady her.

"Easy, Doc," he said in a humor-tinged voice. "Don't want you slipping and breaking a leg."

Then he brushed his lips over her, and she realized that if she *did* slip and break a leg? She wouldn't even care. Not as long as Sebastian drove her over that orgasmic edge first.

Her eyes fluttered closed as she lost herself in pure sensation. Her entire body was hypersensitive—nipples tingling as the lukewarm water sluiced over them, pulse hammering in her ears, sex throbbing from Sebastian's deliberate teasing. He licked her damp folds as if he had all the time in the world, lapping her up, heating her blood, driving her absolutely crazy.

Her hips began to move in a restless rhythm, seeking deeper contact, seeking release, but each time Sebastian brought her close to the brink, he quickly retreated, until her anguished pleas echoed in the shower stall.

"Please," she begged.

His answering chuckle tickled her swollen flesh, but he must have heard the desperation in her voice because a second later, he gave her exactly what she wanted. Pushing one finger inside her, he latched his mouth on her sensitive bud and sucked, unleashing a climax so intense that Julia saw stars.

She'd barely crashed down to earth when she felt herself being turned around. Water from the spray splashed her face, slid down her body and ran over her mound, which was so sensitive from that explosive release that she squirmed away from the shower stream and almost giggled from the tickling sensation.

Sebastian's strong fingers dug into her hips. He pressed his erection into her bottom, rubbing for several excruciating seconds before nudging her forward so that her palms were braced on the tiled wall, and then he plunged into her from behind, eliciting a wild cry from her lips.

The position allowed him to fill her completely, to hit a spot deep inside that had her moaning with abandon. His ragged breathing and her husky noises mingled with the rush of the water. Tightly gripping her hips, he moved inside her in fast, hard thrusts guaranteed to send them both soaring, and it wasn't long before that happened.

Julia's second release came without warning, robbing the breath from her lungs and sending a tornado of pleasure spinning through her body. Shortening his strokes, Sebastian's chest sagged against her back, and then he let out a loud groan and withdrew, drawing her attention to the fact that he wasn't wearing a condom. Warmth tickled the small of her back as he emptied his seed with a hoarse cry.

By the time they stepped out of the shower, the water had grown cold, but Julia's body was still on fire. She'd never experienced such raw, uncontrollable passion. She'd never had sex like this before. Ever.

She was still amazed as they stepped into the main room, where she threw on an oversized T-shirt and some underwear while Sebastian donned a pair of boxers.

"Why do you look like you just struck gold?" he asked.

Julia blushed. "No reason."

"You're a terrible liar, Doc." He lifted the flower-patterned bedspread and slid beneath the white sheets.

After a moment, she joined him in bed. "I was just thinking about how incredible the sex is," she admitted. "It's never been like this for me before."

"Like this, how?" He leaned over to turn off the bedside lamp, then settled on his back and pulled her closer so that her head was resting on his bare chest.

"Passionate." Her cheeks grew hot, and she was glad the room was dark so he couldn't see her tomato face. "I'm not usually so adventurous in the bedroom. And I like being the one in control. But with you…I feel so totally out of control."

"Is that a bad thing?"

She paused thoughtfully. "Before, I would have said yes, but now that I know how extraordinary it can be, how liberating, I think letting go is a very good thing."

She twisted her neck to study the alarm clock on the end table, surprised to see it was almost midnight. But she wasn't tired at all, and Sebastian didn't seem to be in a hurry to go to sleep either.

"What's your favorite place that you've ever traveled to?" he asked.

Julia pursed her lips for a moment. "Toronto."

"Seriously? Out of all the places you've been, you choose a city in North America?"

"I really loved it," she answered with a laugh. "It was so clean and pretty, and the people were so nice. I've always been a city person, and as far as cities go, Toronto was definitely my favorite. What about you?"

"Istanbul," he said immediately. "I love everything about that place—the sights, the smells, the crowds. There's so much to do there, and I like to keep busy."

"Yet you're hiding out on the coast, where you lie around on the beach all day," she teased.

Sebastian snorted. "Does it look like we're lying on a beach right now, Doc? Trust me, I'm the first to volunteer to get the hell out of that beach house. I go stir-crazy when I'm in one place for too long."

"Me, too," she admitted. "I commit to nine months working at one clinic, come back here for three months to regroup, and the second a new cycle begins, I'm on a plane again." She furrowed her brows in the darkness, noting the irony of that. "I was never much of a traveler before. My sister, Mia, was the one with the traveling bug."

"Was?"

"She died." Julia swallowed the lump in her throat. "Mia was five years younger than me. The moment she turned eighteen, she took off to go backpacking around Europe. She wrote short travel pieces that she eventually started selling to travel websites, and she pretty much became a nomad. Three years ago —she was twenty-one by then—she went to South Africa. She was traveling in the north, wound up somewhere in the Limpopo province, where health care is lacking big-time. She fell during a hike, cut her leg pretty bad, and the wound got infected and eventually septicemia set in. There was no hospital she could go to, no antibiotics she could take, absolutely no treatment. A village doctor came by and gave her some aspirin." Julia shook her head in dismay. "Aspirin!"

Sebastian's arm tightened around her. "I'm sorry."

She pictured Mia's smiling face, then thought back to that last phone call from her sister. Mia had invested in a satellite phone, but she rarely ever used it because even a one-minute call cost an arm and a leg. The second Julia heard her sister's tinny voice over the line, she'd known something was wrong.

But she hadn't dreamed that they'd be saying goodbye.

"I wanted to get on the next plane out the second she called me. But she ordered me not to. She knew she was going to die, and she didn't want me to see her like that."

"Christ. I'm so sorry, Julia." He hesitated. "So that's why you went into foreign aid, huh?"

She nodded. "My sister died overseas because there was nobody there to give her proper medical treatment. That's when I decided that I refused to let that happen to anyone else, travelers, locals, didn't matter who. I wanted to save them." A soft laugh slipped out. "And then, to my surprise, I discovered just how much I enjoyed the traveling lifestyle. I don't think I could ever settle in one place nowadays."

"Me either," he agreed. "I love exploring new places and meeting new people."

Do you? she wanted to challenge. She bit her tongue at the last second, but a part of her wondered how much of Sebastian's wanderlust had to do with a genuine thirst for adventure, and how much was about his need to avoid commitment. She'd already figured out that he was deathly afraid of getting too close. The military had been the perfect place for him, offering the opportunity for constant travel, which made it hard to put down roots in one place. She got the feeling that forming roots was something he desperately wanted to avoid.

Silence settled between them. Easy. Comfortable. She'd never felt more at ease with a man before, and as she snuggled closer to his warm body, a contented sigh left her lips.

But when Sebastian spoke again, her contentment faded like an old sweater in the wash.

"This is just sex, Doc." He cleared his throat. "We're still clear on that, right?"

An unexpected arrow of pain sliced directly into her heart. It took her a second to find her voice, to make it sound casual and unruffled. "Of course." Now she tried to sound teasing. "We're not commitment people, remember? We're globe-trotters, explorers, risk takers."

A note of relief crept into his deep voice. "Right, that we are." He gave her shoulder a quick squeeze before rolling them over so that he was spooning her from behind. "We should get some sleep."

"Yeah, we probably should," she murmured.

The motel room went silent again.

Closing her eyes, Julia listened to the sound of Sebastian's soft, even breathing, trying desperately to ignore the little jabs of pain wreaking havoc on her chest.

This is just sex, Doc.

But it wasn't. It wasn't just sex for her.

Not anymore.

Chapter 13

The next morning, Sebastian woke up to the sound of his cell buzzing beside his head. Twelve years in the military—six of them working black ops—had given him the ability to go from a deep sleep to awake alertness in the blink of an eye. As his arm shot out to grab the phone, he slid into a sitting position without skipping a beat.

"Tell me you have some news, Captain," he said instead of hello.

"I do," Tate confirmed. "Not sure if it'll pan out, though. Are you still in Arlington?"

"Yes."

Next to him, Julia stirred in bed. She opened her eyes and glanced over at him, covering her mouth as a yawn overtook it. "What's going on?" she murmured.

"Tate," he mouthed, before shifting his focus back to the call.

"Eva has been burning the midnight oil for the past three days researching everyone who is currently or has ever been connected to D&M Initiative," Tate was saying.

"The lab Dr. Harrison worked at?"

"That's the one. Anyway, she linked a dozen individuals to Project Aries. Some scientists, an epidemiologist, a few lab techs, a research assistant. She managed to hack into one of the technicians' files and found a digital copy of a confidentiality agreement he was asked to sign."

Sebastian snickered. "You talk, you die?"

"Wasn't worded quite that way, but pretty much, yeah."

"Did she find out who hired D&M to develop the virus?"

"Nope. She's still looking, but there's so much red tape that it *has* to be a government contract. For now, we only know the D&M personnel who were involved in the project, and we think we know which one of them sold the virus."

His spine stiffened. "Have you confirmed this?"

"Not yet. That's why I called. We need you to pay the man a visit."

"Who is he?"

"Dr. Stephen Langley. He's a scientist at D&M. We've been vetting all the names and his raised a few red flags. There's some suspicious financial activity in his bank accounts, and he was up to his eyeballs in debt up until two weeks ago. I'm talking millions in credit card bills, unpaid loans, huge sums to several loan sharks. We're thinking he racked up the debt gambling—the man flies to Vegas at least once a month, according to his travel records."

"And now all his debt has miraculously been erased?"

"Yep," Tate replied. "And there's no way his D&M salary was responsible for that. Dr. Langley got his hands on a large amount of money. Eva still hasn't found all of it—he's stashed it in various accounts all over the world, but each and every significant deposit or transfer occurred two weeks ago."

"So he sold the virus to the ULF and pocketed a crapload of cash."

"That's what we're thinking, but I need you to find out for sure. Langley is still employed at D&M, but it'll be next to impossible to get to him there. It's a highly secure research facility, and that building can't be breached, not without a lot of careful planning that we don't have time for. But we have his home address. I'll text it to you after we hang up."

Sebastian slid out from under the covers and stood up, balancing the phone on his shoulder as he grabbed his cargo pants from the chair beneath the window.

"Would this guy really be that stupid?" He couldn't control his skepticism. "To keep working at D&M after stealing a *biological weapon* from the facility?"

"It's actually a smart move," Tate pointed out. "It would look suspicious if he up and quit, and then two weeks later a virus wipes out a small town in New York state. Best course of action would be to hide out in plain sight. Work at the lab for another month or two, avoid suspicion and then take off once the dust has settled."

Sebastian zipped up his pants and fumbled for a shirt. "Good point. Okay, so I'll pay a visit to Langley. Rough him up a bit, see if I can get him to talk."

There was a long pause. "Yeah, I don't know if that'll be an effective approach."

He narrowed his eyes. "What aren't you telling me?"

"Langley was a research scientist for the CIA for two years before he moved to the private sector. They recruited him right out of college, which means he was CIA-trained."

"Which means the concept of keeping his mouth shut was drilled into him in very painful ways."

"If Langley really sold out his country, I'm fairly certain he won't own up to it. Not unless you present him with evidence of his guilt. And even then, he won't talk without trying to strike up some kind of immunity deal."

Sebastian mulled that over. "Fine." A grin stretched across his mouth. "Then let's give him immunity."

"This is the craziest plan *ever*," Julia hissed nearly ten hours later. She followed Sebastian to the front stoop of Stephen Langley's Georgetown brownstone, feeling incredibly ill at ease in her sleek black pantsuit. She adjusted the collar of her white shirt, then smoothed a hand over her hair, which was pulled back in a tight chignon. She felt like a total fraud in the getup, and the newly procured fake ID, clipped to her front pocket, felt like a big, scarlet *L* burning a hole into her breasts. *L* for *liar*.

She couldn't believe they were actually doing this.

Scratch that—she couldn't believe Sebastian actually thought they could pull it off.

"Just follow my lead," he said in a voice so calm she resisted the urge to smack him. How did absolutely *nothing* daunt this man?

This entire day had been one long worry fest for Julia. She'd worried while they waited for her latest false ID, which they'd needed to match the one Sebastian already had on him. She'd worried when they'd left the motel to purchase their snazzy black suits, then at the office depot where they'd printed out the files Eva had emailed. She'd worried as they'd watched Stephen Langley park his silver Mercedes in his driveway and amble into his home.

And now she was in full-blown panic mode, because although she was many things, an actress she was not.

Sebastian rang the doorbell, then rapped his knuckles on the front door, which was a dark-stained oak.

From the corner of her eye, Julia studied his clean-shaven face, a shocking change from his usual stubble-covered look. He appeared younger without all the scruff, but at the same time, far more lethal. The angular lines of his chiseled face were more pronounced, lending him a dangerously sexy vibe. And the man looked incredible in a suit, that was for sure.

Footsteps thudded from the interior of the townhouse. A moment later, the door opened and a short man with brown hair and a slight potbelly appeared in the doorway. "What do you want?" he demanded, narrowing his eyes at them.

"Dr. Stephen Langley?" Sebastian said pleasantly.

"Who wants to know?"

In one swift motion, Sebastian unclipped his ID card from his breast pocket and flashed it at the scientist. "Agent Shane Swanson, Department of Homeland Security. This is my partner, Agent Francis."

Keeping her expression cool, Julia flashed her own

card. Her heart was beating so loudly she was surprised Langley didn't comment on it.

"Forgive me if I request a closer look," Langley said snidely. He held out his hand.

They promptly dropped their IDs in his open palms. He examined them for so long that Julia was convinced he knew they were fake, but Sebastian had assured her that the badges were flawless. They even contained an actual DHS contact chip that was apparently linked to a real file for both "agents." Earlier, when Sebastian had revealed how much those IDs cost, she'd almost passed out.

As usual, Sebastian remained composed as Langley's perusal dragged on. Just when Julia thought the scientist would call them out as liars, the man's lips thinned in distaste and he handed them back the IDs.

"What can I do for you, Agents?" he asked in a clipped tone.

"We'd like to come in and ask you a couple of questions," Sebastian replied, equally terse.

Langley frowned. "May I ask what this is pertaining to?"

"Have you been watching the news today?"

"A terrorist group is holding a gun to our country's head. What the hell do you think?"

"Good, so you're aware that in thirty-six hours, a very deadly virus might potentially be released in one of our fine cities." Sebastian's mouth tightened. "Our questions pertain to *that,* Dr. Langley. So you can either let us in, or we can bring you back to DHS headquarters. It's your choice."

Without a word, Langley opened the door wider and gestured for them to enter.

Julia released the breath she'd been holding. She was so impressed with Sebastian's superior acting skills that it took all her willpower not to high-five him.

They followed Langley down a spacious corridor with wood-paneled walls. The stocky man no longer wore the blazer he'd had on when he'd come home; he'd changed into a blue cable-knit sweater that was a little too snug for him, outlining the paunch of his stomach.

He led them into a large den that smelled of leather, firewood and cigars. The Burberry carpet beneath their feet and the expensive artwork on the walls revealed that Langley liked his surroundings fancy. According to the file Eva had compiled, the microbiologist also owned a villa in Greece, a racehorse he stabled in Kentucky and a yacht that had almost been repossessed before he'd cleared his debts.

Julia wondered if he'd paid for all these luxuries with the money he made from gambling, or if he'd started gambling to support his life of luxury. She suspected it was the latter.

"Look," Langley said as he flopped down in a leather armchair adjacent to a stone fireplace, "the Pentagon already contacted our lab yesterday morning after the Dixie attacks. The director of D&M briefed us about it, and blood samples from the Dixie victims are already being analyzed in our facility. We've been working around the clock to learn as much as we can about what killed those people."

Smirking, Sebastian settled on the brown leather couch opposite Langley's chair. "Around the clock, huh?" He checked his watch. "Huh. Seems to me it's only seven in the evening, and you're here at home rather than at the lab."

Langley's brown eyes flashed with indignation. "I had dinner plans I couldn't reschedule."

Julia sat next to her "partner" and raised a brow at Langley. "And I'm sure the fact that your facility happens to be the lab that engineered the virus also reduces some of the urgency," she added graciously. "After all, you and your colleagues already know everything there is to know about the Meridian virus."

As expected, Langley pretended to look outraged. "That is categorically *untrue,*" he snapped. "D&M had nothing to do with the manufacturing of this virus."

"Of course not." Chuckling, Sebastian leaned over to unsnap the leather briefcase he'd brought with him. He extracted a heavy stack of papers, peeled off the first few sheets, and placed them on the oak table between the couch and the armchair.

Suspicion clouded the scientist's eyes. "What's this?"

"Take a quick peek."

Langley gingerly picked up the papers as if they were laced with anthrax. When he glanced at the first page, his eyes widened for a moment before growing shuttered. "What's this?" he asked, feigning ignorance.

"That's a log of all the researchers involved in Project Aries. As you already know, Project Aries was the code name for the development of this biological weapon." Sebastian paused. "The same biological weapon you sold to a terrorist group two weeks ago."

The scientist recoiled, his face going white as a sheet, but he recovered quickly. "You're accusing me of conducting business with terrorists?"

"It's not an accusation. It's a fact." Sebastian gestured to the stack on the table. "It's all there, Langley. The financial trail that led us straight to you. We've also got photographs of your rendezvous with the man you gave the virus to."

Julia held her breath again as the bluff hung in the air. It was the only piece of information Langley could actually call them on, but they'd needed to make him think they had more than just his shady financial dealings. They'd tried to keep their claim as vague as possible, deducing that Langley would have had to meet *someone* from Escobar's militant group and chances were that contact would be male.

When Langley flinched, she knew they'd hit the nail on the head. So he *had* met with a member of the ULF.

"Now here's the thing." Sebastian hurried on before Langley demanded to see said photos. "Our boss doesn't take kindly to traitors, Doctor. Neither does our boss's boss—who happens to be the *President* of the United States."

There was a brief silence, and then Langley moistened his lips. "I want a lawyer."

Julia and Sebastian exchanged amused looks.

"Uh-huh," Sebastian said good-naturedly. "Of course you do. But you see, when a scumbag American scientist sells a deadly biological weapon to a terrorist cell, there's no such thing as *lawyers.* Or *rights,* if you feel like tossing *that* word around. If you don't cooperate, you'll be detained at a government facility where lawyers and basic human rights don't exist. You're former CIA, so you know exactly what kind of facility I'm referring to, don't you, Langley?"

There was no mistaking the flicker of panic that lit the man's eyes. "Screw you," he hissed out.

"Now, now," Sebastian chided. "We're trying to help you here."

"Help me?" Langley's mouth twisted in a bitter scowl. "It sounds like you're trying to railroad me."

"We're giving you a chance to make this right," Julia spoke up in a soft tone.

"I'm not doing a damn thing," Langley muttered. "I'm no fool, Agent *Swanson*." He glared at Sebastian. "If I really did what you're accusing me of—and I'm not admitting to a goddamn thing—then we both know I'll be executed for those crimes. There is no making it right. Your boss, and your boss's boss—" sarcasm poured from his voice "—will have my head for this. So lock me up in one of your little torture facilities. You won't be getting a confession from me. You won't be getting cooperation from me either. Not unless I'm fully protected."

Julia sighed. "That's what we figured you'd say."

Next to her, Sebastian shoved his hand into his briefcase again and removed a thin stack of documents. He tossed the papers on the table.

"We've been authorized to offer you immunity." He sounded as if he vehemently disapproved of this "offer," and Julia had to hide a smile. Damn, he was good.

On the armchair, Langley blinked in surprise. "Ridiculous."

"We're not fools either," Sebastian retorted. "You're a company man. We knew exactly how you would respond, even when faced with irrefutable evidence of your treason. You'll be granted full immunity for your cooperation. You won't be held responsible for the selling of the virus, or charged with any related crimes. It's all outlined in the agreement."

Langley reached for the papers. Without a word, he read through the documents, then raised his eyebrows when he reached the last page. "This was signed by the secretary of the DHS."

"Trust me, Gallagher didn't like doing it," Sebastian said irritably. "But none of us had much of a choice. Lives are stake. Lives that are far more important than yours."

"It says here I get immunity in exchange for information leading to the *successful* apprehension of the ULF cell and the *successful* recovery of the virus."

"Like I said, we're no fools. If your intel doesn't help us catch these bastards, then what use are you to us? The agreement becomes null and void in that case."

Julia leaned forward and met Langley's eyes. "Your choice, Doctor. You can sign your name on that dotted line, or you can rip up the agreement and come back to DHS headquarters, where I guarantee your lawyer will *not* be waiting to greet you."

Langley scowled again. "What exactly does 'cooperation' entail, Agent Francis?"

"If you were the one who sold the virus, then you would have a protocol for contacting the ULF militant group, would you not?"

"Stands to reason," he agreed, remaining deliberately vague. "*If* I sold the virus, that is."

Julia shrugged. She suddenly realized her pulse was steadier than a metronome, and that she was no longer sweating beneath her pantsuit. This play-acting thing was actually kind of fun.

Deadly virus about to be released?

The ominous reminder snapped her into a somber mood. "We would start there," she told Langley. "You're going to set up a meeting with your contact—tonight."

Langley protested. "I can't arrange a meeting on such

short notice. *If* I was able to arrange a meeting at all," he amended quickly.

"You're damn well going to try," Sebastian snapped. "Thirty-six hours, Doctor. In thirty-six hours, that virus will be released. On *American* soil. Has that sunk in yet, or are you still living in a fantasy world where you think you can sell a bioweapon to a group of psychos and there won't be any consequences?"

When Langley blanched, Julia took control of the conversation once again. "You'll say whatever you need to say to get your contact to meet with you tonight. Our team will be monitoring the exchange, and if we're lucky, your terrorist friend will lead us right to *his* terrorist friends."

"So what's it going to be?" Sebastian asked amiably. He reached into the inner pocket of his suit jacket, removed a ballpoint pen and placed it next to the immunity agreement.

After several minutes of stonefaced silence, Langley reached for the pen.

Sebastian never would've dreamed that this harebrained scheme would go off without a single hitch. Yet here he was, sitting in the front seat of an unmarked sedan and monitoring the movements of a rogue scientist who was about to meet a bona fide terrorist for a clandestine rendezvous.

To Sebastian's delight, Langley had folded faster than a cheap tent in a hurricane, and once the man had signed that forged immunity agreement, the floodgates had opened and his story had poured out. He'd told them about the gambling debts he'd accrued over the past few years, admitted to having a wee bit of a cocaine problem, confessed that he'd been paid a substantial amount of dough for his work on Project Aries, yet apparently not substantial enough to put even a chip in his mountain of debt. When the loan sharks and creditors came knocking, Langley had panicked and done the only thing he could think of—sold a deadly virus to a terrorist group.

Right, because that was *always* the solution to money problems.

Sebastian focused on the corner coffee shop, watching Langley's every move. The scientist was at a table on the outdoor patio, both hands wrapped around a foam cup of coffee. A muffin sat on a napkin next to his cup but he hadn't taken a single bite.

This entire "operation" had come together at lightning speed. Langley had actually impressed the hell out of Sebastian when he'd contacted the man who'd handled the cash exchange for the virus. Like a true former operative, Langley had lied through his teeth as he'd made a case for why he needed a last-minute meeting.

"Nobody told me the virus was going to be released in America!" Langley had raged. "I didn't sign up for this! If I'm going to be indirectly responsible for killing my own people, then I want more money, damn it! And if I don't get it, I'm going to the Pentagon with what I know and telling them all about you and your sadistic little group!"

The speech was so polished that Sebastian had to wonder if Langley had intended all along to hit the ULF up for more money after he'd heard about the Dixie attack.

Langley's contact had agreed to the meeting at the same coffee shop where the original exchange had apparently taken place. Only this time, Langley was wired and Sebastian could hear every word being spoken across the street. The transmitter was the size of a watch battery, expertly sewn into the starched collar of the scientist's button-down, and Sebastian had the option to turn it off with the click of a remote, on the off chance that the ULF man swept Langley for wires. The nifty piece of spy equipment had cost more than Sebastian had earned during his entire military career. Good thing Nick could afford it, Richie Rich that he was.

"This is so cruel," Julia murmured from the passenger seat.

He glanced over in surprise. "What are you talking about?"

She nodded in Langley's direction. "He thinks he has immunity. He thinks he'll walk away from all this scot-free."

"Don't tell me you think he *should*."

"No, of course not. Look, what we did was callous—we pretended to be federal agents, we brought a fake immunity agreement with the forged signature of a government official. We played him, Sebastian, and that was a crappy thing to do." Her delicate features hardened to steel. "But it needed to be done. That man placed a deadly virus in the hands of terrorists who then went on to murder an entire town of people. He deserves to be punished, and he sure as hell deserves to be lied to."

Admiration soared through him, along with a spark of apprehension. He'd never met anyone like Julia. She was no weak-willed damsel. She didn't cave under pressure, or get all self-righteous when they were forced to employ less-than-honest tactics to accomplish their goal. Despite her initial trepidation, she'd given an Oscar-worthy performance for her role as "Agent Francis," and now here she was, refusing to apologize for their underhanded ploy.

No doubt about it, this woman might actually be his perfect match.

But the realization only deepened his apprehension, bringing a tremor of fear and quickening his pulse. Christ. He couldn't be thinking things like that. Julia was confident and brave and sarcastic and wonderful, but this was a temporary affair. A few days or weeks heating up the sheets, enjoying each other's company, and then they'd go their separate ways.

That was the only way to keep her safe. The only way to protect her from the goddamn curse he'd been burdened with.

"I think that's him," Julia suddenly whispered.

A nondescript black SUV had pulled up at the curb in front of the café. Ignoring the No Parking signs featured prominently all over the street, the SUV stopped a few yards from the outdoor patio, and then a man with tanned skin and a goatee emerged from the driver's seat. He was clad in khaki pants and a white button-down, but he carried himself like a soldier. Sharp gaze, aggressive stride, precise movements.

"He got here fast," she added, and Sebastian could see the wheels turning in that sharp brain of hers. "The group's base has to be close, then. Either an hour's drive or a short plane ride."

"Maybe. Or they might have men stationed all over the country, which means the virus could be anywhere."

Julia bit her lip. "Good point."

"We don't have time for your hysteria," an accented voice crackled in Sebastian's earpiece.

Across the street, the ULF representative had joined Langley at the table. Sebastian couldn't see the man's expression, but the anger staining his tone revealed his precise thoughts about this meeting.

Sounding equally pissed off, Langley recited the same speech he'd given over the phone, ending with, "I want another million. Otherwise I go to the Pentagon with what I know."

A Spanish expletive echoed in Sebastian's ear.

"What are they saying?" Julia demanded, looking frustrated that she didn't have her own link to the feed.

"Arguing about money," he told her, then held up one finger to silence her. "Wait, the ULF rep is actually agreeing to pay up. Wow. That was fast."

But Sebastian suspected the decision was more about getting Stephen Langley out of the ULF's hair than the belief that the scientist raised legitimate concerns.

"Enough," the soldier snapped. "Stop sniveling. You'll get your money."

"Same transfer instructions as before," Langley ordered. "I expect the funds to be in my account when the banks open tomorrow morning."

When he noticed the ULF terrorist shifting on the wrought-iron chair in impatience, Sebastian turned to Julia and placed a firm hand on her cheek. "It's time for you to go."

She nodded, her expression all business. "Be careful, Seb."

Leaning close, he lifted up the bottom of her fitted black jacket and gestured to her holstered Beretta. "I know you took an oath, but if Langley tries anything, you shoot the bastard, you hear me?"

She gave another quick nod. "All right."

Conversation continued to buzz in his ear, one line in particular making him take notice.

"And do yourself a favor, take the money and get out of town. You won't want to be in this city thirty hours from now." Sebastian could practically hear the smirk in the terrorist's voice.

"What is it?" Julia demanded. "What did he say?"

"He told Langley to get out of town." Sebastian's jaw went rigid. "Holy hell. I think they plan on releasing the virus in D.C."

He cut off her answering gasp by planting a hard kiss on her lips. "Go, Doc. I'll contact you on the prepaid when I know more."

Without another word, Julia slid out the passenger door of the sedan and casually headed for the unmarked Crown Victoria they'd rented earlier today, which was parked on the curb a dozen yards away. He watched her for a moment, then shifted his gaze in time to see Langley's contact impatiently rise to his feet.

Sebastian started the engine and tapped his fingers on the steering wheel, a rush of adrenaline entering his bloodstream. When the black SUV drove away from the curb, he began his pursuit, hoping this stakeout would actually amount to something. The hours in Escobar's deadline were slowly dwindling away, and it didn't seem like the Pentagon was making any headway in finding Escobar and his men.

Sebastian had checked in with Brent earlier in the day, but the DoD agent admitted to having no leads. Video experts were attempting to pinpoint Escobar's location based on the video he'd sent to the media, but they hadn't made any progress, and apparently the White House had dozens of scientists racing to develop an antidote in the unwelcome chance that the virus was released to the public. No progress on that front either, but Brent had thanked Sebastian profusely for the sample and research notes he'd provided. He'd also yet again urged Sebastian and Julia to come in as official witnesses, which they'd yet again refused.

Now, as he tailed the SUV through the streets of D.C., he considered bringing Brent into the loop again, then decided it might be prudent to wait. Might as well make sure this entire evening didn't turn into a wild goose chase before he brought Davidson in on it.

"Come on, man, where the hell are you going?" Sebastian muttered.

He stayed two cars behind the ULF man, growing warier by the second as they headed toward the northeast end of the city. The farther they drove, the worse the neighborhoods became. Dirtier streets, more graffiti, less upkeep of the homes and buildings. They ventured into one of the poorest areas in the city, maneuvering through residential streets bathed in shadows thanks to numerous broken lampposts. Finally, the SUV slowed in front of a dilapidated clapboard house with a saggy roof and an overgrown front yard.

As the SUV pulled into a gravel driveway overrun with weeds, Sebastian drove directly past the detached home, keeping a diligent eye on the rearview mirror. Langley's contact had hopped out of the SUV and was stalking toward the green front door of the house.

"Have we found your official lair, boys, or is this

just a safe house?" Sebastian murmured to himself as he steered toward the end of the street.

He executed a U-turn, parked the sedan at the curb underneath a busted streetlight and rummaged through the go bag he'd stashed in the backseat. He removed his suit jacket and hurriedly unbuttoned his white dress shirt, exchanging them for a snug black long-sleeve made of lightweight material. Then he strapped on a belt and attached the sheath of his bowie knife to it, shoved a pair of field glasses in his pocket and tucked two nine-millimeters into his waistband.

Armed and ready, he slipped out of the car and darted toward a narrow ramshackle house with all its lights off. He disappeared into the shadows, hopping fences and sneaking through yards as he made his way toward the ULF safe house. The street was surprisingly quiet considering it was located in a poverty-stricken, high-crime area. Sebastian heard the faint sounds of rap music wafting from one of the houses in the neighborhood, along with loud laughter and male voices in one of the backyards, but he didn't encounter any problems as he neared his target.

He initially positioned himself across the street, pressed against a tall wooden fence between two detached houses, also in run-down condition. The field glasses revealed three dark-skinned men brazenly walking past the large bay window at the front of the clapboard house. Interesting. So they weren't concerned about snipers being perched outside.

He watched for nearly twenty minutes, but he didn't see anyone else. There were at least four men in there, though. The trio he'd spotted, and Langley's contact.

Let's see how many more of you there are.

He abandoned his post and moved several houses down. As he climbed the roof of a darkened home, he prayed that the lack of lighting and no car in the driveway meant the residents were out, because the roof creaked like crazy, making him cringe with every step. Stealth was impossible to achieve when you were scaling walls and roofs that hadn't seen any maintenance in decades.

The new vantage point provided him a clear line of sight to the side of the house. Two more windows, and a side door. This time he caught a glimpse of Langley's contact, talking with another stocky, bearded man who didn't belong to the window trio. The tally went up to five men. Sebastian waited, then relocated once more.

During his third sweep, he spotted none other than Raoul Escobar himself.

A shocked hiss flew out of his mouth.

Fishing his cell phone from his pocket, he quickly dialed Tate's number. Despite the late hour, Tate picked up on the first ring. "What's up?"

"I'm pretty sure I just found the location of the ULF terrorist cell," he murmured, keeping his voice lower than a whisper.

Tate barked out an amazed curse. "You serious?"

"I'm looking at Escobar's face as we speak. He's holed up in a house in D.C. with five other ULF soldiers. There could be more, but six total is the current head count."

"You think the virus is in the house with them?"

"I'm thinking yes. No matter what these bozos call themselves, we both know they're not real terrorists, at least not in the same league as al Qaeda or other terrorist cells. They released their demands to the press instead of the White House, for chrissake. And honestly? A part of me wonders if they even have a real protocol for *releasing* the virus."

"Well, they found a way to release it in Dixie," Tate pointed out.

"Yeah, a tiny town with a tiny water treatment facility that anyone can walk into. They'll need a lot more planning if they want to release this thing into D.C.'s water supply."

"D.C.?"

"Makes the most sense. Why else are they holed up here in the city?"

Tate was silent for a second. "This could be a decoy house. Make us think that they're keeping the virus here and that they plan to release it nearby, but really, there's another cell in L.A. or New York or God knows where, ready to contaminate the city's water supply on Escobar's order."

"Could be, but Escobar's presence makes me think otherwise. He's the leader of this wacko ULF splinter group and my gut tells me he would want to stay close to the virus. It's his ticket to demolishing the American influence in San Marquez and his quest for national purification, or whatever the hell he was preaching about in that video."

"Well, either way, Escobar needs to be taken into custody. Can you handle it?"

Sebastian's gaze drifted to the ULF house, such a small, innocuous structure yet too damn big for one man to tackle on his own, even a man as well-trained as he was.

"No can do, Captain. We're looking at nine potential escape routes—front, back, side doors, six windows. If

I burst into the place guns blazing, I might take down a tango or two, but I won't get them all, and there's no guarantee I'll get Escobar. With all those exit points, these tangos will have multiple places to flee like rats. And I should note—I have no idea what kind of hardware they're packing. I counted six or seven assault rifles inside, AKs and M16s, but there aren't any guards posted at the exterior, and no perimeter whatsoever."

"Which means they're confident about the interior security measures they've employed," Tate finished. "My guess? The entire place is rigged to explode."

"That's what I was thinking." Sebastian released a heavy breath. "I can't breach this house on my own, Captain. Not without the risk of Escobar or one of his men escaping with the virus."

"I could send Prescott."

"Still won't be enough." Clenching his teeth, he stared at the house in the distance, then sighed again. "There's only one thing I can do."

"Which is?"

"Officially come out of hiding and turn myself in."

Chapter 14

When Sebastian strode into the motel room several hours later, Julia had never been happier to see anyone in her entire life. He'd kept his promise and called her on the prepaid phone to let her know he was on his way back, but she still hadn't been able to breathe easy, not until she saw him in person, saw with her own two eyes that he was okay.

And he looked more than okay. Her warrior was back, his gray eyes glittering with menace as he spotted Stephen Langley sitting stiffly at the kitchenette. Julia had brought Langley back to the motel room after his illicit rendezvous, claiming that it was for his own protection and that he needed to stay out of sight while the DHS conducted reconnaissance. She'd led Langley to believe that Sebastian and an entire team of special agents were pursuing the terrorist, when in fact it was a solo recon mission on Sebastian's part.

Yet he was no longer working solo, she realized once two men in dark suits followed him into the room.

Federal agents. *Real* ones, she thought, noticing the Department of Defense ID cards affixed to their suit jackets. The taller of the men, a light-skinned African-American with piercing brown eyes, removed a pair of handcuffs from his pocket as he headed for Langley.

"Please come with us, Dr. Langley," he said in a monotone voice.

Langley instantly shot to his feet. "What the hell are you talking about? What's going on?"

With a shrug, Sebastian went to Julia and brushed a kiss on her lips before turning to the scientist. "These gentlemen are going to escort you to the Pentagon. I believe every alphabet agency in existence is interested in talking to you."

Like a wild animal about to be trapped in a cage, Langley backed into the wall, eyeing the handcuffs with misgiving. "Why does he have the cuffs?" Accusation rang in his tone. "I signed the agreement, damn it! That means you can't place me under arr—"

Sebastian interrupted. "Oh, that. Well, you see…" He offered a what-can-you-do? gesture. "We weren't authorized to make any sort of deal with you. In fact, Agent Swanson and Agent Francis don't exactly exist."

Langley's face turned redder than a fire truck. "You lied to me?"

"Sorry." Now Sebastian merely shrugged.

"You're not Homeland Security?"

Another shrug. "Not really."

The real federal agents advanced on the livid scientist. As the metal cuffs snapped around his wrists, the man cursed up a blue streak and proceeded to hurl threats at every single person in the room. Suppressing a sigh, Julia watched as the federal agents escorted Stephen Langley out the door. She could still hear his incensed shouts even after the door closed, and a few minutes later, a car engine roared to life.

She turned to Sebastian with a quizzical look. "You called the DoD?"

"I had no choice."

Taking her hand, he led her to the bed, where they sat down so he could bring her up to date on what he'd discovered during his surveillance. "I couldn't have infiltrated that house on my own," he finished. "So I contacted Brent. He's sending a car for us in two hours."

Confusion spiraled through her. "Where are we going?"

"We'll be debriefed at the Pentagon, and Brent promised to keep you safe while I'm gone."

Now a rush of fear chilled her body. "What do you mean, 'when you're gone'?"

Sebastian clasped her suddenly frozen hand, gently stroking her palm. "I'm going to be part of the assault team. They're dispatching an elite military force to apprehend Escobar and secure the virus if it's on the premises."

To her mortification, tears stung her eyes. God, what was the matter with her? She was a doctor who'd seen unimaginable horrors. She wasn't programmed with silly feminine responses like bursting into tears for no good reason.

She quickly attempted to collect herself and rein in her emotions. "Brent's letting you do that, even though you're no longer active-duty?"

"He suggested it. In fact, he was adamant that I be

on the team, because I just spent the entire evening staking out the place." Sebastian squeezed her hand. "Don't look so worried, Doc. Chances are, this op will go down without a single hiccup."

"Chances are?" She choked out a laugh. "That's not at all reassuring, Sebastian."

His features softened. "You know I'm not one to offer false assurances. So yes, there's also a chance there *will* be hiccups. A lot of them."

When he hesitated, Julia's guard shot up. "What aren't you telling me?"

"There was a disconcerting lack of external security at the house," he admitted, rubbing his hand over the five-o'clock shadow darkening his jaw.

She frowned. "What does that mean?"

"It means there's a possibility that we'll encounter some nasty surprises when we get inside. Explosives are the likeliest option."

Her throat tightened with fear. "You mean you might get blown to smithereens once you enter the house?"

"Maybe."

"Or walk into some booby trap straight out of the *Saw* franchise?" Julia's heart was beating so rapidly that she started to feel light-headed.

"I'm fairly confident we won't encounter any horror-movie contraptions."

Sebastian had the nerve to laugh, but Julia couldn't bring herself to feel an ounce of humor about any of this. He was being so damn cavalier about the notion that he might get blown up and it made her want to kick him.

"Hey, come on now." He slid closer. "Get that crease out of your forehead." His fingertips massaged the worried groove beneath her hairline. "Chances are, I'll be just fine."

"Stop saying *chances are!*"

He chuckled, then brushed his lips over hers in a tender kiss. "Don't go all scaredy-cat on me, not this late in the game." He peppered more kisses on her mouth before dipping his head to press his lips to the hollow of her throat. "You've been so ridiculously brave since this all started, and it's impressed the hell outta me. So show me that iron strength of yours."

A ribbon of emotion uncurled in her chest, circling her heart, sending rays of warmth through her body. She leaned forward and rested her cheek on Sebastian's muscular chest, listening to the steady beating of his heart. "I don't want you to get blown up," she whispered.

The sound of his laughter vibrated in her ear. "I don't particularly want to get blown up either."

He rubbed her back, then reached up and started pulling out the pins holding her hair up. When her hair was free from its confining chignon, Sebastian threaded his fingers through her long brown tresses, his touch sweet and soothing. Eventually he broke the contact, hopping to his feet and dropping the pile of hairpins on the table before heading back to the bed.

He just stood there for a second, sweeping his gaze over her, his gray eyes softer than she'd ever seen them.

"Take off your clothes," he said gruffly.

She snapped into action. She slid her jacket off her shoulders and began unbuttoning her white blouse. As she hurriedly undressed, Sebastian did the same, and soon they were both naked, standing at the foot of the bed, watching each other.

She'd never really considered herself beautiful, but

somehow Sebastian made her feel that way. When he looked at her, it was with such reverence, such wonder, such passion. Like she was the most appealing creature on the planet.

And he was equally appealing to her. She stepped closer and ran her hands over the hard planes of his chest, skimming his defined pecs and washboard abdomen and the trail of dark hair that arrowed down to his groin.

He groaned. "I love it when you touch me, Doc."

Smiling, she continued to explore, petting and caressing and teasing until her hand finally made its way south to encircle his erection.

"So is this why the car isn't coming for a couple of hours?" she teased. "Were you the one who asked Brent for the two-hour window?"

"Yes," he admitted.

She laughed. "Well, I hope you didn't tell him why."

"No, but I'm sure he knows. All anyone has to do is take a good look at my face whenever you're around and they'll know *exactly* how much I want you."

Her breath caught. "And how much is that?"

"A lot," he said simply, and then his eyes grew heavy-lidded and he crushed his mouth over hers.

The kiss made Julia's head spin. Hot, passionate, demanding. He kissed her like they had only a minute to live and he needed to make every second count, every thrust of tongue and glide of lips and nip of the teeth *had* to count. That same urgency was present when he scooped her into his arms and lowered her onto the mattress.

His warm, naked body covered hers, callused hands exploring her feverish flesh and stoking the fire of arousal smoldering inside her. Tension gathered between her legs. Her heartbeat accelerated like a Formula 1 race car. Her breasts tingled. Nipples puckered. A knot of restless desperation started to build, until she was digging her nails into the hard sinew of Sebastian's back and begging him to enter her.

With a husky laugh, he grabbed a condom from the nightstand and sheathed himself. She expected him to plunge deep, to fill her with one passionate stroke, but his urgency seemed to have dissipated, replaced by slow tenderness.

His eyes shone like gray diamonds as he peered down at her, awe overtaking his handsome face. "How do you do this to me?" he murmured.

She swallowed. "Do what?"

Rather than answer, he kissed her again, his tongue sliding into her mouth at the same time his cock slid into her core. Her body stretched to accommodate him, and the feeling of sheer completion overwhelmed her. She didn't know what was happening between them, but something felt…different.

He made love to her with such exquisite tenderness she wanted to cry again. Each slow, gentle stroke stirred her senses and brought her closer to the precipice. When he slid one hand to where their bodies were joined and feathered his thumb over her swollen bud, she moaned and rocked her hips, welcoming the rush of pleasure. Her climax sent her soaring, and as her heart pounded like a drum and her body trembled with bliss, she heard Sebastian's hoarse cry, felt him grow still, felt his muscles tense as he let himself go.

Afterward, he rolled over and got rid of the condom, while Julia stared up at the cracked plaster ceiling. Stunned. Confused.

And happier than she'd ever been in her life.

Sebastian returned to bed and stretched out beside her. He fumbled for her hand and intertwined their fingers, keeping their locked fingers between their naked bodies as they lay in contented silence.

"Julia." His voice was gravelly.

"Yeah?"

"If for some reason I don't come back from that op tomorrow…"

Panic constricted her heart. "Hey, don't say that. You're not going to get blown up, damn it."

"I know." He paused. "At least I hope not." Another pause. "But just humor me, okay? If I don't come back, there's something I need you to know."

Unsettled, she moved onto her side and studied his profile. She couldn't decipher the strange expression on his face, and that only troubled her more. "What is it?" she asked.

After a long moment of hesitation, he breathed in deep, then exhaled in a fast rush. "If I could offer you more than a casual affair, I would."

Surprise lifted her eyebrows. Okay. Well, she hadn't been expecting *that*.

But he wasn't done surprising her.

"I could fall in love with you, Doc."

Now her mouth fell open, and with her brows up at her hairline and her jaw down at her feet, she knew she must make a comical sight. She had no clue how to respond to either of those revelations, so she opted for, "Huh?"

Sebastian sighed. "I'm not making any sense, am I?

I…I'm cursed, Julia. I'm totally freaking cursed, and that's why I try not to get close to people." An endearing crack broke his voice in half. "I can't love you. Do you understand?"

Sheer and utter confusion left her speechless for an entire minute. And then she shook her head repeatedly and sat up. She wasn't even self-conscious of her nudity, that's how bewildered she was.

"No, I don't understand," she burst out. "What do you mean, you're cursed, and you *can't* love me?"

He moved into a sitting position, too, leaning his head against the wall. His expression conveyed nothing but anguish. "I get people killed, Doc. Everyone I love dies. Because of me."

The odd confession caught her off guard. "I'm sure that's not true."

"It is." His powerful body emitted thick waves of sorrow. "I had a twin brother, you know. Michael,"

She blinked. "You did?"

"Mmm-hmm. We were identical twins. He drowned when we were twelve years old." Sebastian turned his head to meet her eyes. "It was my fault."

Julia instantly slid closer and reached for his hand. She found it was trembling. "I don't believe that," she said firmly.

"It's true." He gave a bitter shake of his head. "Michael and I couldn't have been more different. He was the serious, studious type. I was the reckless thrill seeker. I always talked him into doing the craziest stunts, though I think half the time he agreed to come along so he could keep an eye on me. He always warned me I'd get seriously hurt one day."

When Sebastian went quiet, she didn't push him to

go on. The pain in his eyes sent an ache to her heart, and the dull note in his voice brought the fresh sting of tears to her eyes.

"But he was the one who got hurt in the end," Sebastian mumbled. "One night I convinced him to sneak out of our house after midnight so we could go late-night fishing at the lake about half a mile from our property. He bitched and moaned, but ended up coming with me, and we grabbed our rods and tackle boxes from the porch and ran off to the lake. After fifteen minutes without a single bite, I got bored of fishing and decided it would be fun to go skinny-dipping."

Another silence descended. Julia suddenly felt queasy.

"So we shucked our clothes and jumped in the lake. Swimming, splashing, seeing who could hold our breath underwater the longest. I won with a time of ninety seconds. But me being me, I got bored of swimming as fast as I tired of fishing. Michael wanted to stay in the water for a bit, so I left him in the middle of the lake. When I reached the shore, I turned around to look at the water, and he was gone."

A ragged breath wheezed out of his mouth. "He was just *gone.* At first I thought he was playing a prank on me, so I stood there for a few minutes, grumbling and pouting and shouting for him to quit being such a jerk. I was wearing my waterproof watch—that's what we were using to time our underwater game, and suddenly I realized he'd been under for more than three minutes."

Julia sucked in a breath. "Did you go in after him?"

"Without hesitation. I swam like I was being chased by a damn shark, but I couldn't find Michael anywhere." Sebastian's voice cracked again. "I don't know how long

I was in that lake, Doc, searching for my twin brother. I dived as deep as I could, but I couldn't see a damn thing. It was too dark and the lake was full of these pesky weeds that made it even harder to see. Eventually I went back to shore and ran home as fast as I could. I woke up my folks, and they got the police and fire department there in record time."

One final silence, this one heavy with regret. She squeezed Sebastian's hand, urging him to continue. "What happened?"

"The divers found Michael's body in the morning. His legs were tangled up in some weeds, but I don't know if that's what caused him to go under or if it happened after the fact. For all I know, he had a cramp, or got dizzy and passed out, or..." Sebastian trailed off, and then an angry expletive left his mouth. "It was my fault he drowned. It was my fault he was at the lake. I was the one who turned my back on him in the water, and I was the one who couldn't save him when I realized he was gone."

Julia had done her residency in the ER, which meant she'd spoken to countless survivors, hundreds of men and women who were rushed in after a horrific accident, an accident that *they* survived but their friends or loved ones didn't. She knew a case of survivor's guilt when she saw it, but she feared that if she raised the issue, Sebastian might shut down on her.

Still, she couldn't humor him, not about something this important. "It wasn't your fault," she said softly. "You weren't responsible for Michael's death."

"My parents thought I was," he muttered. "Dad openly blamed me. Mom was more subtle about it. And Michael's death destroyed them both. He was their favorite, and after he was gone, they both sort of… checked out. My dad got meaner, colder, and I suspect he got careless in the field. I think that's why he died, because he just didn't give a damn anymore."

Julia let out an unhappy sigh. "And now you believe you get the people around you killed? Because Michael drowned and your father died in combat?"

A harsh, cheerless laugh echoed in the room. "They weren't the only ones."

"What are you talking about?"

"It took me a long time to get over Michael's and my father's deaths. Throughout high school, I was friends with this kid Greg, but it wasn't until junior year that I finally opened myself up to the guy. We were inseparable after that. Practically lived at each other's houses, went everywhere together, double-dated all the time. And we both planned on enlisting in the army after high school. But Greg didn't get the chance." Sebastian's jaw tightened. "A few weeks before graduation, we were at a party, and reckless ol' me challenged Greg to a drinking contest."

Julia's heart sank to the pit of her stomach. Crap. She didn't like where this was heading.

"And guess what I did afterward?" he said sarcastically. "I let him *drive*." He laughed again, an absolutely ravaged sound. "I let him drive to his death, Doc. So that was Greg. Want to hear about Lynn? Christ, I loved Lynn. I met her when I was twenty-one, right after I got home from my first tour of duty. She was a freaking angel."

"Sebastian—"

"We were together for a year. I wanted to marry her. I was going to ask her the night she got mowed down by a car on her way to meet me. She was supposed to work that night, but I convinced her to call in sick so we could have dinner together."

Her heart officially broke in two.

"Oh, God," she whispered.

"Do you get it now? Do you see? Everyone I love is destined to die."

Before he could resist, she threw her arms around him. After a moment, his shoulders drooped and his head sagged, falling into the crook of her neck. Cursed. Yes, she supposed she understood why he'd reached *that* particular conclusion.

"I'll get you killed." His voice was muffled against her skin, thick with torment, and his naked body trembled in her arms.

"No, you won't." She used the tone she normally reserved for hostile patients, the one that said *Don't mess with me. I know best.* "If anything, you're the reason I'm alive, for Pete's sake."

He stiffened. "That's not true."

"Are you kidding me?" She pulled back, gripped his strong jaw and forced him to look at her. "You rescued me from those soldiers in Esperanza. You talked me out of going back to the clinic and saved me from being burned alive. You gave me shelter in Ecuador, safe passage to the States, protection from Davidson and the DoD." Now she was the one laughing, each breathy sound ringing with disbelief. "*You* are the reason I'm not dead."

His gray eyes filled with shock. "You're in danger because of me."

She arched one brow. "And now you're just grasping at straws and straight-up rewriting history. I was in danger before I met you, Sebastian. I'm in danger because Kevin radioed me from Esperanza and I rushed to his rescue. *You* didn't put me in this position. *You* have protected me from day one, and guess what? I'm still here. I'm still alive. Doesn't that prove that you're capable of getting close to someone without their dying?"

Sebastian looked stricken, as if he truly hadn't considered that he might actually be responsible for her current state of *alive*.

The room got so quiet you could hear fifty pins drop. Julia continued to run a soothing hand over his rugged face, her other hand solidly perched on his shoulder. She wanted to offer more words of comfort, but instead she chose to say nothing, knowing that Sebastian needed the time to think, to reflect, to understand that some things were beyond his control.

As she sat there in silence, it suddenly occurred to her that Sebastian wasn't the only one who'd gotten too close. She'd known for a while now that this thing between them had evolved into more than just sex, but she hadn't been able to put a label on it until this very moment.

She was falling for him.

She'd spent every waking minute with him these past seven days, shared more of herself, both physically and emotionally, than she'd ever shared with another man. She'd given Sebastian Stone free rein of her body, control of her safety, access to her heart…and in the process, she'd fallen in love with him.

Sebastian was grateful as hell when the sharp knock sounded on the motel room door, indicating that their ride had arrived. He'd been fighting the need to flee ever since he'd told Julia about his past. He hated talking about all those ancient tragedies. Hated thinking about them. Normally he kept the memories locked up tight, yet he hadn't been able to stop himself from spilling the sordid details to Julia.

He'd felt himself getting too close. His heart had been in his throat when he'd made love to her earlier. He'd felt so damn vulnerable, his emotions so close to the surface that he'd decided to remind himself what happened when he let himself love someone.

But his plan had backfired. He'd told Julia about his past, his fear, his curse, and she hadn't batted an eye.

You're the reason I'm alive.

Her quiet words buzzed in his head and he pushed them away as he went to answer the door. Brent had sent his aide, Paul Waverly, to deliver Sebastian and Julia to the Pentagon, and Sebastian opened the door to find a frazzled young man standing on the other side of it.

"Sergeant Stone?"

He nodded. "Waverly?"

The man nodded in return. He had pale blond hair and even paler white skin that washed out his face and lent him a ghoulish vibe, but he was very friendly and polite as he escorted them to a black sedan with tinted windows.

Julia didn't say a word as she slid into the backseat next to Sebastian. She'd put on a pair of jeans and a loose gray sweater, and her hair was in its trademark braid, which meant that her fingers were toying with the end as usual.

He resisted the urge to put his arm around her or hold her hand, though he desperately wanted to touch her. He'd been thinking the craziest thoughts since their heart-to-heart. Crazy, terrifying, liberating thoughts that he wasn't quite ready to vocalize, and so he kept a physical distance, needing more time to let everything settle.

The ride to the Pentagon was a short one. Paul had already arranged for a pair of visitor's passes, and he handed each of them a navy blue lanyard with the passes affixed to the end. Sebastian shoved the lanyard around his neck, then kept a firm hand on Julia's arm as they followed Paul to the elevators.

They found Brent Davidson in a large conference room that housed a long mahogany table, padded chairs, several telephone lines and an enormous flat screen mounted on the wall.

"Good, you're here," Brent boomed when they walked through the door. "Paul, get Dr. Davenport a cup of coffee and get her settled in my office. Stone, come with me. The team is about to be briefed."

"Is this goodbye?" Julia spoke up, her voice swimming with uneasiness.

Sebastian shook his head. "I'll come find you before we head out," he said gruffly.

With a nod, she followed Paul out of the room, while Sebastian went with Brent. They navigated through an endless series of hallways, walked through several secure doors that required the swipe of Brent's key card, and eventually wound up in an enormous elevator that took them to the lower levels of the massive compound.

"You did a good job handling Langley," Brent remarked during the walk, his tone more than a little grudging. "But you just couldn't let us handle it, huh?"

"You government folk move much too slow," Sebastian answered with a grin. "My way allows for quicker results."

Brent chuckled. "Nice move with the immunity agreement, by the way. Fax me a copy of it. I'm curious to see how good your forgery guy is."

"Damn good. And you're not getting anywhere near him."

They turned another corner, entering a spacious corridor with bright overhead lights.

"Has Langley started talking yet?" Sebastian asked.

"Nope. He's still hoping to save himself. Now he claims he's got an antidote to the virus. Apparently he stole it along with the virus when he robbed D&M."

He raised his brows. "You think he's telling the truth?"

"Who the hell knows? This scumbag sold a biological weapon to a terrorist group. He knows there's no way out of that, and I suspect he'll say anything to save his own skin. We've got agents with him now. If there really is an antidote, they'll get it out of him. Anyway, Langley's not a priority at the moment. Right now our primary objective is neutralizing the cell and securing Meridian."

Sebastian nodded. "Got it."

The briefing that followed was one he'd been a party to numerous times before. The commanding officer was a bulky man by the name of Darius Foster. Foster had been heading up this elite Delta unit for years, and he looked less than thrilled that Sebastian would be joining them for such a sensitive operation. He seemed appeased once Brent explained Sebastian's former training, and when aerial photographs of the ULF nest flashed on a large overhead screen, Foster turned to Sebastian first for the details he'd amassed during his recon.

It took more than an hour to plan the assault. Every last detail was discussed, every available photo scrutinized, every contingency accounted for. When Foster clapped his hands to signal the end of the meeting, the men filed out of the room and marched toward the equipment locker to gather their gear. It would be a ten-man team: Foster, Sebastian and eight other highly trained operatives who'd been working black ops for most of their careers.

Preparations were made at lightning speed. Weapons, body armor, earpieces—every piece of equipment they'd need was checked and rechecked before the team reported to the waiting chopper.

But Sebastian had promised Julia a proper goodbye and he wasn't going anywhere until he gave it to her. He quickly scanned the men swarming the helipad, finally spotting Brent's aide amid the crowd. "Waverly," he called.

The blond man hurried over. "Yes?"

"Where's Dr. Davenport? I want to speak with her before we go."

Paul Waverly pulled out a sleek smartphone and dialed a number. "Mary, will you escort the doctor to the launch?" A second later, he hung up and said, "She'll be here shortly."

A wave of gratitude swept through him. "Thanks, Paul."

The young man smiled. "Not a problem."

Five minutes later, most of the team was in the military chopper, and Julia still hadn't showed up. Growing worried, Sebastian glanced over at Foster, who was barking orders at the pilots. Fortunately, the senior officer didn't seem to notice that Sebastian was still loitering on the tarmac.

When a door flew open and Julia burst out, he was overcome with relief. He met her halfway, smiling at the way her long braid was whipped around by the late-night breeze. It was just past three in the morning, and the moon sat high in the black sky, illuminating the unmistakable lines of worry creasing Julia's mouth.

"You okay?" he asked.

"I'm scared," she admitted, but her voice was so frank and steady that it made him laugh.

"You don't sound like it," he teased.

"Well, I feel it." She met his gaze. "Please be careful."

"I'm always careful." He touched her cheek, sweeping his thumb over her silky smooth skin. "Thank you, Doc."

She wrinkled her forehead. "For what?"

"For everything." His voice grew hoarse. "The time we've spent together has been…" He trailed off, unable to find an adjective that did the rest of the sentence justice.

Then he noticed that Julia was glaring daggers at him. "Stop doing that," she ordered. "Stop acting like we're never going to see each other again."

He smiled. "What should I say, then? 'See you soon'? 'Catch you later'?"

"Yes," she said firmly. "You're even allowed to tell me you're going to miss me. But anything that so much as implies this might be the last time we see each other? Forbidden."

Laughter tickled his throat. "Yes, ma'am."

With her chin lifted in defiance and her hazel eyes glittering with true grit, she'd never looked more beautiful.

Crossing her arms over her chest, Julia pinned him down with a stern look and said, "So now give me a hug and a kiss, and go kick some terrorist butt, Sergeant Stone."

Chapter 15

"We've got a visual on Apollo. I repeat, visual on Apollo. Appears to be asleep in the back bedroom, west side, clear shot." The hushed report came from the sniper positioned on the roof of the house bordering the terrorist nest.

"Roger that. Maintain visual." Foster's voice, in that same monotone murmur, echoed in Sebastian's earpiece.

"Visual on two tangos in the back bedroom, east side," the operative covering the side of the house whispered. "Andromeda One and Two. No movement."

"Andromeda Three, Four and Five in the kitchen. Visual on back door," came another whisper. "Awake but no movement."

From his position in the hedges separating the ULF nest from the neighboring home, Sebastian fixed his gaze on the front of the house. The lights in the living room were on, and a body was sprawled on the couch, a male arm pointing a remote control at a television. The bluish light from the TV screen reflected off the glass of the large front window.

"Tango in the living room. Awake but no movement," Sebastian murmured. "That makes Andromeda Six."

Six soldiers and Escobar, who'd been dubbed Apollo, making that a total of seven bodies inside the house. Four awake, three potentially sleeping.

Sebastian looked at the stoic-faced operative next to him. They were both decked out in the same getup— all-black uniform, utility vest, protective helmet, sturdy boots, and their faces were smudged with dark polish for them to blend into the shadows. Protected by a layer of Kevlar and body armor, Sebastian was carrying an MP5 submachine gun and two nine-millimeter side-arms, not to mention strategically placed knives and several grenades clipped to his vest.

"Get in position," Foster's voice murmured. "Maintain visual."

Using standard operation hand signals, Sebastian's teammate, a man who'd introduced himself only as Boswell, gestured for Sebastian to fall in line. The two soldiers silently crept toward the house, flattening themselves against the exterior wall and inching toward the edge of the bay window. They slid down to the ground and assumed a crawl position, neither one making a sound as they slithered beneath the window toward the paint-chipped front door.

One by one, the other team members checked in with a quick "Ready," including the two snipers positioned on the roofs of the neighboring houses. Once Sebastian and his partner were in position, they murmured their status, then awaited instructions. The plan called for a simultaneous ambush on every point of entry, but not until they received the go signal from Foster.

Time stood still as Sebastian waited in the darkness. The entire street was quieter than a church, though he did make out the sound of a car engine in the distance. Other than that, there was virtually no residential traffic at four-thirty in the morning, and the unit had been able to infiltrate the area without any trouble.

Foster's voice hissed over the transmission again. "Remember, lethal force if necessary, but the objective is to apprehend, not eliminate. Priority on Apollo. We move on my count. One."

Sebastian tightened his grip on his MP5.

"Two."

He breathed deeply through his nose.

"Three."

He and Boswell sprang to action, spraying the front door with bullets before kicking it in and bursting into the house. Boswell went straight, Sebastian ducked left into the living room. Noise exploded in his ears, coming from all parts of the house. Deafening gunfire, shattering glass, urgent shouts and brisk commands to lay down weapons.

The ULF soldier in the living room dived off the couch, firing an AK in Sebastian's direction. Ears ringing, Sebastian rolled behind the arm of the tattered polyester sofa and unloaded a round. Glass exploded. More gunshots continued to rock the house.

The soldier was hunkered down behind a brown armchair with its stuffing coming out. Sebastian's gaze followed the movement of the man's arm, which appeared to be trying to reach the splintered wooden table.

"¡Ahora!" The frantic Spanish order broke through the *rat-tat-tat* of machine gunfire. *"¡Ahora!"*

Now.

Sebastian glanced at the coffee table and instantly realized what the panicked ULF rebel was attempting to grab. A silver remote the size of a cigarette pack, with a blinking red light and black button.

Son of a bitch. A detonator. Evidently, the responsibility of blowing the house to kingdom come was this little bastard's job.

Making a move for the detonator meant exposing himself to the barrel of that AK-47, but Sebastian had no other choice. Saying a silent prayer, he left the cover of the sofa and executed a flying leap toward the table. Bullets whizzed by his head. Something hit him in the gut, hard, knocking the wind right out of him. He made a mad grab for the detonator, his fingers colliding with it just as the ULF soldier lunged at him.

The remote slipped out of his hand and clattered to the weathered hardwood floor. Both men went after it, Sebastian dropping his MP5 in the process. Christ, he wasn't going to reach it first. Fear and adrenaline seized his blood. He fumbled for the Glock at his hip.

With a wild cry one might hear from an injured animal, the terrorist flung out his arm, his fingers inches from the detonator.

Sebastian pulled the trigger and put four bullets in the back of the man's head.

Thump.

The terrorist's arm dropped to the hardwood. His body went motionless.

Breathing hard, Sebastian climbed over the dead

man, ignoring the puddle of blood forming around the man's head.

He grabbed the detonator, then shuddered out a sigh of relief as he touched his earpiece and said, "Andromeda Six KIA. Detonator confiscated. South quadrant clear."

He tipped his head up to examine the ceiling for any signs of wiring, but whatever explosives this house had been rigged with, they weren't visible to the naked eye. He expected they'd find a mountain of C4 in the basement, maybe even concealed in the walls.

"Andromeda One and Two apprehended. West quadrant clear," a brisk voice reported.

"Andromeda Three, Four and Five KIA. North quadrant clear," another voice barked.

"Apollo apprehended," a triumphant voice announced. "East quadrant clear."

Pocketing the detonator, Sebastian picked up his fallen MP5 and stepped into the hallway, where he found Boswell. It was hard to make out the man's expression beneath all that black face paint, but it was easy to discern the glint of victory in the soldier's eyes.

They headed for the back of the house toward the bedroom where Escobar had been holed up. There, they found two Delta operatives looming over Raoul Escobar, guns trained on his forehead. The ULF leader wore an expression of pure defeat, looking so upset that Sebastian had to swallow a laugh.

Your dastardly plan didn't work out the way you wanted, huh?

"Any sign of Meridian?" Foster's voice barked in everyone's ears.

"Doing a sweep of the premises," one operative barked, and he was echoed by three similar responses.

Sebastian removed the detonator from his vest pocket and held it up. "House is rigged," he said, clicking on his earpiece. "Get a bomb squad here. We don't know what we're dealing with."

"Meridian virus secure."

Silence rippled through the feed.

"Say that again?" Foster ordered.

"Meridian virus is secure."

Sebastian glanced at Escobar, whose dark eyes had taken on a hard, resigned light. He was beaten, and he knew it.

"I repeat, the Meridian virus is secure."

An hour later, Sebastian was still riding the adrenaline high of a successful op as he hopped out of the chopper with the rest of the team. A ground unit was bringing Escobar and the two surviving ULF soldiers in for interrogation, while the deadly vials discovered in the basement of the nest were being airlifted to the CDC. A search of the house hadn't turned up any more vials, and according to one of Escobar's men, who was singing like a canary, all the vials in the group's possession had been in the house.

That only spoke to the disorganized and highly unprofessional tactics of the ULF splinter sect. Escobar's planning had been shoddy, his security weak, his goals unrealistic.

"Very nice work," Brent Davidson boomed as he greeted him at the helipad.

He slapped Sebastian's back, and the two men headed for the door leading into the building. The rest of the team stalked past them, Foster barking orders at his men as he wiped the black polish off his face with a cotton rag.

Sebastian did the same, running a cloth over his skin as he fell into step with Brent, who was still spitting out details.

"A joint task force is being organized in San Marquez. Every known ULF hideout will be raided. We can't take the chance that Escobar has another vial of the virus stashed somewhere in that country."

"Honestly? I don't think he does," Sebastian answered. "Escobar didn't strike me as the brightest bulb in the bunch. I think he was tired of Luego not producing any results, convinced a handful of idiots to join his cooler and more extreme ULF sect, and half-assed a scheme that unfortunately got those people in Dixie killed. He was successful on a small scale, but I doubt he would've been able to pull off an attack on a major city, and I doubt he'd risk letting that virus out of his sight, not if there's a chance of it being released in his own country."

"Valid points," Brent agreed. "We'll see what the searches turn up."

They strode down a fluorescent-lit corridor, and Sebastian unsnapped his helmet and tucked it under his arm. "I want to see Dr. Davenport. Where is she?"

"She's in my office. The couch in there is comfortable as hell, but I suspect she didn't listen to my suggestion that she get some sleep. She was wearing a hole in the carpet the last time I checked on her."

He suppressed a grin. Yep, no surprise there. No way would Julia do anything other than pace—she'd been too damn worried when they'd parted ways on the helipad.

"You want something to drink?" Brent asked as they entered the elevator.

"Some water would be great. Feels like my mouth is filled with sawdust."

Brent grinned, reaching out to punch two different level buttons. "I could use a cup of coffee myself. I'll grab you a bottle of water and meet you and the doc in my office for debriefing."

"Sounds good."

The elevator doors dinged. Sebastian stepped into the hall and made his way toward Davidson's office. His pulse sped up the closer he got, and he suddenly realized just how eager he was to see Julia. The last time he'd felt this excited to see a woman had been… nine years ago.

When he'd been falling in love with Lynn.

He came to an abrupt stop in the middle of the corridor. Before he could stop it, the image of Lynn's big blue eyes and silky blond hair floated into his head, and his heart clenched in response. Christ, she'd been so delicate. Barely over five feet, with soft ethereal features and the prettiest smile he'd ever seen.

Lynn's face quickly transformed into Julia's—those stubborn hazel eyes and angular jaw and sassy mouth. There was nothing delicate about Julia. She possessed an unyielding amount of strength. She was hotter than molten lava. Smarter than he'd ever be.

And he loved her.

He freaking loved her.

Rather than the icy rush of fear he expected, pure

liberation soared inside him like a bird taking flight. He set off again, his strides long and determined.

He marched into Brent's office without knocking and found Julia on the couch, absently flipping through a copy of the day's newspaper.

She shot to her feet when he walked in, blurted out "Thank God!" and threw herself into his arms.

He wrapped his arms around her slender body and held her, breathing in her familiar scent of soap and orange blossoms. Christ, he could get high off that sweet feminine fragrance, and he held her even tighter, never wanting to let go.

"I'm so glad you're okay," she murmured, gazing up at him with those big doe eyes that suddenly seemed so unsuited to a woman who had nerves of steel.

"I'm so glad you're here," he replied huskily.

Ignoring the surprised look on her face, he swiftly bent his head and kissed her, all the pent-up tension of this unbelievably tense day pouring out and transforming what was supposed to be a gentle kiss into a passionate domination that had Julia moaning against his lips. He nibbled on her bottom lip for a moment, then pulled back with a grimace. His mouth was now officially devoid of any moisture, parched to a whole new level.

"I'm so damn thirsty," he said with a sigh.

Laughing, Julia grabbed a bottle of water from the desk. "Here, drink," she ordered. "We can't have you getting dehydrated."

"Yes, Doctor." He untwisted the cap and chugged the entire bottle in one long gulp, eliciting another laugh from Dr. Davenport.

The cold liquid hit the spot and eased the dryness of his mouth, but when he tossed the empty bottle in the wastebasket by the door, he saw Julia eyeing him with disapproval.

"What?" he said sheepishly.

"You really couldn't save a teeny little drop for me?" She rolled her eyes. "Because now *I'm* thirsty."

"Er, I'm sorry, Doc. Let me make it up to you." With a wicked grin, he advanced on her, intending on resuming that hot makeout session, but Brent foiled that plan by striding into the office.

Holding a foam cup of coffee in one hand, the black-haired man tossed an Evian bottle in Sebastian's direction before rounding the desk and sitting on the commanding leather chair.

"Here," Sebastian said, handing the water to Julia. "This one can be all yours."

Smiling, she uncapped the bottle and took a long sip. "Thanks."

"Have a seat, guys," Brent said, gesturing to the two plush chairs in front of the mahogany desk. "We've got a few matters to discuss, and some statements for you to sign."

They spent the next twenty minutes being debriefed and discussing their options. With a frustrated sigh, Brent leaned back in his chair and said, "I recommend you remain stateside. I can offer both of you round-the-clock protection and—"

"Not gonna happen," Sebastian cut in. "I need to rejoin my men as soon as possible. I'll discuss it with them, but I suspect they'll want to avoid the States until we know for sure who murdered the rest of our unit."

"I promise I will do everything in my power to figure that out," Brent answered. "I'm certain that once we discover who authorized the creation of the Meridian virus in the first place, we'll find that the same person was the one responsible for the deaths of your men. A task force is already being assembled, and an internal investigation of every government agency and every government worker, as high up as the White House, will be conducted. Finding the person responsible for Meridian is now a matter of national security."

"Good," Sebastian said. "But until you find that person, I can't stick around."

"Me neither," Julia spoke up.

He glanced over in surprise. They hadn't discussed what her plans were, but he was happy to hear she wasn't foolishly insisting on returning to Boston or sticking around in D.C. He knew exactly where he wanted her to go, but that required the long, mushy discussion he wasn't sure he was ready for.

"For now, Julia stays with me," he said, hoping he wasn't overstepping his bounds.

But she didn't seem at all bothered by the declaration. "If I decide to accept your protection, I'll let you know," she told Brent.

The older man sighed. "Well, short of placing you in protective custody against your will, I can't force either of you to stay. But you will need to come back at some point if your testimony is ever required."

"We'll see," Sebastian said, his tone intentionally vague.

Brent chuckled. "Uh-huh. I know what *that* means." He rose from the desk and stuck out his hand. "It was good to see you, Stone. Do me a favor and leave me a number where I can contact you?"

He offered a gracious nod. "That I can do."

The two men shook hands, and then Brent gave Julia's arm a gentle squeeze before walking them both out. "The country owes a great debt to you both," Brent said seriously. "The CDC is already working on developing an antidote based on the sample and notes you gave us, and Escobar won't be releasing a damn thing into any water supply thanks to you, Sebastian."

When they stepped into the hall, they bumped into Brent's aide, Paul, who gestured to Sebastian's combat uniform. "You'll need to stop at the equipment locker before you leave the premises, Sergeant. I can take you there."

"Thanks, Paul."

He took Julia's hand, and the two of them followed the blond man down the corridor. As they waited for the elevator, Julia dropped her water bottle in a nearby trash can before walking back and bringing her lips close to Sebastian's ear. "Thanks for not getting blown up, Seb."

A smile tickled his lips. "You're very welcome, Doc."

Rather than return to their motel room, Sebastian and Julia checked in to a hotel on the other side of the city using Sebastian's false identity. The only available room ended up being a suite with a huge Jacuzzi tub that brought a delighted grin to Julia's face.

Sebastian loved seeing her so happy. She'd had a spring to her step ever since they'd left the Pentagon, and she was much cuddlier than usual. Linking arms when they walked, snuggling close during the car ride, planting a spontaneous and unbelievably passionate kiss on his lips in the hotel elevator. That kiss had succeeded in getting him harder than concrete, but neither of them had been in the mood for sex as they got settled in the suite.

They hadn't slept for twenty-four hours, which was probably why they collapsed on the huge bed the moment they got to the hotel.

When Sebastian's eyes opened hours later to find that it was pitch-black beyond the floor-to-ceiling window, he groaned with unhappiness.

Julia stirred beside him, her warm ass wiggling into his groin. "What's wrong?" she asked sleepily.

"We've been sleeping for sixteen hours."

"You're lying." She gave a loud yawn. "What time is it?"

"Eleven."

"That's not too bad. We checked in only at six."

"Eleven at night, Doc."

That got her attention. Propping herself up on one elbow, she twisted around and stared at him in horror. "We wasted the entire day and night?"

"I wouldn't call it a waste," he pointed out. "We did need the rest."

"Yeah, but…"

He cocked a brow. "But what?"

Julia's cheeks went pink. "I was looking forward to spending all those hours in bed with you."

"Technically, we *were* in bed."

"You know what I mean."

Before she could blink, he flipped her onto her back and slipped his hand underneath her T-shirt and inside her bra. When he found her nipple poking straight up, he groaned in approval. "I know exactly what you mean, baby."

She let out a little laugh before squirming and shifting out from under him. "Well, now you can wait a bit longer. I'm hungry. Let's order some room service.

Oh, and I feel super-grimy and I kind of want to try out that Jacuzzi."

He injected a seductive note into his voice. "How about we try out that Jacuzzi together, and we'll peruse the room service menu while we do it?"

"Oooh, sounds like a plan."

Five minutes later, they were doing precisely that. The tub was big enough for them to stretch out at opposite ends, but now Sebastian was the one feeling cuddly. Leaning against the porcelain tub, he opened his legs and pulled Julia into the cradle of his thighs, so that her back rested against his chest, her round bottom pressed into his groin and her legs tangled with his.

After they studied the menu, Sebastian set the plastic sheet on the edge of the sink and began running his hands over Julia's slippery body. The jet directly behind him placed steady pulsing pressure against his back muscles. A naughty idea involving positioning one of those jets between Julia's legs sent all the blood in his body down to his groin, a transformation that didn't escape the woman in his lap.

Rubbing her butt on his growing erection, she let out a throaty laugh that echoed in the bathroom. "Food first," she chided.

"Fine. Then at least let me get out so I can place our order."

Her hands latched onto his thighs before he could move. "No way. I'm nice and comfy. We'll order when we get out."

She let her head fall back against his chest and sighed with pure and utter contentment. Sebastian rested his hands on her flat belly and let out a sigh of his own. The hot water felt incredible as it lapped over their naked bodies, and Julia's loose hair floated around like strands of silk, tickling his shoulders and collarbone.

"I could stay like this forever," she said happily.

His throat tightened. "Me, too."

Christ. He really *could* stay with this woman forever. And maybe, just maybe, that was actually possible.

All the thoughts he'd put out of his mind before the takedown now came rushing back.

You're the reason I'm alive.

It was true, wasn't it? He'd been protecting Julia from the moment he'd heard the general say her name in Esperanza. Every dangerous situation they'd encountered, she'd come out of alive. And here she was, still safe. The woman he loved was safe in his arms, and for the first time in his life, he truly believed it could stay that way.

"Will you come back to Ecuador with me?" His gruff voice hung in the hot, moist air rising from the Jacuzzi.

"Yes."

No hesitation. That one syllable left her mouth swiftly and without an ounce of uncertainty.

Sebastian had to smile. "You will?"

"Of course I will." A note of sarcasm crept in. "Where else would I go?"

That gave him pause. "Wait—are you coming with me because you think you have nowhere else to go?"

"No, I'm coming with you because I can't bear the thought of being *away* from you, dummy."

A laugh popped out of his mouth. "You're really mean sometimes, you know that?"

"I am not. I'm just honest." She changed positions, turning around to straddle his lap, while those hazel eyes bore into his face, unwavering. "And because I'm being honest, I might as well tell you that this is about more than just sex for me. It stopped being about that a long time ago."

The joy that streaked through his chest caught him by surprise, but once it registered, he realized he couldn't deny it. Julia's declaration made him happy.

Because he felt the same damn way.

"I understand why you're scared of commitment," she went on, her voice gentle, "but you need to know that you're *not* cursed. You're not the only one who's lost people, Sebastian. I lost the two people I loved most in the world, and I'm sure if I try hard enough, I could link their deaths to something I'd said or done. Like Mia went to South Africa because of that one time I had PMS and told her she'd never cut it as a travel writer—" her expression grew pained "—which I totally regret saying, by the way, because she was an *amazing* writer. And I could easily say I'm to blame for my dad's death because the night before his heart attack, we were at a restaurant for dinner and I talked him into ordering a sixteen-ounce steak, even though he was on a strict no-red-meat diet."

Sebastian exhaled in a weary rush. Christ. It did sound ridiculous when she put it that way. And yet…yet he wasn't ready to let go of that guilt. Wasn't ready to admit that the burden of responsibility might fall elsewhere—or nowhere.

"We can take it slow," she said, her hazel eyes shining with what he could only describe as faith. Faith in him. Faith in *them*. "No promises, no weddings. We'll just see what happens. How does that sound?"

It was damn difficult speaking through the monstrous lump in his throat. "It sounds perfect."

With a smile, Julia leaned in and brushed a fleeting

kiss on his mouth. "Good. Now let's get out of this tub and order some food. I'm ready to pass out if I don't put something in my stomach."

They stepped out of the Jacuzzi and dried off, slipping into a pair of complimentary terry cloth robes rather than getting dressed. Sebastian was all over the robe situation—he didn't plan on letting Julia wear a stitch of clothing for the rest of the night. Or maybe ever again.

They both ended up ordering cheeseburgers and fries, along with a plate of onion rings to share. Probably wasn't smart to eat such a heavy meal at midnight, but they were both starving, and Sebastian was just happy to see Julia eating. She'd filled out since he'd met her, which was ironic considering they'd been doing nothing but traveling and hiding out in motel rooms. Still, no matter where they'd been, he'd encouraged her to stuff her face, and his efforts showed in the rounding of her cheeks and the fact that he was no longer able to count each of her ribs.

"When you get a new assignment with the foundation, you're not allowed to overwork yourself anymore," he announced as he watched her munch on a French fry.

She raised her eyebrows. "Oh, really? Who's gonna stop me?"

"I will." He shot her a mocking look. "I won't be in hiding forever. Sooner or later, me and Tate and Nick will figure out who killed our unit and attempted to kill *us,* and once we find those bastards, I'll be free to travel the world with you, Doc."

The moment he said it, he realized just how much he wanted to do that.

Julia looked as surprised as he felt. "You really want

to follow me all over the globe while I work for Doctors International?"

"Why not?" he said with a shrug. "I've never wanted a boring old nine-to-five job. My only ambition was to join the military, but I'm a tad soured by the United States Armed Forces at the moment. My military career is over, which means I'm free to do whatever the hell I want. And I told you, I've got a case of wanderlust."

She tilted her head, intrigued. "But what would you do when I'm at the clinic?"

"Anything. Everything. Take pictures. Explore. Pick up odd jobs here and there if we run out of money."

After a beat of silence, Julia's beautiful face broke out in a smile. "I kind of like the sound of that."

So did he. In fact, he couldn't wait to start a life with this woman. Julia Davenport was the smartest, sexiest, kindest, sassiest woman he'd ever known. She'd fascinated him from the second he'd met her in Valero, and during their time together, she'd managed to breach his defenses. Make him yearn for something he hadn't yearned for in years. Companionship. Laughter. Love.

As a wave of emotion swelled in his gut, he helped Julia gather up their empty plates, then dropped them on the room service cart and rolled it out to the hall.

He returned to the suite to find Julia lying in the center of the bed—and she wasn't wearing her robe.

This time, as he made love to her, he didn't hold back or fight those intense emotions. He opened his heart and welcomed all those feelings in. He thrust into Julia's tight heat with long, languid strokes, gripping her upper thigh to prop her knee up so he could drive deeper. She moaned, and the glazed look in her eyes told him she was close.

Capturing her mouth, he gave her a long, reckless, tongue-tangling kiss that made her gasp, then quickened his pace and sent her flying over the edge. As she came apart beneath him, he threw himself over that same cliff, pleasure seizing his lower body before shooting out in all directions, until he was gasping, too.

Afterward, they lay tangled in each other's arms. Sebastian didn't remember falling asleep, but when his eyes blinked open, it was suddenly morning again. Sunlight streamed into the room, blinding him, bringing a sharp ache to his head.

With a groan, he rubbed his temples, hoping the massage would soothe his headache.

"You're like a furnace," Julia mumbled.

Yeah, he did feel hot. And slightly lethargic, too, as he climbed out of bed so he wouldn't disturb Julia. The clock on the night table read 7:39 a.m. Last time he remembered checking the clock it had been 3:00 a.m., which was probably why he was so exhausted. Sixteen hours of sleep the night before, then four and a half hours the next night. Clearly his REM cycle was all screwed up.

Sebastian left the bedroom and wandered to the other room of their suite, which featured a kitchenette, a living area and a dining table. Fortunately, the kitchen had a coffee maker, and a few minutes later, he was happily sipping on a cup of coffee, almost instantly feeling more alert.

Drifting toward the bedroom, he stood in the doorway and watched as Julia tried to find a comfortable position. One slender leg was poking out from the covers, and she was hugging a pillow as she rolled around on the white sheets, making soft little noises that brought a smile to his lips.

But the smile faded when a flash of red caught his eye.

"Julia," he blurted out.

She stirred but didn't open her eyes.

"Julia." He spoke louder this time—it was the only way he could hear himself over the deafening pounding of his heart.

Those hazel eyes focused on him, sleepy and annoyed. "What?" she mumbled.

"You're bleeding."

Her ability to snap into a state of alertness was as honed as his. She sat up like she'd just been shot out of a cannon, fixed her gaze on the crimson stain marring the stark white pillow, and then her hands flew to her face. She touched her nostrils, her eyes widening, her lips parting in shock.

As icy-cold fear paralyzed every muscle in his body, Sebastian stood frozen in the doorway, seeing nothing but the two trails of blood pouring out of Julia's nose.

Chapter 16

Shock pummeled into Julia's body. When she touched her nostrils, the blood dripping from them seemed to flow faster. Horrified, she launched herself out of bed, then halted when a wave of dizziness overtook her. Her legs felt like they were made of lead, and her torso suddenly weighed three hundred pounds, making it difficult to support her own weight.

Sebastian was at her side in a flash, steadying her with his strong arms.

"Hey, you need to sit down." His voice held an unambiguous note of terror.

He was scared.

Oh, God. *She* was scared.

Why wouldn't her nose stop bleeding, damn it?

She allowed Sebastian to lead her back to the bed. He forced her to sit down, then hurried into the bathroom and returned a moment later with a box of tissues. He ripped out a handful and brought them to her nose, staunching the blood flow. With his other hand, he touched her forehead, then her cheeks and then her neck. "You're burning up," he said hoarsely. "You're on fire, Doc."

Julia didn't doubt it. She felt like she'd been dropped in a vat of boiling water. And that sluggish wave of exhaustion continued to slither through her veins.

"In the first hour, it's a fever, lethargy and bleeding from the ears, nose and eyes," she said weakly.

"Don't." Sebastian's voice was as sharp as a razor blade. "We don't know if this is…if you've been…"

"Infected by the virus? Let's not kid ourselves, Sebastian. I was perfectly healthy when we went to sleep, and now I'm exhibiting all of the initial symptoms Frank described." Swallowing a lump of panic, she forced her brain not to shut down on her, no matter how tired she was. "If humans react to the virus the same way as the mice, then symptoms start after twenty-five hours. That means I ingested the virus…" It became impossible to do basic math, so she simply gave up and quit talking.

"Six-thirty yesterday morning," Sebastian supplied.

"Right, six-thirty. We were…at the Pentagon. Brent's office."

The tissues were almost completely soaked from her bloody nose. Sebastian tossed them on the floor and replaced them with a new batch.

"You were drinking a bottle of water," he reminded her. "Remember? You gave me the rest."

"Not the rest, the whole thing. I never opened that bottle." She struggled to search her memories. "I had a cup of coffee when we first got there, around three in the morning. I didn't have anything else to drink after that." She frowned. "Maybe my symptoms are showing up later for some reason? I guess the mice had a more accelerated reaction to—"

"The coffee wasn't the last thing you drank," Sebastian cut in. His face had gone white, and his hands trembled as he pressed the tissues beneath her nose. "I gave you my water bottle after I drank yours."

"Right. Right, I remember."

"And that was around six-thirty, so the timing of the symptoms fits." An anguished curse flew out of his mouth and then he started mumbling. "Brent got me that water bottle, Julia. It was *my* freaking water. It was meant for *me*."

His low mutterings made her head spin. Battling a rush of disorientation, she staggered off the bed. Sebastian shot up without delay and put his arm around her.

"Hospital," she wheezed out. "We have to get to the hospital. Seizures will start…in an hour or two."

Oh, God, and the paralysis soon after.

Terror seized every muscle in her body. She was going to die.

Holy mother of God, she was actually going to *die*.

The next ten minutes were a total whirlwind. She didn't remember getting dressed, but somehow she was wearing jeans and a tank top when they stumbled out of the hotel. She didn't remember getting into the car, but somehow she was in the passenger seat while Sebastian murmured soothing words in her ear and kept a firm hand on her thigh.

Her skin was on fire. Her nosebleed refused to ebb; she could taste the coppery blood in the back of her throat and she almost gagged.

In the driver's seat, Sebastian wasn't saying a single word.

"Maybe…maybe the CDC developed an antidote already," she said feebly.

He sucked in a breath. "An antidote."

"Maybe," she murmured again. "Sometimes they can develop one fairly fast."

Yeah, right. It would take weeks, months, years even. She knew that, yet she refused to give up hope. After everything she'd been through, this couldn't be the way it ended.

Lissa. Simone. Marcus.

Kevin. Marie-Thérèse. Kendra. Nadir.

Me.

"No," she mumbled. "I don't want to die, Seb."

His fingers curled over her denim-clad thigh. "You're not going to die, Doc. I won't let you."

Julia started to laugh. Of course he'd say that. Her warrior, always coming to the rescue, always looking out for her.

"There's a team of medical professionals waiting for you at the hospital," he went on. "Doctors and CDC folks and federal agents and researchers. You'll be in good hands."

She squinted, as if that would somehow help her make sense of what he'd said. "What are you talking about?"

"I arranged everything before we left the hotel. You'll be taken care of, baby."

She didn't remember him making any phone calls. Then again, she was so out of it she couldn't be sure.

But she certainly hadn't missed his continued use of the word *you'll*.

"You're coming with me, aren't you?" she whispered.

"Not yet, baby. I just have one little thing to do first, and then I'll come right back to you."

Her pulse sped up. "No, don't leave me."

The world started to spin again, and suddenly she wasn't sitting anymore. She was lying down on a hard surface and loud voices were floating all around her. Panic squeezed her chest, then eased when Sebastian's face hovered over hers.

"You're going to be just fine, Doc. Just fine." His gray eyes glittered with determination. "So now close your eyes and get some rest, okay? I'll be right back. I'll come right back to you, I promise."

And then he was gone.

It was meant for him.

The water was meant for him.

The virus was meant for him.

Those three simple truths were all Sebastian was capable of concentrating on as he drove like a madman in the direction of the Pentagon. He'd already called Brent and told him he was on his way, and if that son of a bitch wasn't waiting for him outside like he'd promised, Sebastian might actually consider shooting his freaking way into the freaking building.

Julia couldn't die. It had ripped his heart in two, leaving her back there at the hospital. Alone, scared, *dying.* But what other choice did he have? He wouldn't let her die. He couldn't lose her. He'd already lost everyone else.

It was meant for him.

The water was meant for him.

The virus was meant for him.

He'd been the target. Not Julia.

The sedan's tires screeched as he executed a hard right into the parking lot. He was ready to tear his own hair out as the guards in the security booth forced him to follow protocol. Checking the name and picture on his fake ID, which Brent had added to the visitor's list. Asking him pointless questions. Confiscating his Beretta and his knife.

By the time the lot barrier swung up, Sebastian was seeing red and prepared to dropkick the next person who got in his way.

Brent met him at the building's entrance, his expression creased with concern. "What's going on? How did Dr. Davenport get infected?"

White-hot fury spiraled through him. So that was how they were going to play it, huh? Well, fine. Let the son of a bitch play dumb. At the moment, Sebastian didn't have time to deal with Brent Davidson. He'd rip the man's throat out later. No, he'd do a helluva lot more than that. He'd torture the bastard, bring him within an inch of death only to yank him away from the light and begin the torment all over again.

If Julia died, Brent would meet that same fate.

Only his road to death would be a lot longer, and a lot more painful.

Clenching his teeth, Sebastian ignored the other man's inquiry. "Have you gotten anything more from Stephen Langley about that antidote he claims to have?"

"No, but—"

"I want to see him." He marched toward the front entrance.

Brent raced into the building after him, his voice tinged with disbelief. "You can't. Langley is being detained. Only authorized federal employees are allowed anywhere near him."

Sebastian halted in the middle of the lobby. "Are *you* authorized to talk to him?"

"Yes, but—"

"Then take me to him," he snapped.

"Sebas—"

Before Davidson could get out that third syllable, Sebastian had slammed the older man into the wall and was gripping him by the collar of his white shirt.

The armed guards posted all over the lobby immediately stormed the elevator bank, weapons drawn.

"Call them off," Sebastian ordered.

Gasping for breath, Davidson held up a hand, making a signal to fall back. The guards immediately went still.

"Now, listen, I don't have the time to argue with you," Sebastian hissed out. "You're going to give me five minutes with Langley. Call it a reward for finding that ULF nest yesterday. Call it my pat on the back for being part of that op. I don't care how you explain it to your superiors—just get it done, you understand?"

"Why?" The word came out on a wheeze.

He loosened his grip on the man's collar. "Why do I want to see him?" When Brent nodded, he set his jaw. "Because if that bastard is telling the truth and has an antidote stashed somewhere, then I'm going to get it out of him. And if there *is* an antidote, it goes directly to Julia. You understand me?"

"Stone, you need to calm down. Langley has been undergoing interrogation for a day and a half. He refuses to talk unless we give him immunity."

"He'll talk to me," Sebastian said in a deadly tone.

He abruptly let go of Davidson, and the man nearly fell over before managing to steady himself.

With a wave of his hand, Brent dismissed the guards who were warily monitoring the entire exchange. "Resume your posts, men. Everything is fine here." He glanced at Sebastian. "You know I could have you arrested for this, right?"

"Five minutes, Brent. I need only five minutes."

Indecision flashed across the other man's face. "I know you're worried about Dr. Davenport. Hell, I'm worried, too. I don't know how she got infected, but I promise you, the last thing I want is for that woman to die."

Sebastian fought the urge to grab a gun from the hip holster of one of those guards and empty an entire clip into Brent Davidson's chest. Son of a bitch had given him that water, and now here he was, acting like he had no idea how Julia had gotten infected? Acting like he actually *cared* about her well-being?

"Take me to Langley," Sebastian muttered. "Now."

There was a long moment of silence before Brent finally nodded. "Follow me."

Sebastian's hands were uncharacteristically shaky as the two men stepped into the elevator. He was so wired he felt like he might black out, but he forced himself to breathe, to find his center and keep his cool. The need to confront Brent, to *strangle* Brent, was so strong his mouth watered from the temptation, but he restrained himself.

Right now, he couldn't afford to focus on anything but saving the woman he loved.

Stephen Langley was being held in a small interrogation room in the lower levels of the building. Armed guards lined the fluorescent corridor, remaining expressionless as Sebastian and Brent stalked past.

They reached a heavy steel door with an electric keypad mounted to the wall beside it. Brent swiped his key card and the door buzzed open.

Sebastian followed the DoD agent into a room with a wall of security cameras and dozens of beeping machines that provided readings on the subject's heartbeat, blood pressure, facial expression and whatever else was deemed relevant to catching a subject in a lie. Two federal agents manned the large desk, monitoring the various screens in front of them. Four of the screens revealed a hunched figure sitting on a metal chair in a small, windowless room. The four different angles allowed Sebastian to easily identify Langley, whose head was bent low, hands resting on the tabletop.

"Has he said anything?" Brent asked the agents.

"Nothing. Haskell and Rhodes just left," one replied. "They're going to give it another go in an hour or so."

Brent nodded. "Sergeant Stone has requested five minutes with him. I'm allowing it. Will you buzz him in, please?"

The second agent leaned forward and clicked a button on the electronic panel on the desktop. The door leading into the interrogation room clicked loudly.

"And turn off the cameras," Sebastian said in a low voice.

The agents immediately turned to Davidson, who quickly turned to Sebastian with visible wariness. "Wasn't part of the agreement," Brent said tersely.

"Don't care. Cameras off."

He and Brent eyed each other for several tense seconds. Finally the older man cursed under his breath and said, "Cameras off."

Sebastian arched a brow. "Sound, too."

The agent at the desk clicked another button and the monitors went black.

"Thank you, boys." With a pleasant smile, he marched over to the door and pushed on the handle.

He entered the airless room, wrinkling his nose when the scent of urine, sweat and fear met his nostrils. "Those a-holes didn't even bring you a bathroom bucket?" he said in surprise. He glanced around the room, which was barren save for the table and three chairs.

Langley's head snapped up, and then red-hot rage exploded in his eyes. "You! You goddamn bastard!"

"Nice to see you, too, Doctor."

Unbothered by the cold reception, Sebastian sat in the chair across from the scientist and casually folded his hands on the tabletop. When his gaze snagged on the clock hanging on the wall behind Langley, panic seized his insides. Nearly thirty minutes had passed since he'd left Julia at the hospital.

Seizures. The seizures would start soon.

Then paralysis.

Then death.

His heart burned with agony. No. *No.* He was *not* going to let her die.

"Let me just cut to the chase, Langley." Sebastian met the scientist's eyes. "You're going to tell me where the antidote is."

Langley smirked, then crossed his arms over his chest. "Who says there's an antidote?"

"Oh, there is. That's why you're sitting there looking so damn chipper. This is your leverage. Your ticket to freedom."

"If that's true, then do you really think I'm going to tell *you* where it is?" Langley laughed loudly. "You think I'll throw away my *ticket to freedom* by confiding in a lying son of a bitch like you? An unimportant foot soldier who has no authority to get me what I desire? Sorry, *Agent Swanson,* or whatever the hell your name is. I'm not telling you a damn thing."

"Yes, you are," Sebastian said softly.

Another laugh. "Uh-huh. Sure."

"Scoff all you want, but you're still going to tell me where the antidote is." Slowly, he rose from his chair and rounded the table, stopping when he was standing over the other man.

Langley snorted with genuine amusement. "Gonna torture me now? Go ahead. Do your worst. We both know they—" he gestured to the cameras positioned in every corner of the ceiling "—won't let it go on for too long. They'll stop you before you rough me up too bad."

Now Sebastian was the one laughing. "Sorry to disappoint you, but the cameras are off. See how those little red lights aren't blinking anymore?"

Langley's face turned a shade paler as he glanced at the cameras again and saw that Sebastian was telling the truth.

"Oh, but don't worry, I don't plan on torturing you," Sebastian added with a feral smile. "You're going to tell me where the antidote is, Langley. Because if you don't, I'm going to kill you."

Silence crashed over the room. Langley's expression was a cross between suspicion and amazement.

He stared at Sebastian for a moment, then released an unsteady breath and shook his head half a dozen times.

"No, you won't," Langley finally said. "You won't kill me." More head shaking. "You won't."

"You can see it in my eyes, can't you, Doctor? You know I'm speaking the truth right now." He inched closer to Langley, and the man flinched.

"You won't," Langley repeated, but the conviction was slowly draining from his eyes. "If you kill me, you'll never get away with it. They'll either throw you in prison or put a bullet in your head."

"And do you honestly think I care?" He squatted down so they were at eye level. "Look at my face, Doctor. Look into my eyes as I tell you that I will *absolutely* kill you if you don't tell me where the antidote is. You know why? Because without that antidote, the woman I love is going to die. And if she dies, then I've got nothing left to live for, now, do I?"

The scientist's pulse throbbed in his throat.

"If you don't talk, I'm going to snap your neck, Doctor, and if I go to prison for the rest of my life because of that, then so be it. If the people behind that door burst in and riddle me with bullets, then so be it. Frankly, I don't give a damn what happens to me. As long as I snap your greedy little neck first, I'll die a happy man."

Langley gulped.

Rising to his full height, Sebastian cracked his knuckles. The sickly sound bounced off the concrete walls, bringing a glimmer of fear to Stephen Langley's brown eyes.

"So what's it going to be, Langley?" he asked quietly. "Are you going to tell me where the antidote is, or am I going to have to kill you?"

Chapter 17

After four minutes of the allotted five, Sebastian marched out of the interrogation room and tossed an impatient look in Brent Davidson's direction. "The antidote is stashed in a locker at his health club. Locker number four-nine-six. Key is on the key ring you confiscated along with his personal belongings."

Davidson sucked in a breath, his face awash with shock.

"Get me that damn key ring," Sebastian snapped on his way to the door.

"Stone, wait."

He heard Brent's footsteps behind him but didn't stop.

"I'll dispatch a team to fetch it. You don't have to do it yourself."

He kept walking.

"Damn it, Sebastian. Stop!"

The next thing he knew, Brent was right up in his face, shaking him by the shoulders.

As a wave of rage crashed over him, he shoved the other man away. "Don't touch me," he hissed. "And don't tell me what to do."

Brent got in his path again. "You need to be at the hospital. With *Julia*. For chrissake, Sebastian, she's all alone there."

His heart lodged in his throat.

"I'll send people to the health club," Brent went on. "They'll find the antidote and have it airlifted to the hospital."

"Or you'll betray me and make sure the antidote never reaches her," Sebastian spat out. "So forgive me if I'm not willing to take that chance."

Brent's jaw fell open. "What the hell are you talking about? I would *never* betray you."

"You already did, you son of a bitch!" As a red haze consumed his field of vision, he slammed Brent against the wall for the second time in less than twenty minutes.

And yet again, several guards hurried to Brent's rescue.

"Call. Them. Off." Sebastian spoke through clenched teeth.

With a ragged breath, Brent signaled the approaching men to stand down.

"You think I don't know how Julia got infected?" Sebastian was so infuriated that the thought of murdering Brent in front of all these guards was actually beginning to seem like a totally reasonable idea.

"H-how?" Brent stuttered.

"She drank the damn water! The water intended for *me*. The water *you* brought me."

Those blue eyes widened. "What…what the hell are you—"

"Don't patronize me," he interrupted. "We did the math. We know exactly when she would've had to be infected for the symptoms to show up when they did. It was in the water bottle *you* brought me."

Brent's mouth slammed shut. Silence hung over the corridor. The guards littering the hall didn't move, but every single gun was still trained on Sebastian.

"Not gonna deny it, huh?" he said bitterly.

"I…" The other man shook his head. His dark brows furrowed, his mouth pinched in uncertainty, and then realization dawned in his eyes. "Paul."

Sebastian faltered. "What?"

"My aide, Paul Waverly," Brent said urgently.

As wariness climbed up his spine, he released his grip on Brent and took a backward step. "What about him?"

"He's the one who brought me my coffee yesterday, and he's the one who gave me the water bottle."

"No, I was in the elevator with you. You got off alone and went to the cafeteria yourself."

Brent shook his head again, his blue eyes intense. "I needed to use the john. Paul found me in the corridor, and I told him to grab me a coffee and get you some water while I took a leak. He was waiting for me outside the men's room. With a cup of coffee and that damn bottle of water."

Sebastian sucked in a breath. Paul? Paul Waverly had tampered with that water?

He searched Brent's expression and found nothing that indicated the man was lying, but that didn't mean a damn thing. Brent Davidson had once worked black ops. He knew how to lie. He knew how to deceive.

But he'd also been there for Sebastian his entire life, especially after his dad died.

"Go to Julia," Brent said gently. "Trust me to have the antidote delivered to the hospital. Trust me to save her, son."

Son. That one quiet word triggered his surrender.

With a weary breath, Sebastian nodded. "Okay."

Eyes shining with sympathy, Brent touched his shoulder before giving it a quick squeeze. "Come on. Let's see about arranging for a chopper to take you to the hospital."

Her brain hurt. Her muscles hurt. Her fingernails hurt. God, *everything* hurt.

Was this how it had been for Kevin? Had everything hurt for him, too?

Julia closed her eyes, hoping that if she shut out her surroundings, she could pretend she was somewhere else. On an island maybe. Lying on a beach, breathing in the scent of sand and salt and coconut, feeling Sebastian's strong hands rubbing sunscreen all over her naked body....

She shivered in pleasure. And shivered. And shivered some more.

When her teeth began to rattle around in her mouth, Julia realized she wasn't shivering—she was seizing again.

Urgent voices shouted above her head, and her arms and legs seemed to be weighted down with anvils. Confusion swarmed her brain, confusion and fear and completely inappropriate amusement because she must look so silly flopping around like a fish out of water. She started to laugh, except she suspected she wasn't really laughing because no sound left her mouth, at least none that she could hear.

When the episode finally faded, she felt like she'd been beaten with a baseball bat, then poked with hundreds of little needles.

Her skin hurt. Her back hurt. Her toenails hurt. God, *everything* hurt.

"It's okay, Doc. I'm here now."

At first she wondered if she'd dreamed Sebastian's voice, but when she took a deep breath and inhaled his woody, masculine scent into her aching lungs, she knew this wasn't a dream.

"You're here," she whispered.

The world dipped and rocked and spun, and then she found herself nestled against Sebastian's muscular chest, his warmth seeping into her tired limbs.

"Sorry I was gone for so long," he said roughly, his fingers stroking her hair with infinite tenderness. "I had to take care of some business."

"S'okay. S'long as you're here now." She could hear his heart beating beneath her ear, a steady *thump-thump* that sent a wave of tranquility rippling through her. "Glad you're here, Seb. Now we can say a proper g'bye."

The hard muscles of his chest went even stiffer. "We're not saying goodbye, Julia. You're going to be okay."

She didn't answer. Might as well humor him. But really, who was he trying to kid? He wasn't a doctor. *She* was. She knew exactly what was happening to her central nervous system at the moment. The virus was attacking it one cell at a time. Soon she'd be nothing but a motionless lump of *dead,* just like those mice in Frank's cages.

Another giggle bubbled in the back of her throat, and soon she was shuddering with laughter because this was all so funny and—nope, she was seizing again. God, she was tired.

Those same shrill voices assaulted her eardrums again. Those same anvils crushed her body.

This time she decided to try and close her eyes. Maybe get some sleep. She succeeded in the closing-of-the-eyes part because everything went black, but when she heard Sebastian's husky voice again, she realized that sleep was a bad, bad idea.

Because what if she never woke up?

"Sleep," he urged.

"No," she protested.

"It'll take some time to kick in. You need to rest."

"No."

But she couldn't keep her eyelids open anymore. They were too damn heavy.

"I'll be here when you wake up."

I won't wake up.

She knew it with a certainty that went bone-deep. If she went to sleep right now, she would never wake up.

Which was probably why she couldn't stop her next words from floating out.

"Love you, Sebastian."

Everything went quiet. She couldn't hear him anymore. She couldn't see him anymore either. Had he left? She didn't have the energy to open her eyes to check.

But she could have sworn that right before she drifted into a state of unconsciousness, she heard him say, "I love you, too, Julia."

* * *

Sebastian found himself in a relentless cycle of pure torment over the next three hours. He'd been sitting at Julia's bedside ever since the doctor had injected the antidote into Julia's vein, feeling like he was riding a roller-coaster ride that never seemed to end. Up and down. Up and down. Julia's fever rose, then fell. Her blood pressure soared, then plummeted. Up and down. Up and down. Making it impossible to know if the antidote was doing a goddamn thing.

They'd administered the exact amount Stephen Langley had said to administer, but was it working? It had to be, Sebastian assured himself. It had to be working because the nosebleeds and seizures had stopped. Or at least that was what he kept telling himself. Considering that three hours had passed and Julia still hadn't regained consciousness, he had no idea what to think anymore.

He lifted his head when he heard a soft rap on the door.

"How is she?" Brent asked, stepping into Julia's private hospital room.

"Unconscious." He raked both hands through his hair. "The doctors think she's stabilizing, that the antidote worked, but I don't know. I'd feel better about her prognosis if she'd just wake up."

"Her body probably needs to regroup. I'm sure she'll come to soon."

"I guess." He swallowed. "Thank you for getting the antidote here so fast. I'm sorry I ever doubted you."

"I understand why you did." Brent shook his head in anger. "I can't believe I cheerfully handed you a bottle contaminated with that damn virus."

"You didn't know." And he truly believed that. He'd known Brent his entire life, and now that he wasn't operating on fear and panic, he realized that Brent would have nothing to gain from killing Sebastian. And no doubt about it, Sebastian *had* been the target.

Clearly someone still wanted him dead.

"Any leads on Paul?" he asked, absently stroking Julia's palm.

"None. He's disappeared and no one can get in touch with him. We put out an APB, placed men at his apartment, but somehow I doubt I'll ever see my trusty aide again."

"I don't imagine you will," Sebastian agreed wryly. "He probably took off right after he gave you that bottle. He had to know it would eventually be traced back to him."

"Speaking of that bottle, we found it in the trash can where Julia tossed it," Brent said, looking relieved. "The CDC should have received it by now. And we sent them a sample of the antidote, too. So if for some unforeseen reason Meridian gets released again, we'll be able to administer the vaccine before the virus kills any more people."

"If the vaccine even works," Sebastian murmured.

As his gaze drifted to the unconscious woman on the bed, he nearly broke down and wept. Julia had an IV in her arm and was hooked up to a heart monitor, her body so small and fragile beneath that blue hospital gown. These past three hours, he'd memorized every square inch of her face, down to the last freckle, and now he needed her to open her eyes so he could complete the mental picture he planned on taking with him when he left.

He squeezed her hand again before glancing at Brent. "Your aide's involvement proves that someone in our government authorized the development of Meridian. That same someone was able to get a sample of the virus into Waverly's hands, and that same someone probably whisked Waverly away to some beach in South America."

"And that same someone still wants you dead," Brent finished with a sigh. "So I suppose once Dr. Davenport recovers, you still plan on leaving the country?"

"If she recovers," he mumbled.

"If?" came Julia's outraged voice.

Sebastian nearly fell off the chair. His heartbeat took off in a gallop when he saw Julia's hazel eyes focused on his face, her expression a combination of fatigue and indignation.

"You're awake," he blurted out. Happiness shot through him, followed by a jolt of pain so strong his stomach clenched.

"And Nick was right—you're so damn pessimistic," she shot back. "You really thought I was going to die, didn't you?"

"You thought the same thing," he said defensively. "You even said goodbye."

"I was clearly under the influence of the Meridian virus," she huffed. "I'm usually far more optimistic."

Groaning, she tried to sit up, and Sebastian was instantly at her side, helping her move into an upright position.

In the doorway, Brent looked like he was fighting a laugh. "Good to see you looking well, Dr. Davenport. I guess I'll say my goodbyes now, in case I don't see you before you and Stone take off." He paused. "You need me to arrange air transport for you?"

"Nah, we'll find our own way," Sebastian said vaguely.

"I have no doubt." Brent moved to the door. "Good luck, you two."

After Brent left, Sebastian focused all his attention on Julia, whose cheeks were regaining some color. "How are you feeling?" he asked gruffly.

"Surprisingly good. I take it you miraculously got your hands on an antidote?"

He nodded. "Langley stole a vial from D&M at the same time he stole the virus. I paid him a visit and got him to reveal where he stashed it."

Julia's lips twitched with humor. "And how did you manage that?"

"I'm very persuasive," he said with a shrug.

When she reached out to touch his cheek, he flinched despite himself, bringing a startled look to her eyes. "What's wrong?" she demanded.

"Nothing's wrong." He kept his tone light. "You're alive. That means everything is *right*."

A wrinkle appeared in her forehead. "Okay."

"I should go tell your doctors that you're awake."

He started to stand up, but Julia latched her hand on his arm and forced him to stay put. "Not yet. First tell me what I missed when I was unconscious."

"Not much." He filled her in on Paul Waverly's disappearance, then hesitated. Wanting to say more but unsure how to proceed.

Julia, of course, immediately narrowed her eyes and said, "What the hell is going on, Sebastian?"

He met her eyes. "I'm leaving."

"Leaving," she echoed.

He nodded.

Wariness washed over her face, which was beginning to look ashen again. "Leaving *me?*"

Ignoring the agony clutching his heart like a vise, he managed another nod.

Her lips tightened. "I see. And why is that?"

"You know why," he said hoarsely.

"Do I?"

His cheeks hollowed in frustration. "You know exactly what I'm talking about, Julia. That water was meant for *me*. You almost died because of me."

"But I didn't die," she said smugly. "I lived. And yet again, I lived *because* of you. You got the antidote here in time."

Anguish clamped around his throat, nearly suffocating him. Christ, she didn't get it. Why didn't she get it?

"*I* gave you that water," he said softly. "If you'd died, it would've been my fault." His eyes began to sting. "I told you, the people I love are destined to die."

Julia stared at him with wide eyes, though he couldn't figure out whether she was shocked or hurt or angry. Or all three.

Probably all three.

But he couldn't allow himself to back down. He couldn't take any more risks with this woman's life.

"You're better off without me." Regret burned a path up his chest. "The best thing I could do for you is let you go."

She still didn't utter a word.

Sebastian used her silence as an opportunity to move closer. To brush his lips over her cheek in the sweetest of kisses.

"I'll stick around long enough to help you figure out where you want to go, but once you do, we'll go our separate ways. It's for the—"

Julia slapped him.

As his head snapped back from the surprisingly strong blow, Sebastian's jaw dropped. A second later, righteous anger coursed through him. "What the *hell*, Doc?"

"You're asking *me* that? Are you frickin' *kidding* me, Sebastian?"

He blinked a few times, then reached up to rub away the sting on his cheek.

"You just moved heaven and earth to save my life, and now you're abandoning me?" she went on, her voice dripping with outrage. "Well, you know what? I'm not letting you go *that* easily, you big dumb jerk!"

Sebastian opened his mouth but no words came out. Maybe that slap had rendered his vocal cords useless or something. Either way, all he could do was sit there and gape as Julia gave him a tongue-lashing that even his own mother would have felt guilty delivering.

"You're my perfect match, Sebastian, do you not get that? You treat me like an equal, you respect my career, you understand what drives me to work abroad. You excite me mentally and sexually and emotionally, and I'm not afraid to lose control around you! And if you really think I'm going to let you walk away from us, you're frickin' nuts."

An unwitting smile tugged at his mouth.

"And you know what? Your fears are completely unfounded. It wasn't your fault Brent's aide tried to kill you, and it certainly wasn't your fault that you lost your brother and your best friend and your girlfriend.

Bad things happen sometimes. It's a fact of life. But good things happen, too, and this thing between us? It's *good*. No, it's more than good. It's *spectacular*. So suck it up, Sebastian—you're not getting rid of me. I'm not going anywhere."

Her speech came to a breathless end, her chest rising and falling from each hurried breath. As he looked at her flushed face, he was reminded of all the reasons he loved this woman. Her fearlessness, her take-charge attitude, the way she refused to take crap from anyone, especially him. And when a gleam of stubborn determination lit her hazel eyes, he realized that there was no way in hell he could ever walk away from this woman. If he was her perfect match, then she was his. Her courage floored him. Her strength soothed him.

And her love? Her love had healed him.

"Wow," he finally remarked. "I really messed up, huh?"

She raised her eyebrows. "By thinking the right thing to do was *leave?* Uh, yeah."

"I'm sorry. I guess I just panicked."

Genuine remorse trickled through him, and Julia must have seen it on his face because she slid closer and looped her arms around his neck. The IV dangling from her left arm caught on his shoulder, and he gently moved it out of the way.

"I know you're scared," she said. "I am, too. Ever since I lost Mia and my dad, I've been focused on helping other people, but I don't usually help myself. I barely remember to feed myself half the time."

"I've noticed."

"So, yeah, it'll be hard for me to have a partner, but I'm willing to make this work." She leaned in and brushed a sweet kiss on his mouth. "And you have to be willing to let go of your fears and give us a chance. Can you do that?"

He gazed into her eyes, which were brimming with confidence, warmth and encouragement, and it was like a wake-up call. Christ, why was he even hesitating?

He'd succumbed to a moment of weakness, but he didn't feel weak anymore. He felt strong. As strong as the woman sitting in this hospital bed.

"I can do that," he said roughly.

She beamed. "Yeah?"

"Yeah." He touched her cheek, sweeping his thumb over her bottom lip. "I love you, Doc."

"And you're going to stay?"

"Right here by your side," he vowed.

"Forever?"

"For as long as you'll have me."

Julia's eyes twinkled. "Forever it is."

Epilogue

"Sebastian and the doctor are catching a flight with Ricardo." Tate strode onto the back patio of the beach house, where he found Nick standing by the rail, gazing out at the peaceful ocean.

Nick glanced over his shoulder. "When?"

"They're landing early tomorrow morning."

"I'll pick them up," the young lieutenant said with a nod.

Tate nodded back. "Thanks. I'd go, but you know I don't like leaving Eva and Rafe here alone."

"You know they're not alone if I'm with them, right?" Humor rang from Nick's voice.

With a sheepish shrug, Tate approached the railing. "Fine. I guess I should say, I don't like leaving Eva and Rafe. Period."

And who would've ever seen *that* coming. Captain Robert Tate, the man who'd once had nothing left to live for, now head over heels in love and the father figure of a three-year-old. It only went to show how your circumstances could change in the blink of an eye. Tate suspected Stone's circumstances had evolved, too, if Sebastian's reverent tone when referring to Julia Davenport was any indication.

"You know what I don't get?" Nick spoke up, sounding troubled. "Why did that DoD aide try to kill Seb? News of the virus had gone public by then. And that's why we had targets painted on our backs, no? Because they didn't want our unit to figure out that the villagers' deaths in Corazón were because of a virus and not the rebels, right?"

"Right."

"So whoever authorized Project Aries didn't want anyone to know about it. But now *everyone* knows about it," Nick pointed out. "Yet someone deliberately slipped Seb the virus *after* the news broke. Why? It couldn't have been about shutting him up—he's no longer a threat in terms of going public about the virus, because the news is already out."

Tate rested his elbows on the wooden ledge and focused on the waves lapping against the shore, mulling over everything Nick had just said.

"You're wrong," he realized. "Sebastian still *is* a threat. We all are. See, all these people who now know about the virus—they *just* found out. They haven't been hunted down, haven't been forced into hiding. They'll act horrified and rave about the injustice of it, vow to find out who was calling the shots about the testing of Meridian, but in the end, they'll run out of steam and quit looking for answers."

"But we won't," Nick said slowly.

"Not a chance. And I think the man in charge knows that we won't stop searching for the truth." Tate set his jaw. "I don't know about you, but I plan on finding the bastard who green-lighted the tests, the bastard who thought it was a good idea to treat those villagers like lab rats, the bastard who ordered someone to blow my brains out when I walked out my front door."

"Oh, trust me, I'm also looking forward to meeting the bastard in question."

"And he knows that. He knows we're after revenge, and the only way for him to keep his identity hidden is by getting rid of us before we find him." A deadly smile stretched across Tate's mouth. "Damn shame for him that he won't succeed."

"You saying what I think you're saying, Captain?"

"Damn right I am. We're going hunting, Nicky."

Nick broke out in a grin. "Can't. Frickin'. Wait."

* * * * *

REQUEST YOUR FREE BOOKS!
2 FREE NOVELS PLUS 2 FREE GIFTS!

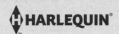

ROMANTIC suspense

Sparked by danger, fueled by passion

YES! Please send me 2 FREE Harlequin® Romantic Suspense novels and my 2 FREE gifts (gifts are worth about $10). After receiving them, if I don't wish to receive any more books, I can return the shipping statement marked "cancel." If I don't cancel, I will receive 4 brand-new novels every month and be billed just $4.49 per book in the U.S. or $5.24 per book in Canada. That's a savings of at least 14% off the cover price! It's quite a bargain! Shipping and handling is just 50¢ per book in the U.S. and 75¢ per book in Canada.* I understand that accepting the 2 free books and gifts places me under no obligation to buy anything. I can always return a shipment and cancel at any time. Even if I never buy another book, the two free books and gifts are mine to keep forever.

240/340 HDN FVS7

Name	(PLEASE PRINT)

Address	Apt. #

City	State/Prov.	Zip/Postal Code

Signature (if under 18, a parent or guardian must sign)

Mail to the **Harlequin® Reader Service:**
IN U.S.A.: P.O. Box 1867, Buffalo, NY 14240-1867
IN CANADA: P.O. Box 609, Fort Erie, Ontario L2A 5X3

**Want to try two free books from another line?
Call 1-800-873-8635 or visit www.ReaderService.com.**

* Terms and prices subject to change without notice. Prices do not include applicable taxes. Sales tax applicable in N.Y. Canadian residents will be charged applicable taxes. Offer not valid in Quebec. This offer is limited to one order per household. Not valid for current subscribers to Harlequin Romantic Suspense books. All orders subject to credit approval. Credit or debit balances in a customer's account(s) may be offset by any other outstanding balance owed by or to the customer. Please allow 4 to 6 weeks for delivery. Offer available while quantities last.

Your Privacy—The Harlequin® Reader Service is committed to protecting your privacy. Our Privacy Policy is available online at www.ReaderService.com or upon request from the Harlequin Reader Service.

We make a portion of our mailing list available to reputable third parties that offer products we believe may interest you. If you prefer that we not exchange your name with third parties, or if you wish to clarify or modify your communication preferences, please visit us at www.ReaderService.com/consumerschoice or write to us at Harlequin Reader Service Preference Service, P.O. Box 9062, Buffalo, NY 14269. Include your complete name and address.

Angry faces and moving bodies whizzed above her. Rebecca
braced both palms on the hot pavement and tried to stand
up, only to fall backward when someone bumped into her.
Someone else stepped on her foot, bringing a jolt of pain. Uh-
oh. This was bad. Her eyes couldn't seem to focus and shapes
were beginning to look blurry.

The fear finally hit her, clogging her throat and making her
heart pound.

She was going to get crushed in a stampede.

With a burst of adrenaline, she made another attempt to hurl
herself to her feet—and this time it worked. She was off the
ground and hovering over the crowd—wait, hovering *over* it?

Blinking a few times, Rebecca realized she *felt* as if she was
floating because she *was* floating. She was tucked tightly in a
man's arms, a man who'd taken it upon himself to carry her
away to safety, Kevin Costner style.

"Who are you?" she murmured, but the inquiry got lost in

the rioters' shouts and the rapid popping noises of the rubber bullets being fired into the crowd.

She became aware of the most intoxicating scent, and she inhaled deeply, filling her lungs with that spicy aroma. It was *him,* she realized. God, he smelled good.

She glanced up to study the face of her rescuer, catching glimpses of a strong, clean-shaven jaw. Sensual lips. A straight nose. She wanted to see his eyes, but the angle was all wrong, so she focused on his incredible chest instead. Jeez, the guy must work out. His torso was hard as a rock, rippled with muscles that flexed at each purposeful step he took. And he was *tall.* At least six-one, and she felt downright tiny in his arms.

"You okay?"

The concerned male voice broke through her thoughts. She looked up at her rescuer, finally getting a good look at those elusive eyes.

Boy, were they worth the wait. At first glance they were brown—until you looked closer and realized they were the color of warm honey with flecks of amber around the pupils. And they were so magnetic she felt hypnotized as she gazed into them.

"Ms. Parker?"

She blinked, forcing herself back to reality. "Oh. I'm fine," she answered. "A little bruised, but I'll live. And you can call me Rebecca. I think it's only fitting I be on a first-name basis with the man who saved my life."

His lips curved. "If you say so."

**Don't miss SPECIAL OPS EXCLUSIVE
by Elle Kennedy, available May 2013 from
Harlequin Romantic Suspense
wherever books are sold.**

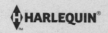

ROMANTIC suspense

CAVANAUGH ON DUTY

by *USA TODAY* bestselling author
Marie Ferrarella

Will the quest for justice lead to
unbridled passion?

When Esteban Fernandez suddenly found
himself pulled out of his undercover work and
partnered with unrequited love Kari Cavelli, he
thought his life was over. Little did he realize
that it was just the beginning.

Look for *CAVANAUGH ON DUTY*
by Marie Ferrarella next month from
Harlequin Romantic Suspense.

Available wherever books are sold.

Heart-racing romance, high-stakes suspense!